TO TELL YOU THE TRUTH

TO TELL YOU THE TRUTH

A NOVEL

GILLY MACMILLAN

WILLIAM MORROW
An Imprint of HarperCollinsPublishers

TO TELL YOU THE TRUTH. Copyright © 2020 by Gilly Macmillan. All rights reserved. Printed in the United States of America. No part of this book may be used or reproduced in any manner whatsoever without written permission except in the case of brief quotations embodied in critical articles and reviews. For information, address HarperCollins Publishers, 195 Broadway, New York, NY 10007.

HarperCollins books may be purchased for educational, business, or sales promotional use. For information, please email the Special Markets Department at SPsales@harpercollins.com.

FIRST EDITION

Library of Congress Cataloging-in-Publication Data has been applied for.

ISBN 978-0-06-287558-7 (hardcover)
ISBN 978-0-06-304037-3 (international edition)

20 21 22 23 24 LSC 10 9 8 7 6 5 4 3 2 1

To my family

TO
TELL
YOU
THE
TRUTH

Fiction isn't just what you find in books, it's the lies we tell ourselves. They can be sturdy lies we use as scaffolding, lies with an abrasive edge to scour our consciences clean, lies that settle over things we'd rather not see like a pure drift of snow. There are many other permutations, but whatever form they take, these are lies that we love and loathe.

The only way to avoid creating your own fiction is not to think at all.

—Lucy Harper, *The Truth*

There are the facts, and then there is the truth.

These are the facts.

It is the summer solstice, June 1991.

You're only nine years old. You're short for your age. The school nurse has recommended that you lose weight. You struggle to make friends and often feel lonely. You have been bullied. Teachers and your parents frequently encourage you to participate more in group activities, but you prefer the company of your imaginary friend.

We know you spend time that night in Stoke Woods because when you get home, leaves and pine needles are found on your clothing and in your hair, there is dirt beneath your fingernails, and you reek of bonfire smoke.

Home is number 7 Charlotte Close, a modest house identical to all the others on a short cul-de-sac built in the 1960s on a strip of land sold for development by a dairy farmer. It is situated adjacent to Stoke Woods, a couple of miles from the famous Suspension Bridge that links this semirural area directly to the city of Bristol.

We know you arrive home at 1:37 A.M., three hours and six minutes before dawn.

As for the rest of what happened, you describe it many times in the days that follow, and you paint, of course, an exceptionally vivid picture, because even at that age you have a facility with words.

You tell it this way:

The stitch in your side feels like a blade, but you daren't stop or slow as you race through the woods toward home. Trees are gathered as far as you can see with the still menace of a waiting army. Moonlight winks through the canopy and its milky fragments dot and daub the understory. The shifting light shrinks shadows, then elongates them. Perspective tilts.

You drive forward into thicker undergrowth where normally you tread carefully but not tonight. Nettles rake your shins and heaps of leaf mold feel as treacherous as quicksand when your shoes sink beneath their crisped surface. The depths below are damp and grabby.

It's a little easier when you reach the path, though its surface is uneven and small pebbles scatter beneath your soles. Your nostrils still prickle from the smell of the bonfire.

It's easy to unlatch the gate to the woods' car park, as you've done it many times before, and from there it's only a short distance to home.

Each step you take slaps down hard on the pavement and by the time you reach Charlotte Close, everything hurts. Your chest is heaving. You're gasping for breath. You stop dead at the end of your driveway. All the lights are on in your house.

They're up.

Your parents are usually neat in silhouette. They are tidy, modest folk.

A bonus fact: including you and your little brother, the four of you represent, on paper, the component parts of a very ordinary family.

But when the front door opens, your mother explodes through it, and the light from the hall renders her nightgown translucent so you have the mortifying impression that it's her naked body you're watching barrel up the path toward you, and there's nothing normal about that. There's nothing normal about anything on this night.

Your mum envelops you in her arms. It feels as if she's squeezing the last of your breath from you. Into the tangled mess of your hair she says, "Thank God," and you let yourself sink into her. It feels like falling.

Limp in her tight embrace, you think, please can this moment last forever, can time stop, *but of course it can't, in fact the moment lasts barely a second or two, because as any good mother would, yours raises her head and looks over your shoulder, down the path behind you, into the darkness, where the street lighting is inadequate, where the moonlight has disappeared behind a torn scrap of cloud, where the only other light is rimming the edges of the garage door of number 4, and every other home is dark, and she says the words you've been dreading.*

"But where's Teddy?"

You can't tell them about your den.

You just can't.

Eliza would be furious.

Your mum is clutching you by your upper arms so tightly it hurts. You have the feeling she might shake you. It takes every last ounce of your energy to meet her gaze, to widen your eyes, empty them somehow of anything bad she might read in them, and say, "Isn't he here?"

I typed "The End," clicked the save button, and clicked it again just to make sure. I felt huge relief that I'd finished my novel, and on top of that a heady mixture of elation and exhaustion. But there were also terrible nerves, much worse than usual, because typing those words meant the consequences of a secret decision that I'd made months ago would have to be faced now.

Every year I write a new book, and the draft I'd just finished was my fifth novel, a valuable property, hotly anticipated in publishing houses in London, New York, and other cities around the world. "Valuable property" were my literary agent's words, not mine, but he wasn't wrong. Every day as I wrote, I imagined the staccato tapping of feet beneath desks as publishers awaited the book's delivery, and this time I felt extra nervous because I knew I was going to send them something they weren't expecting.

"Brave," Eliza had said once she'd figured out what I'd done.

"I'm sorry," I told her, and I meant it. Her voice had a new and nasty rasp to it, but everything has its price. Under different circumstances, Eliza would be the first to point that out, because my girl is pragmatic.

I knew what I had to do next, but it was scary. I had a routine for summoning courage, because it was always hard to find, frequently lost in the scatter and doubt of writing a novel.

Counting to thirty took longer than it should have because I decelerated—I am a master of avoidance—but when I got to zero, I focused like a sniper taking aim. One tap of the finger and the novel was gone, out there, 330 pages on their way to my agent, via email, and it was too late to change anything now.

I waited as long as a minute before refreshing my inbox to see if he had acknowledged receipt. He hadn't. I deleted emails from clothing retailers offering me new seasonal discounts because I thought they were traitorous messages, reminding me of my internet shopping habit at a moment when something more significant was happening, though I did glimpse a jumpsuit that I thought I might revisit later. It was a buttery color, "hot this spring" apparently and "easy to accessorize." Tempting and definitely worth another look, but not now.

I drummed my fingers on my desk. Refreshed again. Nothing. I clicked the back button and checked if they had the jumpsuit in my size. They did. No low-stock warning, either. Nice. I added one to my shopping cart anyway. Just in case. Went back to email. Refreshed again. Still nothing. Checked my spam folder. Nothing there from Max, but good to see that hot women were available for sex in my city tonight. I deleted all spam, re-refreshed my inbox once more. No change.

I picked up the phone and called. He answered immediately. He has a lovely voice.

"Lucy! Just a second," he said, "I'm on the other line. Let me get rid of somebody," and he put me on hold. He sounded excited and it made me feel a little fluttery. Not because I'm attracted to him, please don't get the wrong idea, but because he's the person I plot and plan my career with, the gatekeeper to my publishers, negotiator-in-chief of book deals, firefighter-in-chief when things go pear-shaped, and recipient of a percentage of my earnings in return.

Max and I need each other; I'm his most successful client by far, so it was no surprise that he'd been trying to contain his impatience as my deadline for submitting the first draft of this book had approached, delivering pep talks and confidence boosts via phone and email. Whenever I met him, I noticed his nails were bitten to the quick.

He came back on the line after just a moment. "I'm all yours."

"It's done."

"You. Bloody. Miracle." I heard his keyboard clatter as he checked his email. "Got it," he said. There was a double-click as he opened the document. I imagined his eyes on the first page. Seconds passed. They felt like millennia.

"Max?"

Was he reading it? Was he gripped by the first few lines of my story, or had he scanned a few pages ahead and already felt the cold wrap of horror, the clutch of disappointment? My nerves were shredded enough that I could catastrophize a three-second pause.

"I'll read it immediately," he said. "Right away. You must put down the phone and go directly to celebrate. Do not pass go. Treat yourself. Have a bath, open a bottle of something delectable, tell that husband of yours to spoil you. I'll call you as soon as I've finished it."

At the very start of my career, before I had visited Max's office, I used to try to imagine what it was like. I thought he was the type to have a leather chair well-stuffed enough to cradle his buttocks in comfort and a big desk, its surface large and polished so that it reflected light from the window it faced, which was probably ornate, containing leaded glass perhaps, or framed with elaborate stonework. That's the sort of person Max seemed to me to be, in spite of his bitten nails: a puppet master. Only a puppet master would have a desk like that. I shared that thought with him once—we must have sunk a few cocktails, or I wouldn't have been brave enough to say it out loud—and he half smiled, the expression aligning his asymmetric features.

"But you're the one who has the power of life and death," he replied. "Fictionally speaking," he added after a beat.

True.

Beyond the chair, the desk, and the architectural features, I also imagined that Max's office would be messy. Beautiful bones framing disorder was how I saw it and it was a very attractive image, to me.

I could find beauty in surprising things. You have to when violence reverberates through your work. I imagine every thriller writer will have their own way of handling this.

And, by the way, when I finally got to visit Max's office in person, I found it to be nothing at all like what I had expected.

2

After Max, Daniel, my husband, was always the second person to know when a book was finished, but I wanted a few moments to myself before I told him, moments when I didn't feel watched, because I felt like people watched me all the time.

My first novel had been published four years ago and exploded onto the crime fiction scene (my publisher's words, not mine) and high onto the bestseller list, where it stayed for months. And I was introduced to the concept of a book a year—something Max and my editors insisted on as being of paramount importance. Since then people had taken extreme notice of me. They watched what I was writing next and learned to deduce how quickly I was writing it. They watched me at events. Online. They watched like hawks. They bombarded me with messages on social media. I even had one fan, so far unidentified, who had located the house in which Dan and I rented our flat—a modest building in a graffiti- and coffee-shop-speckled neighborhood of Bristol—and left gifts on the doorstep.

The presents weren't really for me, though. The heroine of my novels was Detective Sergeant Eliza Grey. She was based on my childhood imaginary friend. (*Write what you know*, they say, and I did.) People were mad for Eliza and those gifts were for her. They included her favorite condiment (cloudberry jam—discovered when she was working on a case in Oslo in book two) and her favorite beverage (a caffeinated energy drink). They made me uneasy, I won't lie, however well-intentioned they were. I asked Dan to get rid of them. They felt like an intrusion into my private life.

It had profoundly shocked me, how suddenly and completely I had become public property after the publication of my first Eliza book. I hadn't anticipated it, and had I known it would happen, I might never have sent my novel out to literary agents in the first place. The minute I'd signed over the rights to that book, nobody cared that my natural inclination was to curl around my privacy as tightly as a pill bug.

My moment of aloneness in the office was disappointing. Instead of basking in a sense of peaceful privacy (as opposed to the fraught loneliness that usually characterized my writing days), I could only see the mess.

I'd shut myself in that room for weeks to get the book finished, working on a crazy schedule of late nights and dawn starts, sometimes a frenzy of typing in the early hours, interspersed with snatches of fractured sleep. My circadian rhythm had been more tarantella than waltz and it showed. Even my printer looked tired, its trays askew, fallen paper on the floor beneath it: A courtesan whose client has just left. She dreams of marrying him. (But I mustn't personify my printer. What will you think of me?) The floor and coffee table were hardly visible beneath a townscape created from piles of printed drafts and research materials.

"Should you really dump your stuff on an authentic Persian rug?" Dan had asked from the doorway a few weeks ago, when the surfaces could no longer contain all the clutter and it had begun to creep over the floor. I hadn't thought of it that way. I was more used to soft furnishings from IKEA, we both were, it's all we had ever known, but we were at a point where Dan was getting accustomed to the finer things in life and growing into the new wealth my books had brought us more quickly than I was. He had the time to luxuriate in it and to figure out how to spend it; I didn't. My writing schedule saw to that. I couldn't afford to look up from my work and enjoy the change in our lives. I was barely aware it was happening.

It wasn't just the fancy rug that took some getting used to. The cottage we were renting was also a reflection of what we found ourselves newly able to afford. The weekly rate had seemed eye-watering to me when Dan first proposed the idea, an insult to my natural inclination to be economical and un-flashy, but Dan had insisted that we needed to be here.

"You can't do the final push on this book in the flat," he'd said with an irritating air of authority, honed for years on the subjects of writing and the creative process, but recently applied more frequently to our domestic life. "It's too claustrophobic. We'll be on top of each other."

He was right, and I knew it, but I loved writing in our cozy one-bed flat with its views of the little row of shops opposite, and the smells from the bakery wafting across the street every morning. And I felt superstitious. I'd written all my books so far in that flat. What if a change of routine affected my writing? What if it signaled that I had gotten above myself? Everyone knows that tall poppies are the first to be decapitated.

But even as those anxieties raised a swarm of butterflies in my stomach, I knew I had to take Dan's wishes carefully into consideration because he worked full-time for me now, and it made the issue of who had the power in our household a delicate one. I tried to think of how to frame my objections to renting the cottage in a way that wouldn't upset him, but I got tongue-tied. Words flow for me when I'm writing, but they can stick in my throat like a hairball when I have to speak up for myself.

Dan softened his tone to deliver the winning line: "We can easily afford it, I've looked at the numbers, and imagine being in the countryside . . . by the ocean, too. It'll be so good for us."

I was susceptible to emotional blackmail, and to the poten-tial for romance. Writing is a lonely job, as I've said. I also had to trust him on the money, because he managed my finances for me. Trying to grapple with taxes and columns of numbers plunged me into panic.

I agreed to rent the place and watched him click "Book Now," but as he did, I had the strange feeling that life had somehow just shifted a little bit beyond my control.

There's something else I should mention, in the spirit of full disclosure.

On paper, ours was a nice, mutually beneficial, privileged arrangement where I would write a thriller each year and continue to rake in the money, and Dan would provide all the support I needed, but there was a large and rather revolting fly stuck in the ointment, its legs twitching occasionally.

The fly was this: Being my assistant wasn't the life Dan had dreamed of. He'd wanted to be a bestselling author, too.

*O*n the night Teddy disappears, you wait until midnight before trying to leave the house. You're eager to get going because dawn will break in just a few hours and it's only until then that the spirits will be out, moving among real people, making mischief, playing tricks.

You know what happens on the summer solstice because you researched it in the library. You are a very able nine-year-old. "Exceptionally bright," your teacher wrote in your report. "Reading and writing to a level well beyond her age."

Your bedroom door creaks and the noise cuts right through you. You count to ten and nothing happens, so you think you're safe, and you step out onto the landing, but Teddy's door opens when you're right outside it.

"What are you doing?" he says.

You shush him, hustle him into his bedroom, helping him back into bed, nestling his blankie by his head the way he likes it.

"Go back to sleep," you whisper. You stroke his hair. He puts his thumb into his mouth and sucks. His eyelids droop. You force yourself to stay there until you're sure he's gone back to sleep.

You've just crept over to his bedroom door when he says, "Lucy, I want you."

Your fingers clench. You very badly want to go out into the woods. You've been planning this for weeks. You turn around. He looks sweet, lying there.

"Do you think you can be really quiet?" you say.

"Teddy can be quiet." He refers to himself in the third person more often than not. Later, someone will say it's as if he always knew he wouldn't be with us for long.

"Don't take him with you," Eliza says in your head. Your imaginary friend always has an opinion.

"He'll cry if I don't," you reply silently, "and wake up Mum and Dad."

"Then you can't go."

That's not an option you want to consider. You hold out your hand and Teddy's eyes brighten.

"Do you want to come on an adventure?" you ask him.

Sitting in my office alone, I didn't just feel disappointed, I also felt guilty, because the end of a book was happy news and Dan deserved to share it right away. My schedule was punishing for both of us, and he needed these moments of celebration just as much as I did.

I levered myself up from my seat, left my lair with a sense of traversing a portal, and found him in the kitchen, stirring a casserole. I watched him for a moment before he sensed me. He seemed preoccupied by something, the wooden spoon doing little more than troubling the surface of the food.

"Hi," I said from the doorway. He turned and half smiled, evidently trying to assess my state of mind, his first instinct at this stage of a book to be wary of me. Here I was, his very own Gollum whose precious obsession was a novel. Had she finished? Finally? Or had her glazed and bloodshot stare been fixed on a blinking cursor at the top of a blank page, while at the far end of her optic nerve, her mind shredded itself with doubt?

I saw those questions in his eyes and had the stupid idea that it might be fun to break the tension by conveying that I had good news to share by doing a little victory dance. I tapped one fist on top of the other, twice, then swapped over. Got my hips swaying. Kept it jaunty. It took a lot of concentration in the exhausted state I was in, and I might have been frowning, but I wanted to try it because it was the sort of thing that he and I used to do all the time, a frivolous language we shared with one another that made us giggle.

But Dan's eyes widened. It was as if he didn't know how to speak frivolous anymore—or didn't want to. I stopped, awash with self-consciousness. He flipped the dishcloth he was holding over his shoulder and cleared his throat. "How's it going?" he asked. He was wearing a novelty apron I'd bought him, with the slogan "I can cook as good as I look."

He did look good, sleek and composed, buffed and polished. The Dan I'd met seven years ago, that shabby, pudgy guy running on creative passion and budget groceries, had been transformed by the injection of money. He wasn't just taking care of his appearance but had worked on improving himself in other ways, too. He knew about wine now. He'd invested in a fancy car. He'd even encouraged me to get a stylist, but I hadn't had the time to do that, or to keep up with him in other ways. The only efforts I'd made to improve were my occasional splashy online clothing purchases, and even then, I was never quite sure whether I'd bought the right thing.

I also wasn't exactly certain when Dan's pattern of transformation had begun. While I wrote my second book? The third? After *that* big royalty check? The book-a-year schedule meant that time was sometimes confusing to me, its linearity a deck of cards that could be reshuffled. Creating fiction left no mental space for orderly recollections of reality. I thought of my memories as tall grasses that could be blown this way or that.

"Your memories were like that before you started writing," Eliza muttered. I couldn't deny it. Eliza and I were always honest with one another.

"Earth to Lucy," Dan said. "Hello?" He sounded irritable. He hated it when I zoned out.

"I finished the book. I sent it to Max."

"Truly?"

I nodded and smiled at him, and realized it was probably the first time I'd smiled in a while. The relevant muscles in my cheeks had fallen slack from disuse but making them work was a glorious feeling. Dan hugged me and I felt the adrenaline leave my body in a rush, as if he was squeezing it from me. He smelled of wood smoke and the ragù he was making. The aroma of normality. I was landing back on earth. Coming back to life. Blinking in the daylight.

"Congratulations," he said into the top of my head. The sweet intimacy of it was lovely. "Bloody well done. What can I do? Can I make you a cup of tea?"

I sat down at the table with all the grace of a sack of flour dropped from a height and felt as if I'd been released from a hospital room after months of convalescence. Everything was possible now. Normality was possible. I could make up to Dan for everything he'd been doing for me. We could have some fun. Just so long as they liked the book.

"If you make me a cup of tea, I'll have to kill you," I said, "or at the very least, divorce you. Let's open a bottle of something very cold and very good."

Dan went to find champagne. We'd brought some with us. The good stuff. Nothing fake. Another upgrade. I didn't dare admit to him that I disliked the way champagne sent a metallic sparkle up my nose when I drank it, and how a second glass of it sometimes made me cry, and that part of me missed the cheap alcohol we used to enjoy.

My spirits dipped a little after Dan left the room, because it was impossible to forget the secret I'd been keeping about the new book, and I felt the corners of my mouth droop. When I heard him coming back, I made the effort to plaster that smile back on, though. Now wasn't the time to tell him. First we needed our celebration.

I watched as he filled our glasses. The champagne was the palest, most fragile gold. One of the windows was cracked open, and I could hear the ocean and see the sun creeping behind the edge of the barn, a watery orb, spilling yellow light. Dan placed a bowl of roasted nuts on the table, homemade, my favorite. He kissed me with dry lips and picked up his drink.

"Congratulations," he said. I registered the lovely sparkle in his eye that I hadn't seen for a while, and that made me melt a little, and the gentle tilt of his glass toward mine, but I also had to swallow my nerves because he was giving me a cue and I knew what I should say. I should toast Detective Sergeant Eliza Grey.

I wrote about the Eliza Grey toast for a Sunday newspaper once, describing how Dan and I made it whenever the first draft of a new Eliza book was complete. Fans read the interview and picked up on our little ritual, sending me photographs of themselves raising a glass once they'd finished reading the latest Eliza Grey novel. It became a thing on bookish social media. It had its own hashtag: #CheersEliza.

I couldn't bring myself to say the words Dan was expecting, though, because it would have been tantamount to a lie after I'd effectively removed Eliza from this book completely by incapacitating her. I'll spare you the details. No spoilers. But that was my secret, the reason anxiety was pinching even as I was supposed to be celebrating.

"Why did you do this?" Eliza had whispered when it happened. I found it hard to get used to the way her voice had been altered by her injuries. It made me feel horribly guilty. Nobody wants to hurt their childhood friend. The problem was, she'd become something more disruptive.

When I had decided to base the character of Detective Sergeant Eliza Grey on her, five years ago, Eliza had been a voice in my head, my friend, confidante, and protector. It had been amazing to bring her to life on the page. But she had evolved, somehow becoming more than words. It was as if she had been formed from clay and life breathed into her. When I was writing my third novel, she stepped right out of the pages and into my life.

"I see you everywhere," I told her. "I can't handle it."

At first it had been manageable, but it had begun to happen more and more frequently, until Dan had noticed me being distracted by her. He'd asked awkward questions, accused me of behaving strangely. I didn't know how to explain.

"I'll disappear whenever you want me to," Eliza had pleaded, "you just have to say," but we both knew that wasn't true. She was too much of a maverick and it had been far too long since I'd had her under control. "I don't want to be out of the books. Please don't do it."

She'd sounded desperate but I'd ignored her plea. It wasn't easy, because it hurt me to hurt her, but it was the way it had to be. Honestly, I didn't know what else to do. And it had worked. Eliza hadn't appeared to me in person since I'd written the scene that took her out of the book. I still heard her voice, but that was fine, I was used to it. I couldn't remember a time when that hadn't been the case.

Dan, left hanging, his glass in midair, confusion creasing his forehead, decided to speak for me, though it wasn't his place to, not really, but he said it anyway: "Cheers, Eliza!"

He clinked his glass against mine and I smiled and swallowed my discomfort along with the champagne. How was I going to explain to him what I'd done when I could never tell him the truth about her, because he'd never understand?

After all, what kind of person creates a character who walks right out of their books and into their life?

He would think I'd lost my mind.

Dan didn't notice my discomfort. In his haste to offer me a refill, he knocked over the bowl of nuts, but I'd almost emptied it. He was buzzing.

A completed first draft of the book didn't just mean a measure of freedom for us both, it also meant delivery payments. Not right away—the book would have to be dragged through edits and fully finished for that—but soon. Dan kept spreadsheets tracking my income. The blinking cursor he stared at on a regular basis was the one sitting in the Excel box where he would enter my delivery payment when it landed. He loved to do that.

We took our drinks outside and walked to the end of the garden to watch the sun sink toward the ocean. Waves pounded the rocks mercilessly. The surface of the ocean was a thousand shades of gray and silver, the spray foamy and angry against rocks slicked oily black, their silhouettes slicing the surface of the water after every push and pull of the tide.

I shivered from the cold and leaned into the warmth of Dan's body. It was a balm for my sore muscles and my tired mind, for my nerves. The moment felt incredibly intimate to me after the months I'd spent in the company of fictional people.

Neither of us spoke. Even if we had, the salty wind would have whipped our words away. We sipped our drinks, and I cried after a while. The second glass of fizz guaranteed it, and the creeping feeling of dread that wouldn't go away.

I couldn't stop thinking about how Max felt, or would feel,

when he read the scene in my new book that put Eliza out of action. How shocked would he be? How fast would he scroll frantically on through the pages, imagining money slipping through his fingers as easily as sand, hoping against hope that I had pulled off some kind of novelistic sleight of hand and Eliza would reappear within pages to continue her domination of the market?

I knew he'd be devastated initially, there was no point kidding myself. The question was whether that would abate when he read the rest of the book. My stomach curled. *Hold your nerve*, I told myself, *this book is much better than all your others. It's a fresh start for you.* But my courage was liquefying.

Dan didn't notice I was upset. He had his eyes fixed on the horizon, too. He would have put my tears down to exhaustion, anyway; it wouldn't be the first time I'd wept at the end of a book. Each one found its own special way to drain me.

The wind dried my teardrops as quickly as they arrived and after a while, I laughed to myself, and thought, what was the point of them, really? What was done was done. I should be confident.

I took a bath when we got back inside. Dan went back to the kitchen to finish off dinner. He was still keyed up, energy humming off him. I thought he was happy that the book was finished and that we could finally spend some time together. I got into the claw-footed tub and basked in steaming water so bubbly that it beautifully obscured my white jelly flesh and I emptied my brain by speculating about how much the fancy taps had cost.

I went downstairs afterward in my dressing gown, expecting to eat on the sofa, in front of a movie, our usual ritual at the end of a book, but Dan had laid the kitchen table and it was fancy. There were fresh flowers and another bottle of champagne propped at a jaunty angle in an ice bucket. The apron was off. He was grinning.

"What's this?" I said.

"Are you happy to go back to Bristol tomorrow?"

"Sure. If you want to." I would have preferred to stay here for a few more days, to give myself a chance to decompress, but I was balancing those marital scales, prepared to be acquiescent.

"I've got something to show you when we get there."

"What is it?"

"A surprise."

He popped the cork and I jumped when it flew across the room. The champagne frothed down the neck of the bottle and Dan licked it away.

"What's the surprise?" I asked.

"My lips are sealed," he said. "I could tell you, but I'd have to kill you."

"Tell me!"

"No. You have to wait."

"Is it a good surprise?"

"Oh, yes."

This was exciting. Dan had never done anything like it before. I was grateful I hadn't soured things with the news about Eliza.

I leaned in to kiss him, properly kiss him, but he pulled back and made himself busy pouring. I tried again but he wasn't having it. It was hard not to feel upset. We hadn't been intimate for a long time.

"Don't you want to eat first?" he asked. "Dinner's ready." I supposed I was hungry. Dan pushed a block of Parmesan and a grater toward me. "Your job," he said. "Don't grate your knuckles again."

If he hadn't said that, I swear I would have done it without mishap, but his words made me feel self-conscious about what I was doing, and my fingers were trained to type, not grate, and I was tired, and the accident was inevitable. My knuckles didn't bleed for too long.

It was a good meal, though. We ate spaghetti garnished with

pointy hillocks of dandruffy Parmesan like messy fools, our lips reddening from the sauce. Dan assiduously topped up the champagne. After we had eaten, he insisted on clearing up and while he did, I stretched out on the sofa and was carried off by sleep in a matter of seconds, as if it was a beautiful drug, as if I had nothing to worry about.

I wonder, now, how I had no premonition of what was to come. How I, who could imagine evil in a heartbeat, transcribe it onto the page in ways that chilled the blood of my readers, was able to slip into an unsuspecting sleep so easily, cheek muscles aching from smiling. It's a little bit embarrassing. After all, you don't have to be a rocket scientist to understand that not all surprises are good ones. Especially when you're keeping a secret yourself.

Teddy insists on bringing his blankie with him, but he sits silently while you put on his shoes and he's good at being quiet as you walk down Charlotte Close together. Your excitement infects him. You can feel it in his tight grip, the slick of sweat between your palms, and when he looks up at you, he breaks into a wide smile. Teddy loves to do things with you. His trust is absolute.

The night is humid, the sky crisp, clear, and bright with stars. There is a waning gibbous moon and you have a small torch. Excitement bloats inside you.

Once you're on the main road, you let him talk, but you walk in the shadows in case any passing cars see you. There is only one. It slows beside you and you duck into a driveway and wait there, your chest heaving, your face close to Teddy's, and your finger on your lips. He mirrors you. "Shhh," he says. The car moves on.

You turn into the lane that leads to the woods' car park and as soon as you do, you feel it: the spirits are in the trees.

"Can you feel them?" you ask Teddy. A breeze rustles something, somewhere close.

"Teddy can feel them," he says.

"Come on," you say. You lift him over the stile. It's not easy because he's heavy, but you manage, and you lead him into the woods.

"What does Teddy feel?" he asks when you've walked a little way into the darkness.

"Not scared," you say. Your heart feels as if it has been pumped fuller than usual. Your mind is dancing.

"Not scared," he repeats.

"That's the spirit, Teddy," you say.

Dan and I made the journey back to our flat in Bristol the next morning. I had still heard nothing from Max by the time we left. I emailed to let him know my movements, but he didn't reply. His silence gnawed at me and so did a spiteful little hangover.

The journey home felt like the start of a new chapter. Glittering sea views and trees bent double by gales disappeared in the rearview mirror as we gradually reentered civilization, and soon the motorway beckoned. Three lanes of traffic, roaring between cities. We went north. Dan put his foot down and turned the music up and I gazed out the window and looked forward to being home. I'd thought I might tell him about Eliza on the drive, but I wanted to know what his surprise was first.

My first clue was when Dan didn't take our usual turn off the motorway. I glanced at him and he glanced back at me and raised his eyebrows. He was smiling but I found I couldn't smile back because this road was familiar to me. We were driving toward my childhood, the street where I grew up. Charlotte Close.

I fixed my eyes on the road's center markings and didn't look up. I knew where every landmark on this road was and knew there was nothing I wanted to see here. As we approached the junction with Charlotte Close my chest tightened. Here was where reporters had camped out when I was a child, incessantly calling out my name, desperate to talk to me even after my dad pleaded with them to leave us alone.

When we were almost beside it, Dan said, "It's okay. You're fine. Don't panic."

"Yes," I said. It was the only word I could manage.

"Breathe," Eliza whispered. I listened to her and made myself match the soft rhythm of her inhalations and exhalations, and we breathed in synchrony until Dan had driven past the end of Charlotte Close and on past Stoke Woods, which began where the small gardens on one side of Charlotte Close ended.

Those woods were what I saw from my bedroom window as a child. The old oaks bled oxygen into the air I breathed and enchanted me.

I felt my tension release when we were past the boundary on the other side of the woods, but my relief was premature, because Dan switched on the indicator light and slowed the car before turning into a lane that ran alongside the far edge of the woods. A sign at the junction read "Private Lane."

I had roamed the woods as a child but never explored this far on my own. I vaguely remembered my parents driving us down here once to rubberneck the big houses, but otherwise this place had been meaningless to us. Another country. Until the investigation into Teddy's disappearance, when police had questioned the residents, but nothing had come of that, and we had forgotten it again.

"Why are we here?" I asked.

"Trust me," Dan said. "Will you? Relax. Just be patient for a few more seconds."

The houses were along one side of the lane only, the side adjacent to the woods. On the opposite side was a grass verge and an imposing row of copper beech trees that must have been planted not long after the houses were built. Behind them was more farmland.

I peered down the first driveway we passed and glimpsed an imposing Victorian mansion. The property appeared to have substantial gardens around it, but the overwhelming impression was that it was embedded in the woodland. It made me shudder.

The next driveway offered a view of two homes. One was as

grand as the first place, if not more so. Sharing a driveway with it was a more modern, architect-designed property, probably no more than ten years old. The modern place looked to have been built on land sold off by the bigger house. Though the driveway was shared, the design and distance between the two houses must have ensured reasonable, but not total, privacy for both. These properties, too, were nestled into the woods.

"I don't like it here," I said. Claustrophobia had me in its grip. My hands were trembly and my palms clammy.

"It's okay," Dan said. "You'll see."

"Please turn around," I said, but he kept driving as if I hadn't spoken.

The lane curved and just beyond the curve, it ended abruptly. Posts with barbed wire strung between them signaled you could drive no farther. Beyond them there was more woodland. One more driveway opened to our left, flanked by ornate stone columns. One of them bore a name: Cossley House. Dan turned into the driveway. It was pitted and overgrown.

"Please," I said. "I just want to go home."

Dan stopped the car halfway down. "You have to trust me," he said. His smile had gone, and he cradled my face between his hands. "Look at me," he said. "Pull yourself together for me."

I nodded and he let go. His insistence unsettled me. I felt no better.

We drove the last few yards in silence. At the end of the drive was the finest house of all, a true mansion, but it had been neglected. There was another car in the drive and as we pulled in, the door opened and a man stepped out. He was about our age, with prematurely thinning hair and cheeks that were fatly red with the afterglow of many good lunches. He was an estate agent, I realized, he had to be, though there had been no "For Sale" or "For Rent" sign at the end of the drive.

Eliza came to the same conclusion. "You've been ambushed," she said. "Dan wants to buy this place."

Dan got out of the car without saying anything and before I knew it, he was on the steps of the house shaking hands warmly with the agent. I followed, slowly.

"You must be Mrs. Harper," the agent said, descending the steps toward me, hand outstretched. "Welcome! I'm Henry. It's lovely to meet you."

I suffered Henry's bearlike handshake and knew I was going to have to endure this viewing because it would humiliate Dan if I refused to stay. I thought I would get through the tour as quickly as possible and get out of there because I would never, in a million years, agree to buy this house. Henry unlocked the large front door and held it open for us.

I didn't even want to step through it, but Dan pushed me not-so-gently in the small of my back and I entered the hallway, onto a pale limestone floor, inset with smaller black diamonds. The space was dominated by the staircase, which was dusty, but as elegant as any I'd ever seen. Delicate spindles and dark wooden treads outlined a sinuous climb toward a light well set three stories above us. I stepped into the pool of murky sunlight it cast on the floor and looked up and around. It was obvious that while one or two rooms had been renovated, the rest of the place had not.

This place is way too big for us, I thought. *And way too grand. It's all wrong. We'll rattle around in it. It's almost a total wreck. A money pit. I hate it. And I can never live beside Stoke Woods or Charlotte Close. Never.*

The sound of the door shutting startled me and I swung around. The agent had left us to it.

Dan put his arms around me. "It's one of Bristol's finest mansions," he said, "and one of its most historic. Houses like this only come on the market once in a lifetime."

"I can't live here," I said. "And you know why."

"Give it a chance, for me. Please? Imagine how beautiful we could make it if we finish the renovations. I could project-manage, maybe even do some of the work if we get you a proper assistant. We could put our touch on it."

"He really loves it," Eliza said. She sounded horrified but also intrigued, and I knew it would damage us if I insisted on leaving now.

I was also having to face up to something: the hole in Dan's life that had been left by his failed writing career had clearly not been filled by his becoming my assistant, or by his new, mon-eyed, pursuits. I'd suspected it, but hadn't really thought about what it might mean for us because when I was writing I had no mental space for anything else. However, it felt very real now.

But if Dan wanted another project, it wasn't going to be this house. He was going to have to think of something else.

"Look around at least," Eliza said. "Let him think you're giving it a chance."

It was good advice. "Show me everything," I said, and tried to look interested. Dan beamed. He took my hand and led me into a renovated kitchen where most of the external wall had been punched out and replaced by glass. It overlooked a side garden that was grassed and surrounded by dense hedges. Shiny gadgets had been built or tucked into every crevice of the cabi-netry, and the island was the size of the kitchenette in our flat. It had no charm. There was nothing homey about it.

"We could make the whole house as amazing as this," Dan said. He was practically purring.

"Well, it's something," I said.

"Come," Dan said. He led me back across the hallway and turned a door handle. "Ready for the big reveal?"

I nodded and he pushed the door open with the flourish of a magician pulling a rabbit from a hat.

The room was vast, an absolute dream if you are the type to have pretensions to grandeur. It had an ornate ceiling and the walls were maybe twelve feet high, two of them punctuated by sash windows offering views of a long lawn at the back of the house that was bordered, simply, by the low wire fence that demarcated the edge of Stoke Woods.

I was transfixed by the sight. The oaks were gathered along the perimeter of the property like sentries who have stood still for so long that their flesh has warped and turned to bark. I felt as if my past had walked right up to the boundary and was waiting for me there. Waiting to remind me of Teddy. Waiting to punish me.

I couldn't pretend any longer. I turned to tell Dan that I absolutely could not contemplate living here, that it would be impossible for me to return to this location, but the sight of him stopped me.

He stood in the center of the room, in the midst of the remains of a fallen ceiling rose, which had created a starburst of debris on the parquet. Sunshine cut through the windows and pale light played across his face and his body, burnishing his narrow shoulders, glinting from his glasses. His grin widened as he pulled an object from his pocket and held it up in the dusty shaft of light. It was a set of keys.

"The house is ours," he said. "I bought it for you."

Eliza swore and I felt a powerful wave of nausea before my knees gave out from under me.

Crushed plasterwork was digging into my backside and I could taste fine dust in the air, too. Dan was cradling me. I sat up cautiously.

"Are you all right?" he said. "I got you, I caught you before you hit your head."

I looked at the lofty ceiling, the broken molding, the decayed grandeur, and imagined it all collapsing on us, the stale air choking us.

"How dare you buy this house without telling me?" I asked. "Did you buy it with my money?"

"Lucy, I—" he began, but he sounded bossy, as if he was a teacher and I was a slow pupil, and I didn't want to hear it.

"You've betrayed all the trust I put in you."

"I—" he began again.

"I want to go home. Take me home, please."

We drove into the city across the Suspension Bridge without speaking. When we got home to our flat, we unpacked the car in silence and put as much distance between us as we could in the cramped space.

I lay on our bed, still barely able to process what Dan had done. It was shocking, totally unexpected, frightening. We would have to undo it as soon as possible, sell the house, even if we took a hit. There was no other way and I would have to summon the courage to tell him so.

I checked my email, hoping for some good news to distract

me. My heart leaped when I saw a message from Max, but it was brutally short: Nearly finished reading. I'll call as soon as I'm done.

I reread the message, more than once, but it was infuriatingly hard to read between the lines. Max was good at that. I typed out a needy reply, then deleted it. I typed out another and sent it to myself. I read it and was happy I hadn't sent it to Max. I deleted that one, too.

I gazed around our bedroom. It was too small, like the rest of this place, but I loved every inch of it. I understood the arguments about investing my money sensibly, and knew we'd buy a place eventually, but it should have been a joint decision, a gradual moving on, when both of us were ready.

Eliza said, "You have to talk to him sooner rather than later. Find out exactly what he's done."

I felt nervous. This felt bigger than me, somehow. I sensed it sharply, though even I could never have imagined where it would take us.

Dan was sitting at the kitchen table, doing something on his laptop. He shut the lid when he saw me. He had his wary expression on again.

"Why that house?" I said. "What were you thinking?"

"I thought you'd fall in love with it like I did." There was something in the way he said it, a simplicity and a sweetness, that helped me let go of a little of my anger. He stood up and came to me, cupping my face in his hands, just the way he had earlier, but this time he kissed me, and my body relaxed.

"Are you hungry?" he said.

"Starving."

"Let's go out and get something to eat and we can talk. I want this to work."

We walked to the restaurant but didn't hold hands, as we usually did. Things felt strange. Not unpleasant, but off. Dan was overly solicitous, stepping behind me when the sidewalk was too narrow for us to pass other people. Triple-checking the road was clear before crossing. He seemed hypervigilant.

Eliza said, "Thinking about it, if he's really bought this place, and I think he has, you need to play a long game. You can get out of this, but probably not right away, so be smart and don't be angry. Pick your battles with him. If he went behind your back and used your money to buy it, and I think he did, you need to make sure your name is on the deed. Until then, it's his decision whether you sell or not."

She was right. I listened carefully. But she couldn't resist adding, "I told you not to give him access to your accounts."

I had trusted him, though, and hadn't wanted to handle the money myself. It had seemed like a no-brainer. Now I felt stupid.

Dan held open the door of the restaurant for me. It was a new pizza place he wanted to try. Over *mozzarella in carrozza*, a dirty martini for me, and a lager for Dan, I said, as calmly as I could, "You should have talked to me before you bought the house. We should be making joint decisions about money."

"But if I had, you'd never have agreed to buying it," he said. A string of cheese dangled from his mouth and he sucked it up.

"I'd never have agreed to buying it anyway, because of where it is."

"It was the chance of a lifetime. I didn't want your past to stuff up our future. And no one is going to know who you are. The last time they saw you, you were—what?—ten."

"I was thirteen."

My parents moved away from Charlotte Close then. It took that long for them to believe, finally, that Teddy was not coming home, but it haunted my mother afterward, that we hadn't stayed. She regretted the move because she began to have recurring dreams that Teddy had turned up at number 7 after we left and thought we'd abandoned him.

She couldn't bear to remain on Charlotte Close, but she

couldn't bear to be anywhere else, either. That was the pain she lived with, until she died, only a few months after my dad.

"And you changed your name," Dan said.

I had changed it twice. Once as soon as I became an adult. Lucy Bewley had been a recognizable name and I didn't want my past to be evident to anyone who might care to search for it on the internet. It was a worry even back then, before I became a somebody. I'd chosen to become Lucy Brown because it was a perfectly, beautifully, bland and extremely common name. When I'd married, I'd transformed from being Lucy Brown to Lucy Harper. Nobody who unearthed my marriage certificate would be able to connect me with the disappearance of Teddy Bewley.

I'd reveled in the wonderful anonymity of my married name right up until the point when I'd gotten a public profile. After that, I knew I would never feel adequately shielded from the past and wondered how Dan could sit here in the restaurant now and behave as if he didn't know all too well that this was one of my greatest fears.

I wanted badly to argue the point, but was afraid that I'd become upset, that he'd accuse me of being overwrought, or irrational, of making a scene, so I swallowed my frustration.

"How much did the house cost?" I asked.

He stalled. "I made a good deal," he said.

"How much, Dan?"

"Just shy of two million."

I let out a low whistle. "You should have asked me."

"But then we wouldn't have the house, would we?" Dan took a swig of his beer and I felt confounded, as if he'd flipped my argument against me, and any coherent train of thought I might have had evaporated.

"Exactly!" I said, but I was a bit confused over whether I'd just agreed or disagreed with him. I downed my drink.

"I just don't think anyone's a loser here." He folded a slice of pizza over itself and inserted most of it into his mouth. I watched him chew.

"We should have ice cream after," he added, and I could see the masticated dough and pepperoni in his mouth, and it made me feel a terrific distaste for him. I felt like saying I wanted to leave and denying him ice cream, but I badly wanted some myself so I agreed with him that we should and the conversation about money seemed to be over for now.

He got salted caramel and blackcurrant ice cream. I got chocolate and lemon sorbet.

When it arrived, Eliza prompted me and I asked, "Is my name on the deed of the house?"

"No. Because if it was, I'd have had to trick you into signing to keep it a surprise and I wasn't comfortable with that."

I wasn't sure how this was any worse than buying the house without telling me. Dan seemed to have entirely rewritten the moral code to justify doing what he wanted. He reached across the table and took my hand, turned it over and ran his finger over my palm. I flinched a little, in case my nerve pain flared up, but it didn't. "The paperwork for putting your name on the house deed is ready for you to sign," he said. "We'll see the solicitor and make it official next week."

He went to the washroom while I paid the bill. I wondered if he meant the house would then be in our joint names or just mine. I felt wrung out by the shock of it all, bone tired, incapable of processing it properly until I'd had some more rest.

As we walked home, Dan took my hand again and said, "Will you come back to the house in the morning with me? Give it a fair go? Try to imagine us there? That's all I ask."

The thought made my anxiety resurface, but Eliza said, "I don't think you have a choice," so I said, "Yes."

She had another question, too: "Ask him how he knew about the house. There was no 'For Sale' sign outside, so it probably wasn't on the open market."

I asked the question.

"Sasha told me about it," he said.

Sasha Morell. She and Dan had met at a creative writing course he'd taken at the university. He had talked about her a lot at the time. I remembered he liked her because he felt she understood his "vision." I'd Googled her. She had a website for her writing. The short story posted there was unpublishable. The photograph was of an exceptionally attractive woman. I also remembered that she and her husband lived on the other side of the bridge.

"Sasha happened to mention the house to me, in the context of how pleased she and James were that the place was on the market because it meant it would be rescued from declining completely, and I just knew it would be perfect for us."

I hadn't even known they were still in touch.

"She'll be one of our neighbors, then?" I asked.

"Absolutely. Which is amazing. Apparently, they're a tight group because the lane is privately owned and managed by the owners of the houses, so it'll be nice to have an instant community. We won't be isolated out there."

I disagreed. The house might only be a mile or two from the Suspension Bridge, but it was rural; we would no longer have shops or urban life on our doorstep. Dan said some more stuff, but I didn't listen properly, because all I could do was try to drink in the city sights and sounds that I would soon lose, and all I could hear was her name in my head, repeating in time with the lights flashing in a barbershop window across the street: Sasha, Sasha, Sasha.

You saw the notice advertising the summer solstice celebrations because your outraged neighbor held it up in front of your dad, using his fingertips, as if it was dirty, and said, "We have to put a stop to this."

You thought it sounded amazing. *Summer solstice. A bonfire. Fireworks. Staying up all night. It was an opportunity to do things kids didn't normally get to do and then there was also the chance that you might see the spirits and become a part of real, actual magic.*

You smell the bonfire before you reach the clearing that is on a site where an Iron Age fort once stood. It is deep in the woods, close to the edge of the gorge. The scent of the smoke is both acrid and enticing.

Teddy's nose wrinkles. "I don't like it," he says. He's flagging now. Just when you want to go faster, to get there as quickly as possible, he's dragging his feet.

"You will, Ted. Just wait until you see it."

You're so close now that you can hear crackling and spitting, feel the heat.

At your first sight of the fire flickering against the tree trunks, you gasp and Teddy's mouth falls open. A few steps farther and you are both enchanted. It's a lure you can't look away from. It paints your faces golden. It's huge.

You instantly imagine the spirits gathering around it, invisibly, acrobats and dancers, tumbling through the treetops, wild with freedom, drunk on the possibilities of this night. Your mind is in overdrive.

But you approach carefully. There will be adults here. "Bloody pagans," your neighbor called them, and his tone suggested that there was something wrong with them, so you looked up the word and didn't think they sounded so bad. Even so, you don't want them to see you. They are adults, after all, and all the adults you've ever known insist on bedtimes and rules.

It's easy to stay hidden. You and Teddy crouch on the far side of the huge bonfire from the main camp. You are hidden by the height of the pyre, and the flames. In the heart of the fire you recognize the glowing skeletons of pieces of furniture. Domesticity is burning.

You stare and Teddy does, too. The flames reach higher and higher, licking the darkness. Smoke rises in a twisting, fickle column. It seems to have a life of its own. You're exhilarated by it and by the sense that you have stepped outside of normal life and into a wild night.

There are quite a few people on the other side of the bonfire, but no other children; you are the only ones here. The people seem to exist in a parallel world of their own. The firelight reveals their features to you in fragments. One man has a bare chest, and sways with his arms upraised, facing the fire. A woman wears a crown of foliage and has ivy woven through a plait as thick as your arm. She is singing. Others huddle on the ground in circles.

The people you watch most closely are those who dance with a feral energy that's startling and infectious. You seize Teddy's arms and move them in a mimicry of the adults. He beams, his blankie falls to the ground, and together you stomp and turn until you're both out of breath and then you stand side by side again with heaving chests and through the flames you think you see a face, a painted face, with markings on the cheeks and wild hair, and the face is turned toward you both, watching back, but swiftly it's gone and you say to Teddy, with wonder, "Did you see the fairy king?" because you believe it was him.

7

Lucy," Dan whispered. We were in bed but in spite of my exhaustion, I couldn't sleep, my thoughts were racing. Light from the streetlamp outside our bedroom window filtered through the flimsy curtains.

"Yes."

"When you come back with me to the house, there's something special I didn't get to show you. I think it'll make all the difference."

"Okay," I whispered.

The drive there was just as bad for me as it had been the first time. I sat beside Dan with gritted teeth and clammy palms. When he opened the door, the air inside the house felt as suffocating as before.

"Imagine this house is somewhere else," he said. "Forget the woods. Forget Charlotte Close. Just focus on what you can see."

I tried. It worked, a little. I noticed more of the original features and I saw beauty in the proportions and charm in the details. I managed a small smile, for show.

"Are you ready to see the really good bit?" he asked.

He led me up the staircase. The second-floor landing was broad, room-sized itself, and some of the floorboards were in disrepair, rising at the corners, nails loosened and protruding. At least six doors led off the space, each of them closed. Dan opened one of them a fraction and said, "Do you mind if I cover your eyes?"

"Do you have to?"

"It'll be worth it."

He stood behind me and put his hands over my eyes. We shuffled through the doorway together, awkwardly. Claustrophobia crept up on me again. The only thing worse than being openly watched is being watched when you cannot see.

Just as I felt I needed to escape him, he pulled away his fingers—"You can look now!"—and I found myself in a room almost identical to the one I'd fainted in yesterday.

It also had views on two sides, with one side offering the same outlook into the woods as downstairs, but from this height it was possible to see the spread of the sky and over the top of the tree canopy where evergreens were interwoven with the bare branches of trees that had waited out a long winter and now, early in April, were longing for the weather to warm enough that their buds would burst into leaf. The view from the other set of windows would also have been of the woods, but it was mostly obscured by the boughs of a majestic cedar tree that grew on the lawn of our house.

"Lucy?" Dan said.

I turned away from the view, looked at him, and gradually the rest of the room came into focus around him.

Like the kitchen, it had been fully renovated. The paint smelled fresh, and the moldings had been restored so they were as stiff-peaked, crisp, and white as the meringue on the top of a pie. I took in the polished paneling, a veined marble fireplace with an elegant hearth, and the gleaming oak floor. I recognized a chandelier I'd admired months ago, in a high-end antiques shop that I'd felt too intimidated to enter.

"You got the chandelier?" I asked, though it felt as if I had to force the words out.

"I know you love it. What do you think of the desk?"

"It's huge."

"It's all for you. I made the space for you to write in. I organized it while we were in the cottage."

He looked so proud. I ran my fingers over the desk's surface and felt no attachment to it. It had none of the sweet charm of the desk in the cottage or the unthreatening modesty of the small kitchen table I wrote at in our flat. This room felt like a gilded cage. It was overwhelming, ridiculously grand. *He surely wants me to work*, I thought. *And why has he put me in here, where he knows the view will torment me?*

"Don't you want this room?" I said. "You should have it. You deserve it."

"This is for you. You need it. You have deadlines to work to," he said. How loaded that word had become since I had gotten deadlines, when he was the one who wanted them.

"Okay," I said. My voice sounded small.

He pulled me to him, unexpectedly, and his fingers trailed into the small of my back and slid beneath my waistband. I caught my breath. I was confused. It was so long since we'd been intimate. My body wanted him, but I didn't want this. Physical acquiescence felt like acceptance of the situation, like giving him what he wanted. I wasn't ready for that, and I didn't think he should get it so easily, not after what he'd done, but his hands were insistent, and I couldn't stop myself from responding. I had been so starved of physical affection.

As he kissed me again, more deeply, I thought that perhaps I should be grateful because this house and this beautiful renovation might just be the best and most thoughtful thing anyone had ever done for me. And then I didn't think at all.

We made love in the beautiful renovated office and it felt like it had at the beginning of our relationship, not the first time, because that was like the blind leading the blind, but a bit later, when we got better at it and were still delighted with one another. I forgot myself for those precious minutes and afterward I watched Dan dress and said, "I love you. Thank you for this," and I thought I meant it.

"I love you, too," he said, though it wasn't quite the moment it might have been, because he was struggling to get one of his legs into his trousers. He went downstairs. He wanted to check on something or other. I wasn't really listening. He still had the flushed excitement of a kid in a candy shop.

I put myself back together and stood in the center of the room. I felt myself drawn back to the window, transfixed by the aerial view of the woods.

I imagined the trees dissolving, one by one, until only the understory remained and then that, in its turn, disappeared and all I could see was earth. Protruding from it slightly, almost unnoticeable, even with the landscape stripped bare, was the slightly domed roof of a sunken building.

It was a place I hadn't revisited since Teddy disappeared.

The bunker.

8

Over the next few days the blows kept coming and I had no choice but to keep on absorbing them.

Dan announced that he had given notice on our tenancy of the flat while we were in Devon and a sheaf of flat-pack boxes was delivered there.

"A condition of buying the house was that we complete the sale very quickly. It was buy it or lose it. And you don't want to stay here, do you, when we could be there?"

I did want to stay here. I wanted it more than anything. This was my home. All the belonging I'd ever felt was to this place. My imagination had formed and re-formed wall and ceiling cracks into images that fed into my work. Every surface knew my finger-prints as well as I knew its texture. The daily blend of noises—the ticking pipes, car doors slamming outside, the creak of a cer-tain floorboard beneath the carpet, and all the others—was a soundtrack whose rhythm the clack of my laptop keys, even the beating of my heart, had kept time with. Hearing the soft click of the door behind me sounded like a sweet, safe welcome every single time I returned home. I wasn't ready to leave it.

But we had only a few days to move out, and while Dan sat on the floor and constructed the packing boxes, our land-lady, Patricia, who lived downstairs, called round with a tin of homemade shortbread and cried. Mascara bled down her heavily powdered cheeks.

"As soon as you got famous, I knew you'd go," she said. "Don't forget Patricia, will you?"

She was prone to exaggeration, but I was susceptible to her pout because I felt fond of her. I hugged her tight, catching a faint whiff of alcohol, and we held each other so long that her bony shoulders dug into my chin and strands of her hair fell from their tortoiseshell comb and became entangled with my earring.

Dan asked if he could leave a couple of small boxes in her flat for safekeeping, so they didn't get lost in the move.

"It's only paperwork. I'll collect it in a few days' time," he said.

"Of course, darling," she replied. "Happy to help." But she still looked mournful.

"Don't be fooled," Dan said after she'd gone. "She's already got new tenants lined up."

"What's in the boxes?" I asked.

"Stuff I don't want to lose track of."

"Why don't you just label it? Bring it in the car with us."

"Better safe than sorry," he said.

I thought this was odd, another example of his proclivity for pedantry since he'd taken control of our admin, but I had to pick my battles.

It was horribly painful for me to watch Dan packing our stuff away with brisk efficiency as if the time we'd spent here had meant nothing. Every time he sealed another box, it felt as if the tape was screeching with callous disregard for every memory I'd ever made. I couldn't bear to help him or even be a witness to it. It would be impossible to suppress the great wrench of grief that was building in me.

I told him I needed to check over something in the book. "But I'll get out of your way," I said. "I can go to a café."

"Have you heard from Max yet?" he asked, but he didn't sound worried. I'd never had anything less than an enthusiastic reception for my first drafts before.

"Not yet. I think he had another manuscript to read first." I tried to say it lightly.

Dan frowned. I knew he wanted to ask, "Whose manuscript is more important than yours?" because I was Max's highest-earning client, and I held my breath because I was afraid he was going to start nagging me to put pressure on Max and the conversation was going to go to a place where I'd have no choice but to tell him what I'd done, but he let it go.

I went to my favorite café, where I logged on to the WiFi and visited the Eliza Grey fan fiction page. It was something I couldn't resist doing, a sort of masochism, given what was happening, but I was fascinated by the way people appropriated my creation. I had mixed feelings about it: a queasy combination of flattery and discomfort, but sometimes mixed feelings are the hardest to resist indulging in. They can make us feel alive.

At the top of the page was a banner:

This Is the Fan Fiction Page for Detective Sergeant Eliza Grey, Heroine of Lucy Harper's Series. 10 Million Copies Sold and Counting! Join Us!

I read a few new stories and tutted where they had gotten details about Eliza wrong, but they were fun to read, a good distraction. I never commented on the stories but I visited the page often enough that the people who posted had become familiar to me and felt a bit like a community. I was excited to see a new post there from someone I hadn't spotted on the site for a while: MrElizaGrey. I'd always enjoyed his stories about Eliza. Of all the people who posted, he was the one who really understood her character, who got her. Sometimes to an uncanny degree. I clicked on his post.

Woke up before Eliza today. She slept naked. Ready for me.

"Oh!" I said. I blinked at the screen. What he'd written was partly accurate. Eliza did sleep naked, that was in the books, but she never let anyone stay the night with her. She was a commit-mentphobe, married to her job, in charge of her own life. Her affairs were passionate, but she kept her partners at arm's length. I read on, pressing my fingers against my mouth, which formed an O behind them.

I reached for her, woke her the way she liked the most. She pushed back into me and spread—

"Ew!" I said, out loud. This was Eliza porn, especially shock-ing because MrElizaGrey had never written anything explicit before. I closed the web page and felt my cheeks redden. I glanced around the café, worried I looked as grubby as I felt, but the other customers hadn't noticed a thing, they were all plugged in. What MrElizaGrey had written was grim; it felt like a violation. I wondered how long it would take for the page admin to take it down.

Eliza laughed. "I've had worse from my colleagues," she said, and it was true. If anyone in the Criminal Investigation Depart-ment tried it with her, she gave as good as she got. My girl was braver than I ever would be, quicker with a retort, master of the crushing comeback.

"Oh," she added. "Max is phoning."

I looked at my phone. I'd set it to silent and now Max's name had appeared on the screen. I snatched it up.

"How are you?" he asked. I didn't love his tone. It seemed weighted somehow.

"What's wrong? You don't like the book?"

"We have a problem."

"Why?"

"It's a big problem. We're very worried."

"'We'?" Usually, Max and I discussed the book together be-fore involving my editor. "You talked to Angela before talking to me?"

A beat of silence resonated before he said, "You've delivered a book that's in breach of contract."

"I haven't." Why was he starting with this negativity? Hadn't the book impressed him at all?

"They paid for an Eliza Grey novel. And she's horribly incapacitated by the end of the first chapter. It's shocking."

"No. The contract says, 'a book provisionally titled "The Truth."' There's no mention of it being an Eliza Grey novel."

I heard him exhale heavily. Max had a tic where he removed his glasses and massaged his forehead before replacing them and I imagined him doing it now.

He hadn't checked the contract, clearly, and I guessed that Angela hadn't, either. It was lazy wording. Somewhere at the publishing house, a head was going to roll and there would be a mighty thunk as it hit the floor.

"Did you like the book, though?" I asked because I believed that was the real question. If the novel was as good as I hoped, as I knew in my heart it was, the contractual stuff was a moot point because Angela would be gagging to publish it.

"Why didn't you talk to me about cutting Eliza from the book?" The question sounded reasonable; Max's tone of voice, not so much. "You can talk to me about anything, you know." Except that I couldn't. Nobody knew everything about me except Eliza.

"But did you like it?" I asked. I shouldn't have raised my voice, I'd never raised my voice to Max before, but I did then. *Please say yes, please say yes*, looped through my mind in the silence that followed.

"Okay, I think this conversation got off on the wrong foot," Max said eventually. "I did like this book you've written, it's a very good book, but the problem we have is that your readers want an Eliza Grey book."

My stomach took a swan dive. "Like this book." "Like" was,

is, a supremely dangerous word in publishing, where superlatives are the most common currency. I was being damned with faint praise.

"Lucy." He said my name so slowly and deliberately that I was made acutely aware that he was handling me, and it was one of those times my career felt like a corset being cinched incrementally tighter. "They don't want the book. I'm sorry."

"What about the Americans?"

"Same story."

"But the contract . . ."

"If you're right about the contract, we can *possibly* insist that they accept this book and pay for it, but it will impact hugely on any new negotiations, as in, there might not be any. That's the bottom line."

I blinked back tears. "But did you like it?" I asked one more time. My voice sounded feeble and small.

"In the publishers' opinion, and mine, it's not sufficiently marketable."

Worse than "like," "not sufficiently marketable" were words of terrible doom, words a writer never wanted to hear unless she had another income.

"So, they're not going to pay?"

"Not for this novel in this form, no. I'm sorry."

I had thought the risks through so far as money went, or I thought I had, but clearly, I'd grossly overestimated my value because I'd had no idea it rested so completely on Eliza.

"The house," I said.

"What house?"

"We're moving."

"I didn't know."

"I didn't know about it myself until this week. Dan bought a house without telling me. It's a reno job."

"What?"

I didn't know what to say. It was humiliating. I heard Max exhale.

"So, you need money?"

"We will do."

"The way out of this is to put Eliza back into the book. I have every confidence that it's doable because you're such a talented writer. What do you think?"

"I'll think about it," I said, and hung up. If I'd said any more, I would have broken down and I didn't want Max to hear me like that. It was too shameful. He tried to call back, but I didn't pick up.

I packed up my stuff and went out into the cold afternoon. The city streets were swarming with people. I began to walk home before realizing I didn't want to go back there, not yet, and I stopped abruptly. A woman collided with me, knocking both of us off balance. "Hey!" she said.

She leaned over to pick up her bag. She wore clothing that Eliza might wear when she was off-duty, jeans, boots, and a khaki jacket, and had the same athletic physique, the long red hair, and I held my breath as she turned to me, waiting to see Eliza's eyes, slightly hooded and darkly liquid, just as I had written them, with their slow blink that made you feel as if she had all the time in the world to unpick you psychologically. I had made many characters squirm beneath that gaze. I braced myself to be the subject of it, and also because I was afraid of seeing the injuries I'd inflicted on her.

But it wasn't Eliza. This woman was older, her face entirely different, and the relief I felt made me bark out a laugh. She looked at me as if I was crazy. "Watch where you're going," she said. I apologized and as I walked on, not knowing where I was going to go, all I could think about was how if I put Eliza back in the books, I would see her everywhere again, around every corner, in crowds, sitting beside me on the bus, in bed.

"You won't," Eliza said. "I promise."

I walked on, pushing past more people, but it seemed as if the world around me had tilted a little and I tried to think about how I was going to tell Dan what Max had said, and I had no idea.

It was much later when I let myself into the flat and Dan shouted, "Where have you been? I just heard the vans are coming at nine tomorrow morning. You need to pack your stuff," and I knew this was a moment when I should come clean but all I could say was "Okay, then," because I had no idea where to start explaining and I felt as if I was drowning in all of the change.

We moved the next day, as planned. I had a sleepless night. We both did. Dan mistook my restlessness for excitement, and I let him.

I felt as if I was barely there while our boxes were loaded into the van. When the flat door shut behind us for the last time it was a brutal severance, a final silencing of all the gentle whispers our home and I had exchanged. Leaving the city was horrible. As we drove across the bridge a taut knot of anxiety formed in the pit of my stomach and it tightened as we approached the new house.

When Dan stopped the car, he put his hand on my knee and squeezed. "Welcome home," he said, "and welcome to the beginning of the rest of our lives."

"Put a brave face on it," Eliza said. "You've got no choice now."

"Welcome home to you, too," I said.

I didn't know who to hate more in that moment, myself, or him for bringing me back here.

I stood beside the car for the longest time before I walked into the house. I could see the tops of the trees in Stoke Woods. I imagined their trunks bleeding memories like sap and the rustling leaves whispering accusations, and when I listened harder, I could make out the voices of the search party being carried on the wind, and my brother's name.

It doesn't take long for Teddy to get tired and it hurts when he tries to sit on you. The heels of his shoes dig into your calves and his weight is enough to make your ankles feel crushed. He's just said it for the first time: "I want to go home," and every cell in your body is willing him not to say it again, but his eyes have gone glassy with fatigue and you know you're on borrowed time.

You also know you can't leave now because of the burning inside you, the hot tug of wanting to stay. You think that if you walk away from here now and go back into the woods, then everything around you will go gray again and you'll have to retreat back into your head to find color.

There, it's always Technicolor, kaleidoscopic and packed so full of thoughts and feelings that sometimes it feels as if it might explode.

9

On our first morning in the new house, I crept out of bed quietly so as not to wake Dan. He had been up late, unpacking, moving stuff around, pacing the rooms. I'd heard the drag of furniture and his footsteps on the bare floors for what seemed like hours as I tried to get to sleep.

It was close to dawn and the darkness was tinged blue and friable. I made my way downstairs cautiously, not wanting to turn lights on, because that would make the fact of this house more real, but it meant I was spooked by each unfamiliar feature as it emerged from the gloom.

I sat at the kitchen table facing the expanse of window. It was noticeably quiet here compared to our flat. I was used to waking to traffic noise, a background drone of sirens, the rumble of trains. Here, there was birdsong and it occurred to me that I should take pleasure in it, but instead I couldn't help imagining baby birds in their nests, bald, vulnerable, and needy, beaks stretched wide open to reveal bottomless red gullets.

I wanted to expel that image from my mind and stared hard at the strip of sky I could see above the hedges but it didn't metamorphose as quickly as I thought it would, and it occurred to me this might be a good time to try to locate my friend the coffeepot.

"Why are you sitting in the dark?"

Dan's voice startled me. I hadn't heard him approach.

"I'm enjoying the dawn chorus," I said. It was an answer I

knew he'd approve of. I usually kept a few of those up my sleeve because he liked it when I conformed to his idea of what a creative person should be like.

The light switch snapped, and I blinked as the halogens deluged the room with light.

"Coffee?" he asked.

"I'll make it." Between books, it was important to demonstrate that I was willing to do stuff for myself, or Dan felt taken for granted.

I got up and took over the coffee making and he leaned against the glistening countertop to stretch. His running gear looked brand-new. "Run with me?" he asked.

"No way." I laughed, and he did, too, because he knew I'd say that. I hated exercise.

Once he'd gone, I turned out the lights again, cradled the mug in my hands, and thought, *When did he acquire that gear and when did he get so mad keen on running that he'd be up and out this early on the weekend? Has he been doing this in Devon while I was shuttered in my writing room?*

I was beginning to understand that while I'd been writing, Dan had been doing far more than I had ever imagined.

He texted me a photograph from the Suspension Bridge. The sun was just rising over Bristol, a lurid orange glow splitting the sky at the horizon, silhouetting treetops and rooftops. He wrote:

> Isn't this glorious? Btw I ran into Sasha. She and James say WELCOME (caps intentional by order of Sasha) and are organizing drinks so we can meet the other neighbors. Xxx

It torpedoed my mood. I hated parties. Every aspect of them inflicted psychological torment upon me. I was terrible at small talk and intimidated by big groups of people. I scoffed at the "caps intentional," considering it proof that Sasha was no more substantial than a social media hysteric. And I wondered where Dan had run into her. At the end of her driveway, I supposed. I knew now that she and her husband had the first house on our lane. Perhaps she had been exercising, too. Probably.

I felt my midriff. The end-of-book muffin top wasn't going to disappear anytime soon, that was for sure, nor was my exhaustion. I felt heavy-limbed and sluggish. I didn't reply to Dan but put my phone on the table facedown. Sometimes, the act of prodding at the screen could feel as dumb as a chicken pecking dirt, the gains no more substantial.

The sun still hadn't reached our garden, though the air was visibly brightening, finally. My eyes roved the shadows and caught something unusual. Down at our perimeter, where the lawn met the woods, I thought I saw the silhouette of a man standing, staring straight at me. I froze. Blinked. Refocused. He was still there. He looked tall and solidly built. He stood facing me with his arms hanging loosely by his sides. The posture of someone who is not threatened but could be threatening. I couldn't see any more detail than that, though, and a second later I wasn't even completely sure it was a man and not a shadow, yet I felt the threat viscerally, as a shudder, a premonition of violence, and I couldn't shift my gaze away.

He didn't move and neither did I for what felt like the longest time, until I steeled myself to stand up. I took two paces to the side, my eyes still fixed on the shadow, on him, and as I reached to switch on the outside lights all the tender places in my body felt both tense and intensely vulnerable, as if anticipating the slash of a knife. A bright glare washed the terrace outside, and I realized I'd made a mistake because it was impossible for me to see out now, and that was more frightening than seeing. I switched the lights off again and he had gone. The light had changed, the shadows shifted.

I remained in that spot, immobile. My chest was heaving. I gave myself a talking-to, telling myself that I must have imagined what I saw at the edge of the woods, that it was my past playing tricks on me, but fear rooted me there for minutes until the garden and the edge of the woods were soaked with light. Then it felt safe to move again.

I felt bleak and hollow in the aftermath of this little drama.

"Do you think someone was there?" I asked Eliza.

"I don't know," she said. "It was hard to tell."

When Dan got home, I told him what had happened.

"Where was he standing?" Dan looked toward the spot I pointed to. A bead of sweat crept down his forehead. "It must have been a shadow," he said.

"It didn't look like a shadow. It was more solid than that."

"Who's going to be out at that time in the morning, sneaking around?"

"I don't know."

"I think maybe you imagined it. You know what you're like."

I certainly did. And I needed help.

I said, "We need to talk."

10

They've rejected the book," I told Dan, and the concerned expression fell from his face and shattered on the floor like a piece of dropped porcelain. I stared at the shards until they disappeared. I was afraid to raise my eyes to his. I kept them fixed on the flooring while I explained what I'd done.

"You spent nine months writing a whole new book without Eliza in it, without telling anybody? You didn't tell *me*?"

Dan rarely shouted. Instead, his voice had altered more subtly than that, as if he'd marinated it in disdain overnight.

I snapped back, "You didn't tell me about the house!"

"I wouldn't have bought the house if you'd told me what you'd done. What were you thinking?"

"Maybe I wouldn't have done it if I'd known what you were up to."

"What makes you think you can just do something like that?"

"Because I'm the bloody writer!"

"You have no idea." He shook his head, as if I was irredeemably stupid. "No idea how much I prop you up."

I had an urge to scream at the absolute, total unfairness of that, but instead I said, "Let's not forget that any propping up you do is funded by me."

I left the room and he scrambled to follow, catching me easily, grabbing me painfully by the elbow as I reached the hall. It forced me to halt and we stood there, too close, exhaling contempt right into each other's face, and it felt overwhelming.

I yanked my arm out of his grasp. He surprised me by making a sudden gesture of surrender: hands raised, palms out.

"Hey," he said. "I'm so sorry. I didn't mean to grab you. You scared me. This is a shock. I'm sorry."

He made to touch me again but thought better of it when I flinched. Hurt twitched in the backs of his eyes. I still wanted to leave, but I forced myself to absorb his words, his contrite tone, and the way he looked as if he'd shocked himself by grabbing me. My anger shriveled a little and the frisson of fear I'd felt disappeared. I shouldn't alienate him. I loved him. I would be completely alone, without him.

"It's just . . ." he said, and his brow crinkled as he sought the right words. "What about your delivery payment?"

"There won't be one."

"Fuck."

"I know."

"Then how do we fix this? Can you put Eliza back in the book?"

"No."

"Surely it's not impossible. What have you written? Could you work her into it or even start from scratch? You wrote the draft of book three in just a few months."

"What if I've written the book I wanted to write?"

Anger flashed in Dan's eyes. There wasn't a shred of contrition to be seen in them now, neither was there sympathy. "I thought you said you never wanted to become a diva?" he said.

It felt like a body blow, after all the work I'd done, the times I'd pushed myself to the brink of exhaustion and beyond. I ran upstairs, slamming and locking the bathroom door before he could follow me in there, turning on the taps to drown out the sound of him shouting, then apologizing, then pleading for us to talk about things like adults.

He stopped, after a while. I put the lid down on the loo

and sat there thinking of how naïve I'd been when I first got published. How I hadn't realized what a treadmill I was stepping onto. How the sheer pace of it, and the exhaustion, eroded your confidence and then chipped away at your sanity, how it made you vulnerable because the books crowded every corner of your brain, every minute of every day, until your main character stepped off the page and compromised your real life, which made you feel crazy. How your husband took too much control while you were buried in your fictional world.

How he lost respect for you.

Treated you like a commodity.

Did he even love me anymore? And if not, what did he want? I wondered.

I stood up and looked in the mirror. I smoothed back the skin on my cheeks and the years fell away and I wondered whether Dan was doing something more than just seeking a renovation project. He had to want us here, by Stoke Woods, for a reason. I just didn't know what it was.

My phone rang. It was Max. I didn't pick up. I couldn't face it. A text followed.

> We're coming to see you. Tomorrow. Angela and me. She wants
> to see you in person to talk about how we can turn this situation
> around. I've booked a table somewhere nice.

"Oh, God, no," I said.

This had never happened before. Usually, I went to them, got on the train to London, made a day of it. That they were coming here gave me a sense of shifting power, but it was a slippery sense, difficult to decipher. They wanted an Eliza book. They had used the stick, threatening not to pay me for it, and now this was the carrot, because if they wanted Eliza, they needed me.

I would go, I decided, and listen to what they had to say. A small, hopeful part of me wondered if I might be able to talk

Angela into reconsidering the novel I'd written. I still felt proud of it, hopeful for it.

"Maybe just talk to them about putting me back in the book?" Eliza said.

"I can't."

"You could, you know," she said. "Trust me."

I scrunched my eyes shut and put my hands over my ears and hummed a song that Teddy used to love.

How could I trust anyone else when I couldn't even trust myself?

V

Teddy is still heavy on your lap. He hasn't revived. He says he's too tired to dance any longer, even though you're desperate to keep going. You want to worship that fire like a whirling dervish. But at least you're more comfortable now. You've shifted him to a better position, and the ground where you sit feels soft and dry.

"Take him home," Eliza whispers.

"He's okay," you tell her, and you tighten your arms around him.

The scene beyond the bonfire is more enthralling than ever. The people have formed a circle and are holding hands, their faces turned to the darkness above. Chanting starts up, low at first, impossible to understand, but growing louder, and above the spit and crackle of the fire, words are repeated over and over, and you feel as if they're casting a spell on you, drawing you in, as if something more important than all of you is happening, and it includes you and Teddy and Eliza, and you look up to the skies just like the people do and you understand that they are communicating with the spirits, because that's possible on a night such as this when what is real melts away and the unreal is invited out to play. You've been obsessed with this idea since you read about it. On the summer solstice night there's no need to shut your eyes or open a book to make an enchanted world come to life.

"Can you feel it, Teddy?" you whisper into his hair.

"Teddy can," he says, even though his eyelids are drooping and he's nuzzling his blankie.

11

That night, Dan and I slept in different rooms, and in the morning he made it clear he was still sulking by sighing loudly and a lot.

When I told him—and I purposely waited until late morning because he hated it when I withheld publishing news of any sort from him—that I was going to lunch with Max and Angela, he warmed up and hovered closer, predictably enough. He had questions and he wanted details. I told him the bare minimum.

He helped me put my coat on and picked a hair off my lapel. "You can tell how much you mean to everyone, and how much Eliza means to them, if they're dashing down here to wine and dine you at this short notice," he said. "They wouldn't do that for every author."

I drove into Bristol to collect Angela and Max from the station. I didn't need to, but I wanted to show I was making an effort. It perhaps wasn't the best idea. After a few minutes in traffic, my nerves about the lunch had built, my hands gripped the wheel too tightly, and my head felt so scrambled that I wasn't sure I should be driving at all.

On the way there I found myself at a stoplight outside the cinema where Dan and I had met. So much had happened in the last few years that I sometimes forgot where we had started. He had worked at this cinema. Introduced by a mutual acquaintance, we'd been a match made in heaven and it had been a simple courtship: opinionated, geeky boy meets shy, geeky girl, both are virgins in spite of being a few years into their twenties, both socially awkward, a little bit emotionally needy, but they share a passion for writing, film, art, music, all things creative. They talk and talk. They fall in love and move in together, feeling lucky, full of dreams.

And for the longest time we were settled and happy, with Dan actively pursuing his writing alongside his part-time job, his ambition soaring, me working full-time and writing, too, but more as a hobby, downplaying it so I didn't steal his thunder.

I loved our life then. If you've experienced trauma as a kid, what you want most as an adult is a still pool to bathe in, one where you can see the edges, where the surface of the water is glassy. How ironic it was my writing that had shattered the calm for us; that I had found a literary agent and publisher in just months after Dan had spent years trying to get representation for his work, and that things had moved unstoppably for us ever since then.

Where would we be now, I wondered, if I'd never published a book? Happier? Apart? And what if Dan's dreams had come true and he were in my shoes? It was impossible to know.

Angela, my editor, looked larger than life when she emerged from the station. There was a polish to her plumage, as if she'd brought a little bit of London with her. She stood in the station forecourt and scanned the car park, looking for me. Max, a few steps behind her, was dapper in a peacoat, dark slim jeans, and brogues. His thick-rimmed glasses made me think of Scandinavian architects.

I drove us to the restaurant.

"I've never been to Bristol before," Angela said. "It's very nice." I glanced at her in the rearview mirror. She was in the back seat, gazing out a side window, her view a grimy budget hotel that loomed over the choked traffic lanes, part of its signage missing. I understood that I wasn't the only one here feeling nervous.

The restaurant was on the first floor of a Georgian building with wide views across the floating harbor. It was fancy.

"I have something for you," Angela said, "because I want you to know what you mean to us."

She drew a large envelope from her bag and passed it to me. My name was inscribed on the front in beautiful cursive handwriting. I opened it, ineptly tearing off little scraps of paper that scattered unattractively on the table before I managed to access the contents. I pulled out a card. The front was a montage of the covers of all my Eliza books and inside were dozens of handwritten testimonials from members of my publishing team. Each one began with "I love Eliza because . . ."

I read them all and could sense Eliza reading them, too. The card was a master class in emotional blackmail, I knew that, but it affected me, too. I loved Eliza just as much as they did, in fact more than they did because she'd been part of me for as long as I could remember. The card touched a nerve.

I glanced at Max, wondering if he had known about the card and not forewarned me. He was studying his menu intently, so that was a yes.

"Your books are a very rare thing," Angela said. "Often, I buy a book because I love it, and I find *some* of my colleagues share my enthusiasm, but it's very seldom that I discover an author whose books appeal to *everybody* in the company. And that's you, Lucy. Over the years I've asked myself what the secret of your books is. Why do they speak to so many of us? There's so much to recommend them, obviously, there really is so much to admire, but I think the last few days have brought home to me once and for all that the thing that touches people's hearts is Eliza Grey."

"Wow," I said. It was quite the speech. Angela was usually tersely efficient, speaking of sales figures and other measurable things.

I buttered a piece of bread because I didn't know what to do with compliments from anyone, let alone her, but I felt a little tremor in my hands, and butter smeared my fingers. To wipe it off, I had to dismantle my starched napkin, which had been folded elaborately into the shape of a swan.

"This is what your creation means to us all," Angela continued, oblivious. "This! You did this! You move people." She pointed repeatedly at the back of the card. I understood that she wanted more from me by way of response.

"Thank you," I said.

"I feel the same," Max said. He leaned forward. "Angela and I have an idea. We believe you can make this novel into an Eliza book that'll be as much of a smash hit as the others."

"We don't think it'll take much work," Angela said. "I've put together some detailed notes with Della. We even think Eliza could take a bit of an exciting new direction."

"Della?" I asked. She was my editor in New York. Hearing that she'd been involved made me feel as if the net I was caught in was closing.

"Della loves the idea that we can turn this around," Max said.

"She's really excited," Angela added. "Do you think you can do it?"

I prevaricated. "I'd need to see the notes."

"The notes are nothing you can't handle. You are such a good writer."

"We know you can do it," Max added.

I swallowed. The waitress passed our table and I wished I could follow her into the kitchen and go straight out the back door.

"I probably can," I said, "but should I?"

It was a response so weak and evasive that I hated myself for it, but I had to say something.

"Of course you should!" Angela said. "People love your work.

They love Eliza." She picked up the card again. "These messages are just from us, your publishers, but imagine how many there would be if all the readers out there who love your work and love Eliza had written one, too."

I thought of the fan fiction. "I guess," I said. "Maybe I could."

"Is that a yes?" Angela said. Her voice had risen and the people at the table next to ours were rubbernecking as if it was a marriage proposal they were witnessing. Max was saying nothing, nor was Eliza.

"I could think about it," I said.

Angela put her palm on her chest. "You've made my day. You've made my week, actually. I think this calls for a celebration."

Before I figured out how to stress that I was only going to consider their suggestion and that I hadn't actually agreed to it, she asked the waitress for a bottle of champagne. She and Max were wreathed in smiles. A cold bottle materialized, was displayed and opened and three flutes filled with the same liquid gold that Dan and I had drunk together so recently, though it felt as if that moment had taken place in another world.

I watched, aghast, mute, with the sense that I was observing someone else's life, as Angela raised her glass. "To you, dear Lucy. Author *extraordinaire*. To Eliza. Character *exceptionnelle*. To all of us working and moving forward together. Thank you so much for agreeing to do this. I can't tell you how grateful we are that you've been so understanding. Not all authors are."

We drank. Max and I sipped our drinks, Angela threw hers back and I admired how unashamed she was to display her appetites. She seemed so much larger than me, than anyone else in the room, in that moment. Max was still denying me anything other than the most fleeting eye contact.

After swallowing the champagne I stared at my menu. Even with my reading glasses on, the fine italics swam in front of my eyes. Angela began to talk about what she wanted to order, as if the business end of our conversation was over. I glanced at Max again, still trying to gauge his feelings and the extent of his collaboration with her, which I was coming to think was a full-fledged betrayal of me.

"I think I'm going to have the *boeuf bourguignon*," he said, "with sides of spinach and dauphinoise potatoes."

I looked again at my menu. The letters finally swam into order well enough that I could read the words, but I couldn't process them, not with my heart pounding in my ears.

"You should have the hake," Eliza said, "it's the easiest to digest if you're anxious," and I snapped, "No!" because it was outrageous and upsetting that she was, even at this moment, trying to tell me what to eat.

Angela and Max looked at me, surprised. I realized I'd said it out loud.

"You don't think I should have the *boeuf bourguignon*?" Max asked.

"I think you'd prefer the hake," I said, trying to cover up the outburst. My cheeks were flaming.

"Oh," he said. "I didn't see the hake."

We stared at our menus again. A ripple of laughter rose and fell among the diners at a table across the room. Max cleared his throat and I felt him glance at me but I kept my eyes on the list of entrées.

When the waitress came back, Max ordered the *boeuf bourguignon* anyway and I felt obliged to get the hake and every bite tasted like paper in my mouth and while Angela and Max gossiped about people I didn't know, I imagined myself eating the pages of each and every one of my Eliza novels one by one and I thought, *They can all go to hell, everyone who wants Eliza back in the books.*

It was a pathetic attempt at emotional bravado, though. Hard on its heels I felt a twist of fear because I realized that if they did actually go away, including Dan, I would be left with no one at all except Eliza.

I lifted my champagne glass and drained it in one just as Angela had.

12

I probably shouldn't have driven home. I wasn't sure how much champagne I'd had because Angela had been topping up the glasses freely. She and Max obviously thought I'd drunk enough because they declined my offer of a lift to the station and I stood under the awning outside the restaurant and watched them walk away together, and felt like running after them, even though I didn't know what I would say if I caught up.

I felt wrung out and torn, damned if I put Eliza into the books and damned if I didn't.

At the multistory car park, I put my ticket in the machine, paid the fee, and walked up the concrete stairs to the third floor, each step squeaking sharply, echoing above and below in the stairwell. I was panting by the time I reached the correct floor and paused after pushing through the door into the parking area to catch my breath. Apart from the parked cars, the place looked deserted, but I heard footsteps and felt the hairs on the back of my neck stand up.

"Who's there?" I said, and my voice echoed. The acoustics were strange. I realized the footsteps were probably coming from another floor of the car park, but I couldn't shake the feeling Eliza was there, somewhere, as if the publishers had torn a gap in the wall I'd built around her that was just big enough for her to crawl back through and appear to me in person.

I turned sharply. Was she behind me? I turned again. Was that her leaning against a car? I saw that it was a trick of the eye, a pair of headlamps from a car coming down the ramp, its beams passing across the pillar where I thought I saw her.

"Hey!" she said. "Relax. I'm not out there. See your car? Go and get in."

I did as she told me and leaned my forehead on the steering wheel.

"I don't know if I should drive," I said.

"You're fine. You only had a little more than a glass. I was watching," Eliza said. "Relax."

"You sure?" I felt shaky as I turned on the ignition.

"Just take it easy."

I wanted so badly to drive home to my old flat and felt more and more anxious and depressed as I headed toward the Suspension Bridge. When I reached the bridge, it took me a few attempts to pay the toll. A car behind me sounded its horn. I drove across at a snail's pace. I could see Stoke Woods on the other side.

At the far end of the bridge, I found myself stuck behind a cyclist so I couldn't accelerate away and the car behind began to tailgate me. It was an SUV and I couldn't see the driver because they sat too high up. There was nothing I could do. Ahead, the cyclist was weaving across the lane. Oncoming traffic prevented me from passing. I felt flustered.

The SUV dropped back for a few moments before driving right up behind me again. I tapped on my brakes to show the lights and warn it off, but it had no effect. If anything, the SUV moved closer. The cyclist extended her arm in a signal and I waited for her to make a turn off the road, all the time glancing in my mirror. My lane was coming up and as soon as the cyclist was gone, I accelerated and flicked on my indicator light to let the vehicle know that I was going to turn, in the hope that the driver would back off, but in a break in the oncoming traffic it suddenly lurched out of my rearview mirror and roared up beside me, too fast and too close.

My hands were gripping the wheel and I swerved instinctively away and ran onto the curb at the junction with my lane and bumped over the slim verge into a patch of scrubby grass. I hit the brakes so hard that I was flung forward and back again. I screamed and the sound was swallowed by silence. The SUV had gone. There were no other cars in sight. No one else had witnessed what had happened. I hadn't caught a license plate and wasn't even sure what model the car was or its precise color, beyond pale. I didn't even know whether it had been intentionally aggressive.

I was tempted to get out of the car and walk home, but I was only a few hundred yards away, so I repeated, "Hold it together," to myself until I thought I could, and put the car into reverse and backed carefully onto the end of our lane. Now I could see the patch of ragged and uneven grass where I had ended up, and the large trees butting against it, and I understood how much worse things could have been if I hadn't hit the brakes quickly. The strange thing was that there was no trace that the car had been there. No tire marks.

I felt a tear slide down my cheek and rubbed my neck. I didn't think I had suffered whiplash, but I felt as if my body had been shaken up and put back wrong.

I drove on down our lane very carefully, avoiding the potholes. I imagined I might break into little pieces if I hit one. The copper beeches lining the right-hand side of the lane cast shadows across it at regular intervals. It was like driving through a slowed-down strobe light. Light. Dark. Light. Dark. I had the sense of being in a book, of driving into the woods, becoming a player in a fairy tale where the ending was not going to be good. On the other side, my new neighbors' homes looked immovable and imperturbable.

As I turned into our driveway, I had the disorienting sensation that I wasn't quite sure what had happened, or even whether it had happened at all.

VI

Teddy starts to wriggle unhappily. His elbows dig into you, and his expression collapses from smooth-faced, sleepy wonder into petulance. He whines: he's tired, he needs a wee, he wants to go home. You try everything to change his mind, but it's no use.

"Fine!" you tell him, and you start the walk home, marching too fast for him because you're disappointed, not quite yanking him along but not walking at a pace he can keep up with, either. You don't want to admit it, but you feel a little bit tired yourself. It's not going to stop you enjoying this night you've been dreaming of, though.

You think of the scene you're leaving behind you. It feels like turning your back on something special. Something magical. This is typical of Teddy. He ruins so much of what you want to do. You're sick of looking after him when your mum tells you to, which is all the time, sick of the way they always blame you if there's a sibling argument, sick of Teddy's clinginess. You wanted this night for yourself so badly and now he's wrecking it.

"You're going too fast," he moans. You think he's walking deliberately slowly. "Come on!" you snap. You've been holding on to the hope that you might be able to take him home and sneak back out again, but that idea is fading with the glacial pace of each step he takes. He's hanging on your arm now. He feels twice as heavy as he did earlier. "Teddy!" you say. You yank him and he trips and falls, grazing his knee on the stony path. You help him up and there is a moment of silent shock before his chin quivers and he howls in tired, hurt despair. You cuddle and reassure him. He wants to hold the torch, then he doesn't want to hold it. You cajole him and talk *sternly to him, then cajole him again. He says he's trying to be good, but the leg is too sore to walk on. He starts to hop and cries again. You pick him up. His head droops onto your shoulder. He's very heavy and you know you can't carry him all the way home.*

That's when it occurs to you that you could take him to your den.

"No," Eliza whispers. "It's our special place. He'll tell somebody about it."

"I don't know what else to do," you say.

13

Dan wasn't home when I got in from seeing Max and Angela. Our worn and snug sofa from the flat had been installed in one of the unrenovated reception rooms that didn't overlook the woods. It looked like dollhouse furniture. I lay on it and pulled a blanket over myself.

I was still angry with Dan, but the exhausted, confused, and frightened part of me also wanted him. I fretted that he hadn't left a note to say where he'd gone. I told myself it was because he was still cross with me, but I couldn't help remembering the time that he had gone missing before.

I obsessed over the impossibility of knowing what to do about Eliza. I didn't know if I could ever work out a way to keep her in the books, but out of my life.

I thought about how ironic it was that the first time Eliza appeared to me "in person," it had felt as if something amazing was happening. I was writing my third novel at the time and I actually believed that Eliza's physical manifestation meant that I'd reached a kind of peak writerly success. I could visualize my character in three dimensions! Hold conversations with her in person, not just in my mind! It was more than just a little intoxicating. And, yes, naïve of me.

The truth was that I had been sleep-deprived and under intense deadline pressure for the first time when I had my Eliza epiphany. It wasn't healthy. I was waking up gasping from dreams in which I fought for air, isolating myself from the world, over-eating, drinking too much coffee, too much alcohol, collapsing mentally as I battled my way toward the end of the book, my schedule catching up with me even back then, two books ago.

I didn't recognize that Eliza's appearance signaled a dangerous melding of reality and fiction. She was a gift horse from my imagination and I really should have looked her in the mouth.

I lay under that blanket for so long that I felt paralyzed by my own inertia, by the heaviness of my limbs, by the uncertainty of what might happen next. As my mind skipped from one anxiety to the next and circled them uselessly, shadows crept out of cracks and corners and the house fell dark around me. I'd lost track of time and wished I'd thought to put on some lights, but I couldn't bring myself to move.

I was roused from a semislumber by the slam of the front door and the clink of car keys as they fell on the hall table. I blinked when the hall light snapped on. My limbs still felt leaden.

I saw Dan in the hallway. I should have called out to him, but I didn't. Instead I watched him. He was carrying a plastic shopping bag and his expression was grim. He didn't call for me, either, only glanced briefly upstairs as if he assumed that I was in bed, or in my office, and walked through to the kitchen. Eventually, he returned. As he reached to flip the switch in the room I lay in, I said, "Don't," and he said, "Fuck! You scared the life out of me! Have you been here the whole time? Why are you lying in the dark?"

"Where did you go?" My voice was hoarse. I was afraid of what he was going to say. I didn't know if our row from last night was still at the forefront of his mind.

"To get some food. We've got nothing for tonight. Don't forget we're due at Sasha's for drinks at eight."

I was relieved he didn't seem to want to get stuck back into an argument now, so I didn't provoke him. I supposed it had been hours since I'd gotten back from lunch, if it was dinnertime. I'd forgotten about the party, which at least meant I hadn't spent time dreading it, but I felt my nerves ramp up now.

Dan held up a package. It looked familiar. "Cloudberry jam," he said.

"Delivered here?"

"Yep."

"How did they know we'd moved? It's creepy."

"I honestly don't think it's a threat. Think of it as a house-warming present. I got us some steak. I could bring you a glass of wine while I cook?" My heart tumbled a little, on its relief cycle. Wine followed by steak was a tried-and-true olive-branch substitute in our relationship. Dan had a near-perfect track record of defusing our rows with a display of the sort of domestic prowess I could never manage.

"That would be very nice," I said. "Thank you."

"Make room."

I bent my legs to make room for him on the sofa beside me. He pulled my blanket across both of us, smoothed it down, and took my hand.

"How was your lunch?" he asked.

I shrugged and looked down. He knitted his fingers in between mine.

"What kind of book did you write?" he asked. "If it wasn't an Eliza book."

"It doesn't matter."

"I'd like to know."

"They won't publish it. That's all you need to know."

"They came to Bristol to tell you that?"

"No. They've come up with a plan for how I can put Eliza back into the book."

"Oh, wow. That's great news. Is it manageable in time for publication this year?"

"Shouldn't you be asking if I want to do it?"

"We need the money."

"*You* need the money. I didn't ask for this house."

He looked at me, as if calculating something. A muscle in

his jaw twitched. "I'll start cooking," he said. "You look as if you could do with something to eat."

He was right. I'd hardly managed to eat at the restaurant. He left the room. I stretched out my fingers. He had squeezed them tightly. By the time he called me in, I felt ravenous.

I sat at my place and he served my steak cooked rare, just how I liked it, and poured a generous glass of red wine. I loved the way the crimson liquid slipped into the glass. He told me what the grape variety was and which vineyard it was from, but it meant nothing to me.

"You know what I'm thinking?" Dan said. His steak knife was poised to cut, the serrated edge catching the light.

"What?" I said.

He leaned forward on his forearms, and now the knife was pointed at me, even though he was smiling, and he said, "Thank God you're not a literary writer. It'll be so much easier to put Eliza back into the book. It's not like you've got to tax your brain over big thematic stuff or language or anything. Right?"

"What?" I said.

"Well, I honestly don't think your work is going to win any prizes, do you? Not significant ones, anyway. And it's hardly going to endure, is it? It's only crime fiction!" He laughed.

I was astounded. "What's wrong with that? Readers love my books."

"What's wrong with it is that your work is compromised because it's commercial. You gave up any integrity your writing might have had when you decided to write for the market. It's so disappointing. And don't even get me started on Detective Sergeant Eliza Grey. She's a cliché if ever I met one."

"Are you finished?" I asked.

"Do you not see it? How can you not see it? Don't you ever despair that you've *sold out*? Or perhaps you *can't* see it? I wonder about that sometimes."

I stared at him, hoping there was a way those words could

just retreat right back into his mouth and down into his stomach, where the acid would fry them. I was outraged that he would sit here in this house, which he'd bought with my money, and suggest that writing thrillers was any easier than writing any other kind of novel, that I was a lesser writer because of it. That I was inferior to him. That Eliza was inferior. That my readers were.

I stood and picked up my plate. It gave me sweet pleasure to hurl it at the wall. Dan ducked out of the way dramatically as it flew past him, though it would never have hit him, I'm certain it wouldn't.

My towering outrage flew through the air with the plate, frisbeed alongside it, helped it create a deep dent in the plasterwork before shattering on the floor beside it, creating an uncountable number of tiny shards like sharpened grains of spilled rice. The steak landed on the kitchen countertop with a dull smack and peppercorn sauce dripped down the handmade tiles. I watched with satisfaction, and thought, if this was in a book, depending on the scene, I might describe those as "glutenous rivulets" and that would be okay with my readers and with me.

I hated Dan so very much in that moment.

14

I knew I had to go to the Morells' drinks party, even if Dan and I couldn't exchange a civil word with each other, because it was being held in our honor. I selected an outfit that still had tags on it. Dan had never seen it before. It had been an impulse purchase, shockingly expensive, made in the small hours one night when I'd been working. It was a beautiful tiered silk-chiffon minidress by a big designer. Long sleeves to hide my arms, fitted on my shoulders but a loose drape below to hide my tummy, pretty ruffle details, a stunning floral design on a black background. To match, I'd bought some barely there sandals with a heel and an ankle strap, as suggested by the website. I was aggressively seeking to project confidence and approachability. I wanted people to like my outfit, and me. I wanted my husband to regret everything he'd said earlier.

Dan watched me walk down the stairs with a critical eye. "Is that what you're wearing?"

My heart sank. "What's wrong with it? Should I change?"

"You haven't got time," he said. "We're late already."

He tossed my coat at me.

Self-consciousness prickled me like a full-body case of pins and needles as I walked up the lane, a few feet behind Dan, passing two properties before we reached Sasha's house, the last before the junction with the main road. As we stood and waited for her to answer the door, I felt flushed and flustered and hoped it wasn't too obvious we'd been rowing.

Six guests in total had gathered in Sasha's resplendent living room and it was immediately obvious that Dan had been right to question my outfit. I was horribly overdressed. Sasha wore some skinny jeans, flats, a white shirt, and a gold necklace. The simple outfit looked ravishing on her, complemented perfectly by her complexion, which was exactly the type of creamy English-rose lusciousness that I would give to a woman in one of my novels if I wanted to make other female characters jealous. She greeted me warmly, both her hands clasped around mine, and I felt like mutton dressed as lamb.

The house was as gorgeous as she was. I knew that Dan and I would never in a million years achieve a finish like this in our new home. We wouldn't know where to start. Every detail here had been attended to and a magical atmosphere created just for drinks with the neighbors. Flower displays so sumptuous that the blooms seemed frozen in the act of exploding from their porcelain vases were displayed on polished surfaces. I kept a good distance from the clusters of Diptyque candles in case my ruffled sleeves caught fire.

I was in awe. I had never felt so conscious of my roots in Charlotte Close, so painfully aware of its proximity, and had never felt such a strong urge to flee back to my little flat in the city and be there alone, with my writing for company and Dan as my gatekeeper. But I can't deny that I was also a little bit intrigued to know more about the Morells and my other new neighbors. People might watch me, but I liked to watch them, too.

"You must be Lucy. Hello, I'm James Morell, Sasha's husband." He was tall and leading-man handsome, just the type I would have expected her to marry, but there was also a sweetness to him that took me by surprise. He had dimples when he smiled.

"And let me introduce you to Ben Delaney. Ben, this is Lucy Harper, our new neighbor and a famous author. Lucy, this is Ben, who lives in The Lodge. Ben is a lawyer."

Ben Delaney seemed affable. He smiled easily and had a very

round head, topped with receding blond hair, cropped short around neat ears. Remarkably blond eyebrows framed his pale blue eyes and his belly curved over his belt.

"Sasha has read all of your books," James said. "She loves them. She doesn't even hear me if I talk to her while she's in the middle of one of them. We're very excited to have such a well-known author as our neighbor."

"Brings up the tone." Ben Delaney's laugh sounded more like a hiccup. "My wife, Kate, has read your books, too. She loves your heroine."

"Apparently she's quite the firecracker," James said.

Kate Delaney appeared at her husband's side, was introduced, and hardly took a breath before reeling off a dizzying number of apparently almost insurmountable obstacles she had faced in order to be here tonight, each having to do with one of her children and their myriad commitments or else her business, which she apparently ran from home and was something to do with mail-order baby clothes.

I liked her, though. She was open and warm and didn't start out by making a fuss about the books, so I didn't have to perform for her. She was about my age, medium build, and wore her long, dark hair loose. I wondered if we might be friends and that thought made me think with a twinge about how long it had been since I'd had time to see any of my old friends.

Sasha joined us. "Daniel said you do book clubs, as in visit them to talk about your book," she said.

"I've done one or two." And hated them; I'd felt like the sacrifice at the ritual.

"Would you come to ours? It would be such an honor! We'll have wine! And yummy food! It's a small group—just me and Kate and Vi and a couple of friends! We read one of your books when we found out you were moving here!" Everything Sasha said sounded as if it ended in an exclamation point. Honestly, it would be difficult to write her speech accurately in a book because a copyeditor would want to delete them all.

I felt my temper rise. Dan knew how I felt about book-club visits and I was resentful that he would volunteer me for this, but I smiled and said, "Of course!"

An older couple joined the group, each holding a cut-glass tumbler filled with amber liquid and mounds of ice. They were the sort of people who look as if they've been together for so long that they have begun to grow alike, their faces wearing the same contours of happiness and sorrow. Dan was in their wake, cheeks flushed, clearly enjoying every minute of the attention he was getting as the new kid on the block.

"Veronica Kaplan and her husband, Barry, are the emperor and empress of the street," Kate said. "They've lived here years longer than the rest of us."

Veronica's handshake was firm. She wore no makeup, her only jewelry a single pearl in each ear. In spite of her frumpy clothes—a puffer vest, a pleated tweed skirt in olive green, and sensible shoes—there was a dark elegance to her looks, as if she'd lived a more glamorous life before this one. Her cheekbones were high and sharp, and there was a knowing quality about her that interested me. Here was someone with some layers to her.

"Welcome to the neighborhood," she said. "Please call me Vi."

"Hello, Vi," I said.

"I hear you've just finished your latest novel?" Barry said. He was an ungroomed silver fox. Tall, and seemingly fit, but also carrying a distracted air about him.

"I have," I said.

"Congratulations! What's your detective up to this time?"

Dan, standing beside and just a little behind Barry, raised his eyebrows so that only I could see, as if to say, *Now what are you going to say?*

I felt suddenly sweaty. Usually I was at my most confident

when it came to talking about my books. I knew who I was in those moments, but this was different. "Actually, it's hard to say. I'm a bit close to it still."

"But you've finished the book?"

"Yes."

"So, you must know what it's about."

Dan stepped forward and replied for me. "It's normal for writers to feel that way," he said. "They're superstitious. They believe that if they talk about their ideas, the ideas will disappear. She doesn't even tell me."

"Even after the book is written?" Barry asked, a single eyebrow raised.

"Absolutely," Dan said. "The ideas aren't settled yet. It's part of the creative process." He took a smug sip of his wine, as if he had delivered the last word on the subject and as if he hadn't torn into me earlier that night about my writing. He thought nothing of making authoritative and often incorrect pronouncements on my behalf about writers and their habits.

"I *love* that you're so supportive of Lucy's work," Sasha said. "It's very sweet."

She went on singing Dan's praises until I felt tempted to put my finger down my throat but I excused myself instead and went to the bathroom, where I used the loo, took my time washing and moisturizing my hands with Sasha's lovely products, snooped in the medicine cabinet, and finished my wine, all to delay going back out.

The novelty of meeting and observing my new neighbors had waned and it felt like an effort trying to be functional in front of them all.

When I returned, Dan and Sasha had moved away from the others and were standing together. They didn't see me. I watched as he said something to her, and she laid her hand on his forearm. He fell still, preternaturally so, as if he might break her if he moved. I imagined electricity crackling between them where their skin had made contact. I glanced at the others, to see if anyone else was seeing what I was seeing, but they were focused on one another.

I approached Dan and Sasha and she pulled her hand away. The energy changed, as if they had to make an effort to include me. Sasha started talking about an exclusive interior designer she had used, and Dan responded as if it was a done deal that he and I would hire the same person to do our house.

From where I was standing, her neckline gaped and I could see the fleshy swell of one of her breasts and I was pretty sure everyone else could, too. I began to hate myself, for looking silly in my overly formal outfit, for never owning any situation or looking effortless and elegant like she did, for being ugly, and dull, overweight, greedy, embarrassing, and inarticulate everywhere except on the page. For driving my husband away.

I whispered in Dan's ear that I wanted to go.

"Do you mind if I stay on a bit?" he asked.

I did mind, because I didn't want to leave him there with her, but I also didn't want to make a scene. "It's fine," I said.

As soon as I stepped out of the front door, I took off my horrible heels and walked barefoot. It was bliss, even if the gravel was sharp. I stepped onto the lawn. It was damp and soaked my tights.

"Mind if I join you?"

Vi had followed me. I waited for her to catch up.

"Barry always wants to stay at these things longer than I do," she said. "But I find them so tiring. I'm glad you've got those shoes off. They looked like instruments of torture. Not your usual footwear, am I right?"

"Not unless I'm feeling especially masochistic."

"If there's one thing I've learned it's that you must be yourself, my dear, if it's not too forward of me to say that. Life is too short to be pulling on the costumes of others. Did you enjoy meeting the neighbors?"

"Yes."

"Word to the wise: Ben Delaney is more of a tricky fish than you might imagine. He can be a little bit sneaky, actually. It's worth knowing when you share a boundary with them. He tried to ignore some of the covenants and to slip things past the planners after they bought the land from us. Perhaps you sensed his true nature, though. Writer's intuition."

I hadn't. I wasn't going to lie. "I don't know about that."

She stopped talking and considered me for a moment. "Don't ever undersell yourself to me, dear," she said finally. "I know your books. They are dark and brilliant, and you deserve every accolade you've won."

She squeezed my hand and strode off down her own driveway.

I walked on, around the curve in the lane, but at the end of our driveway, I stopped. I could have sworn I'd left our porch light on, but the drive was a dark tunnel ahead, the laurel hedges horribly dense to either side. I felt a coldness trickle down my spine. Anybody could be hiding in them. I couldn't go down there alone.

I turned and headed toward Sasha's house, the back of my neck prickling. It began to rain. I would pretend that I had forgotten my keys and, hopefully, I could persuade Dan to come away with me this time.

As I walked back down James and Sasha's drive, a security light snapped on in a porch at the side of the house. Dan stepped outside, Sasha with him. She lit a cigarette.

Instinctively, I crouched beside a shrub and watched as they shared the smoke like teenagers. They were talking in low voices, but I couldn't hear what they were saying over the patter of raindrops, which quickly became a downpour, running in rivulets at the edges of the drive and flattening my hair on my forehead. But I couldn't look away. I watched as Dan's head bent lower, toward hers, and I was transfixed, wondering if he was going to kiss her, waiting for it with horror.

A door slammed and their heads parted abruptly. A man had interrupted them. I couldn't see who it was, but I heard the timbre of his voice, low and steady, and after a moment Sasha laughed lightly and threw her cigarette to the ground, stamped on it, and they all went back inside.

I had a strong impulse to confront them, because I knew it was some kind of intimacy I'd witnessed. I began to march across the grass. My dress was drenched and hung heavy; the rain hadn't done the chiffon any good.

"Stop!" Eliza said. I ignored her.

"Stop!" she repeated, and this time her voice wasn't inside my head. I turned.

She was soaking wet, like me, standing on the lawn behind me, though barely. One shoulder was raised unnaturally high as if to ease pain. Patches of her neck were darker than others. Bruised. Sheets of rain fell between us.

"You've had too much to drink," she said. "Come home. Dry off. Sober up. Get something to eat. Don't let everyone see you acting hysterical like this. Don't go in there. You don't know what you saw."

I didn't even know if she was really there or if I was seeing her because I was drunk. I didn't know if I wanted her to disappear or to help me get home and tell me what to do when I got there.

"You're shivering. Your makeup has run down your face. Come with me."

We ran all the way, holding hands, and with every step I thought, *I'm losing my grip.*

VII

It's not easy to get to your den because you have to carry Teddy through the undergrowth. His shoes bang hard against your thighs with each step, his torso and every limb are deadweight. His blankie is wedged awkwardly between you. But the den is so much closer than home. You brush aside the undergrowth and open the door. A few steps lead down into the bunker. Its roof is gently curved, and the floor is of hard cement, but you snuck a small rug and a few other things out here after your mum put them in the bin, and you sit Teddy down on the rug and find the camping lamp you took from the garage. Dad never noticed it was gone.

"Let's look properly at that knee, then," you say. Teddy stretches out his leg and you examine it. "I think you'll be all right after a little rest, Ted," you tell him, though the scrape on his skin is what your mum would call a "nasty scrape." You stroke his forehead, pushing his hair back from his sweaty brow, and he relaxes.

"Do you like my den?" you ask, because you want him to be impressed. You're proud of this place, of what you've made of it. It took you ages to move all the rubbish into one corner and make the most of what was left. You use the old desk to display treasures on, and you keep some library books there, the ones your mum wouldn't have wanted you to take out. You can't sit at the desk because the chair is no more than a metal frame with rags of canvas hanging from it, but that's okay.

You make a nest for Teddy on the little rug, arranging around him all the soft things you have smuggled here from home. A pillow, some garden cushions. "Lie down, Ted," you say.

"Is it camping?" he asks.

"Yes, but only for a little bit, then we'll go home." You drape a thin blanket over him carefully and sit beside him on the concrete.

"Tell me a story," he says.

"Once upon a time," you start, "there was a little boy called Teddy."

"Me?" he asks.

"Yes, you. Teddy went for a walk in the woods with his sister."

"Did they see a fire?"

"They did, but it was a secret just for them. Teddy and Lucy were not going to tell their mum and dad about the fire because they would be cross."

His eyelids droop. He pushes his blankie up over his face. You keep talking, describing the spirits in the trees and their families. You make sure it doesn't sound scary but exciting because you want Teddy to rest for just a short while and then be brave about walking home.

He falls asleep quickly and doesn't wake when the first firework explodes. You open the door of the den and look out into the night. Another firework explodes but you can't see it. You glance back at Teddy. He is deeply asleep, and even though your mum's golden rule is "Never leave your brother alone," you have the most tempting thought.

"Don't," Eliza says.

"I'm only going to run and look quickly, and I'll run back straightaway," you say. "He won't wake up."

You race through the woods toward the bonfire. Without Teddy, it doesn't take long to get there. You creep to the place where you and he were before and are rewarded immediately. Fireworks are exploding every few seconds, large and small. The party has become wilder. Some people hold flaming torches, the smell of the fire mingles newly with the barbecue burn of cooking meat, and a small group are still dancing, with more abandon than ever.

You watch a wild-eyed man heap more wood onto the fire, and it *blazes bigger and hotter in gratitude, sending up a shower of sparks that he must jump to avoid. A group of three shadowy people light sparklers so bright you can hardly look directly at them. Wild, fiery shapes are carved out of the darkness, each one collapsing and lingering as an afterburn deep in your eyes while the next is being made, and you are mesmerized.*

You stand transfixed until the last firework has dissolved among the stars, the last sparkler has burned out, and the afterglow has faded, and only then do you remember Teddy with shock and a dose of guilt that feels like a nasty pinch, because he was gone from your mind for all that time you were transfixed, however long that has been. That isn't clear to you, either.

15

I fumbled with my keys but got into the house. I stripped off my wet dress and took a shower but couldn't stop shivering.

Halfway downstairs, on my way to make tea and find some food, I heard a car and then footsteps on the front drive. I looked out through the window. Panels of stained glass made it hard to get a good view, but a single slim rectangle of clear glass gave me a glimpse. The drive looked empty, apart from a shadow just to the side of it. I couldn't tear my eyes away from it. It was a small child.

"Teddy," I said. He was facing me. He had his blankie. He and it were soaked. He wore the outfit he'd disappeared in.

I could hardly breathe. Every inhalation caught in my chest. I shut my eyes. The doorbell rang. Part of a scream escaped me before I clamped one hand over my mouth. My eyes snapped open. I was panting. It was impossible to move, and my phone was downstairs. I peered out again. A man stepped back from our porch and looked up, as if he knew that I was there. I pulled back, though not before I'd noticed his white-blond hair, and waited a few seconds before peering out again. The man was out of sight, now, and Teddy had gone.

"No," I said. "Teddy. Please come back."

I rubbed condensation from the glass and pressed my eye harder against it and saw that it hadn't been Teddy. A thick segment of branch had fallen onto the lawn, brought down by the rain and the wind.

The doorbell rang more insistently. Now I saw someone

jogging down the drive, a shape emerging from the rain. "Hey!" he called out, and I almost buckled with relief. It was Dan.

He disappeared from my sight when he reached the house. I heard talking and crept downstairs a little way to where I could listen, but only the fact of the conversation was audible, not what he was saying to whoever was there. Their voices sounded low and serious and also tense, if I wasn't mistaken.

Dan opened the door as I heard a car engine start up. It must have been parked around the side of the house. He didn't notice me at first, but he startled when he did. "Why are you lurking there in the dark?" he said, as if I was doing something wrong. "What's the matter with you?"

He had none of the party afterglow I'd expected, and I felt afraid to confront him about Sasha.

"I was upstairs. I just got out of the shower. Who was that?"

"It was a structural engineer. We've been trying to get in touch for days. He was passing so he called in on spec."

"At ten in the evening? And what do we want a structural engineer for?"

"To take down walls in the basement, I want to open it up."

"What for?"

"A cinema," he said. I almost spluttered.

"When were you going to tell me?"

"When you stop freaking out about everything."

"And how much will it cost? It'll be expensive, won't it? How will we afford it?"

"It's nothing we can't handle if you put Eliza back into the book."

I thought of Eliza running back from Sasha's house with me. Of Teddy standing in the drive. "I don't want to live here, Dan. I can't live here."

"I thought we agreed that you would write and leave the rest to me, so why don't you get on with it? Write the bloody book and money won't be a problem."

"I can't do this."

"Get on with it! Start living in the real world and don't be so fucking precious. I'm not giving up this house because you've finally got a creative issue with your work. Listen to yourself!"

The look he shot me was pure poison, but also, somehow, laced with desperation. It cut me to the core. He left the room. I heard him in the one he'd been using as a temporary office, packing things up. Every sound he made left an angry echo. He reappeared with his bag over his shoulder. I said, "Dan," but he shook his head and walked away, slamming the front door behind him, and the whole house seemed to shudder in his wake, as if it had witnessed a permanent farewell, a breaking apart of things.

I touched the door and listened as our car started up and to the tire screech as it left the driveway, and in the silence that followed, I could only hold my breath because it felt as if every tree in the woods was inching a little closer to me.

16

I woke in the night. My dreams had been horrible, the kind that taunt you, torment you, wring every bead of sanity out of you, soaking your sheets with sweat.

Dan hadn't come to bed. I didn't even know if he'd come home.

I called out to him, but there was no answer. Wind battered the house. Outside, through our uncurtained windows, against the sky burned darkest orange by the city lights, I saw the silhouettes of the tops of the trees bent taut as bows. The energy of the wind was ferocious. Windowpanes rattled and from somewhere I heard the steady drip of rain entering the house.

I got up. From the bathroom window I saw that our car wasn't back.

I followed the sound of the dripping. It was coming from downstairs, which seemed strange.

I turned on the light in the hall. At the top of the steps that led from the hallway down to the basement there was a small pool of blood on the limestone tiles. It was roughly the circumference of a tennis ball, with asymmetric edges, and it overlapped two tiles and the grouting between them and dripped onto the top of the basement steps. Its edges were smeared; a partial footprint was visible just a pace away from it. I retched and swallowed convulsively, imagining the tang of blood hitting the back of my throat, though in reality I smelled nothing apart from the stale air that had been incubated by the old walls of the house and the damp air carried in on drafts that chilled me.

The actions I took next were reflexive. My memories of them exist as sensations rather than thoughts.

The loud rush of water coursing from the tap roared in my ears, and the rims of my eyes burned as bleach-filled steam reached them. The wooden back of the scrubbing brush abraded my palms and the limestone stripped skin from the knuckles of my fingers and thumbs as I scrubbed.

I couldn't get rid of the blood entirely. The stone was too porous, the pale grout even worse, though I scraped at that with a knife, until it looked clean. My efforts left a small trough between the tiles, but it was only visible from certain angles. You had to be looking for it.

I saw the other blood spot, then, on the steps, and went through the process again. Then there were more. I scrubbed for hours. Until the knuckles on my right hand bled.

I wrapped up my hand until the bleeding had stemmed.

Hours later, or it could have been minutes, it was still dark, Eliza said, "I don't think Dan's coming back."

The time on my phone was 4:18.

My knuckles were sore and flaked with dried blood.

I could still hear a dripping sound. It was coming from the tap in the bathroom. I turned it off. It hurt my hand to wrench it tightly closed.

"He's not," I said. I caught sight of my reflection in the mirror and felt as if I'd known that for a while.

VIII

You run back to the den, not nimble, you are never nimble, even at that age, but driven to speed by a sense of urgency, worried sick that Teddy has woken up alone and feels frightened.

Eliza is quiet, but you can feel her fear, too, and the weight of her judgment. It's annoying because it's not as if she even likes Teddy. She hates the way he takes up so much of your attention.

The door of the den is open wider than you left it. You go in. The lamp is still on, and everything is as you would expect it to be except that the little nest on the floor where you left Teddy is empty. Your body shakes. You take the lamp outside and search for him, ignoring the tearing thorns and scalding nettle stings, but he is nowhere to be found. It's as if the night has swallowed him up whole. The next thing you know, you are running home through the woods and praying that Teddy will be there, and Eliza's voice is on a loop in your ears, saying, "Don't tell them about the den. Don't tell them you left him alone."

And you didn't tell.

17

I woke in the morning to an empty house.

The hall floor was spotlessly clean, as if last night had never happened. I kneeled down, trying to remember exactly where the blood had been, tracing my fingers along the grouting to see if I could feel a dent where I'd scrubbed, but there was nothing to see, nothing to touch.

"Do you think this is the same as when he went missing before?" I asked Eliza. "Is he punishing me?"

She didn't answer.

"Eliza?"

Nothing. Silence in my head. It was more shocking than anything she could have said. She had never not answered me before.

I called Dan, but he didn't pick up. I left a message asking him to phone me back and tried to sound calm.

I looked through his stuff, unsure what he'd taken with him. I discovered that as well as his phone, he'd taken his laptop. Also his coat. But there was no sign that anything else was missing.

He had to be trying to punish me again, just as he'd done before. It had been a couple of years ago that Dan had first disappeared without warning.

It was after a bad evening that started with a book event.

The evening was memorable for another reason, too, because it was the first time Eliza spoke publicly, in place of me. She stole my voice.

The event was in a bookshop, to celebrate the release of a

new Eliza book. The room was packed. People had queued to get in. I'd been jostled while signing. There had been too many selfie requests. My flight instinct had been building for a while even before they asked me to perch on a tall stool at the front of the room for my reading and interview. It was a challenge. The seat of the stool was the size of only one of my buttocks. I did my reading, got through a short interview with the manager of the shop while sweat soaked the back of my shirt and created half-moons beneath my armpits. The questions dragged on and began to feel very personal. I grew increasingly uncomfortable, emotionally as well as physically. I tried to catch my publicist's eye, but she was taking photographs of the room.

Dan was in the front row, legs crossed, holding a glass of wine. I looked at him, hoping he'd read my desperation and do something to help, but he raised his glass to me and winked. Even in the heat he was wearing the new jacket he'd bought for the occasion. He'd been basking in attention all night.

A man took the microphone. I tried to focus on him, but I was beginning to feel dizzy. The hair around my temples was damp.

He had a speech prepared. It was about Eliza. I kept nodding as he spoke, couldn't concentrate on what he was saying. I zoned in and out, until he finally got to his question: "Can you tell us what's next for Eliza?"

I found I had nothing to say. There was a whiteout in my head. Tumbleweeds scudding. I felt dissociated. Dan looked worried, he made to get up, but before he did, Eliza answered the question for me.

"Eliza Grey is going to be back with a vengeance. She's going to be more vulnerable than ever but also stronger. She's growing in ways you've never seen before. It's incredibly exciting."

The room broke into applause. Dan turned in surprise to look at the faces all around and then clapped, too, his hands held high, angled toward me. "Respect," the gesture said, and

I smiled widely at the room while behind it I was freaking out because I knew I hadn't spoken those words.

We waited to go to the car until after most people had left. Some seemed to linger forever. More books had to be signed. Dan chatted with my publicist and drank wine.

In the car park, he held his hand out for the car keys, which he'd asked me to keep in my bag for the evening.

"He's over the limit," Eliza said.

"No way," I said to him. "You've drunk too much." I kept walking.

"I'm fine." He didn't move. Just stood there, hand out, as if I was being unreasonable. I felt myself weaken, but Eliza spoke for me, again.

"You're pissed."

"But you don't know how to drive her." "Her" was the car. The new Jaguar we'd traded in my old runabout for. One of our first upgrades. Dan hadn't let me drive it yet.

"You can explain what to do," I said.

He shook his head and started to walk toward me, but I had a head start. I ran to the car and jumped into the driver's seat.

"Hey!" he said.

I shut the door. He appeared beside me and tapped on the window, motioned for me to get out. I shook my head.

While I waited for him to get in on the passenger side, I tried to figure out how to start the car. I put my foot on the brake and pressed a button. It roared to life. I looked ahead. We were in a good space. I didn't need to back up, I could just drive forward to exit. I put the car in gear and tried tapping the accelerator. Nothing happened. I could see Dan in the rearview mirror, walking around the back of the car. I tried again, pressing the accelerator harder this time, and the car surged unexpectedly backward and there was a sickening thump.

Time slowed while I opened the car door. I couldn't see Dan.

I took a few paces toward the back of the car. He was on his backside, a few feet away. "What the fuck?" he shouted. "You nearly killed me." The boot of the Jaguar was crumpled against a metal post.

After that he drove home. He was white with anger. "I wasn't drunk!" he muttered, more than once. And the strange thing was, he did seem sober. I leaned my head against the car seat and felt the first stirrings of fear that Eliza had become something I couldn't handle.

Dan disappeared about an hour after we got back to the flat. I heard the door slam, the car engine start up on the street. He didn't answer my texts or calls. I thought I was going to lose my mind from worry.

He turned up after twenty-four hours, sauntering into the flat and dropping his bag casually on the table, as if I hadn't sent him multiple texts and left frantic voice messages.

"Don't ever pull something like that again," he said.

"It was an accident!" I didn't mention how in my darkest hours of waiting for him, I had wondered about that. How it had occurred to me that if Eliza could speak for me, perhaps she could control me in other ways, too. Had I given her too much agency by letting her out of my head and into my books? Was she now ready to take even more for herself?

Or had my foot just slipped?

"I don't want to talk about it any more," Dan said. "Let's put it behind us."

"I missed you," I said. I slipped my arms around him. He was just starting to work out then, and his torso was harder than usual, less welcoming.

He hugged me back. "Missed you, too."

"Where did you go?" I asked.

"Just a crappy hotel."

He began to pick up the used crockery and cutlery from the kitchen surfaces and started to wash up and things had gone back to normal surprisingly easily. We hadn't really talked about it afterward. Eliza had behaved and I'd tried to be better.

But when he disappeared that time, there hadn't been any blood.

And there had been other occasions, since, when I wasn't sure whether Eliza or I had been in charge.

"What's happening, Eliza?" I asked now, in the quiet that felt oppressive, but still she didn't reply. It was just me, and the house, and the woods.

"Are you happy?" I said. "Because he's gone again."

I felt menaced by her silence. It was as bad as feeling her take control.

18

I crept back into bed, where I lay for a while listening to my own breathing as if I needed to remind myself that I was in fact a real person who didn't need Eliza, or Dan, to exist. It was hard to feel confident about that.

After a while, when I grew very hungry, I also got cross. I thought I could try to be functional, that it was the least I could do, to prove to Eliza that I didn't need her and prove to Dan, when he got back, that I'd hardly noticed his disappearance.

I got dressed and looked for something to eat, but we had almost nothing. The nearest shop was a few miles away, in the city. I thought about my new neighbors and decided Kate was the least scary of them. I walked to her house, the smallest on the lane, and the only modern property, and rang the bell. She appeared at the door with a small boy in her arms and it was a horrible moment. Her boy had blond hair, like Teddy, and I recognized my little brother in the way he clung to his mum. He smiled at me in that heartbreaking way little boys sometimes do when they show you how ready they are to love and be loved.

"Hi," I said to him. I did a little finger wave. His smile spread wider. He mimicked the wave.

"Hey," Eliza said softly. "Don't. It'll take you back."

She was right. Memories were stirring and I couldn't let them.

I forced myself to turn my attention to Kate instead, who seemed a bit shocked to see me. I assumed it was because I must look a fright. Shock was a common reaction when deliverymen came to the door while I was writing. I had a tendency to layer up garments to combat the cold that crept in when I sat for long hours at my computer, not really caring what they were, and I could end up looking rather strange. I realized I was wearing one of Dan's hoodies over sweatpants and a baggy old sweater, a far cry from last night's chiffon. I apologized for disturbing her and smoothed my hair down in case it was sticking up.

"Would you by any chance be able to give me a lift into the city?" I asked. "Dan's taken the car today and we forgot to order groceries." I thought that sounded pretty normal. I didn't want to admit that he had left me with no transport and no food in the house. I was ashamed to say it.

She relaxed visibly. "Of course," she said. "It'll be lovely to have some adult conversation for a change."

Her vehicle was filthy. All the detritus of family life was scattered through it. Her boy kicked the back of my seat at regular intervals. He wanted me to pay him more attention. It was hard not to.

"What did you think of the party?" she said.

"It was very nice. I'm sorry I couldn't stay longer."

"You didn't miss much. Barry got drunk, as usual."

She lost her smile. I remembered what Vi had told me about Kate's husband, that he was tricky, and the sense I'd gotten that there wasn't much love lost between the two families.

"Do you get on with Barry and Vi?" I asked.

"Oh, you know," Kate said. "On the surface, we're all civil, but I'm always worried the children are making too much noise, or we're too messy when the kids' stuff is all over the lawn. They make me feel as if we're bringing the neighborhood down, sometimes. I hope you won't feel the same about us."

"Of course not. I love children." I forced myself to say it, but in reality, I dreaded overhearing the shrieks of her little ones. It would be another painful reminder of my past that the new house could inflict on me.

"Oh, good. It's no fun being the poor relations in the little house. Ben says I'm being touchy about it, but I'm stuck here all the time with the kids and my business because I work from home, too, so it gets to me. But do you know what? Not only did they make our lives hell when we were building this place with all the planning restrictions, but Barry only sold us the land because they needed the money, and I'm not surprised. Vi never worked so far as I can tell, and what university professor can afford the upkeep on that house? So, they've got no right to behave as if they're better than us."

"True," I said. I was sensitive to her feelings of inferiority. When we lived on Charlotte Close, my parents had felt the same in relation to the residents of the big houses in the area.

She glanced at me. "Are you happy with your new home?"

Something in the way she said it made me feel paranoid, as if she knew or suspected how I felt, but how could she?

"Yes," I said. "But it doesn't feel like home yet." I didn't trust myself to say more. I was afraid my tone of voice would be flat and would give away my true feelings.

She pulled into a space in front of the shop.

"That house is going to be a lot of work," she said.

"Dan's going to manage the renovation."

"Do you trust him?"

"What?" I said. It felt horribly as if she could see inside my marriage. What did she know?

"I only mean, do you trust him to get it done? Ben is terrible when it comes to anything like that. He leaves it all to me. Sorry if that sounded rude. I can be such an idiot. It's because I only talk to under-tens most of the time."

"Yes, I trust him. Of course I do." I started to get out of the car. "Thanks for the lift."

"Do you want me to wait and drive you home?"

"No, thanks," I said. "I've got some other stuff to do after. I'll get a taxi." It wasn't true, but our conversation had left me too uncomfortable to want more.

"Will you drop round and have a coffee with me soon?"

"I'd love to," I said.

Her eyes narrowed. "Are you all right?" she asked. I didn't know what she saw in me that made her ask and I didn't want to know. It took me a long time after Teddy had disappeared to learn that it was best to keep myself to myself, and that was the way I wanted it to stay.

"I'm fine." I shut the car door and forced myself to wave her off.

In the shop, I put milk, bread, and biscuits in my basket but drew a blank on what else to buy. I was staring at the shelves when I heard my name.

"Lucy, is that you?"

I had no idea who she was, and it must have showed because she said, "It's Melanie. I used to work with Dan at the cinema."

"Of course," I said. "I'm sorry. How are you?"

"Fine. Good. Still studying for my PhD. Nearly finished. You know how it is."

"Yep." I nodded, but I was willing the exchange to be over so I could get away.

"Did Dan ever get the World War Two contact I sent him?"

"What contact?"

"He got in touch via email a little while ago to ask if I could help him get hold of some archival newspaper material around the subject of the English resistance movement and their network of bunkers."

"Bunkers?" I repeated. The word set off a humming in my head. I didn't dare ask for details.

"I put him on to an acquaintance but didn't hear back from him. Just wondered if he got what he needed."

"Yeah," I lied. "He did. Nice to see you, Melanie."

"Sure. Nice to see you, too. Love all your books. And how proud of you Dan is."

"Thanks," I said.

When she walked away, I put down my basket and left the shop without buying anything and I didn't even notice what direction I was walking in because all I could think was: *Why is Dan digging around in the most terrible and sensitive area of my past without telling me?*

This, and our move to the edge of Stoke Woods, so close to Charlotte Close, could not be a coincidence.

I had the horrible feeling that I had become a pawn in a game that he was playing. But even as I had the thought, I felt ashamed of it because I knew what he would say if I voiced it.

You're paranoid.

IX

You found the bunker the autumn before Teddy went missing. It was a spectacular year for leaf color. On a beautiful, sunny afternoon you slipped away from the other kids playing on Charlotte Close and wandered into the woods. You had watched the leaves transform into a blaze of oranges and yellows from your bedroom window. It was better than any sunset you had seen. Stepping among them felt like being inside a kaleidoscope. You lost yourself in the colors. Your mind danced with stories. Time disappeared.

By the time you came to the edge of the dip in the landscape, where the trees were slightly less dense, the light was brighter, and the ground was carpeted with acid-yellow leaves, you had gone farther from home than ever before.

You began to ease yourself down the side of the incline but lost your footing and landed hard at the bottom of it. A curtain of ivy hung beside you. You grabbed a handful to help you get to your feet, and if you hadn't, you would never have seen the door hidden behind it.

It stood partially open, far enough for you to see inside. What you saw was a dark tunnel. It was hard to know where it ended, but it didn't frighten you because a beautiful cylinder of sunlight broke through its roof and sliced through the space below, showing you the golden, sun-kissed outlines of familiar things: a desk and chair, bedframes, books.

You stepped inside. The air here felt closer, as if it had wrapped itself around you. As your eyes adjusted you saw that the space wasn't very long. At the far end was a corrugated metal wall with *another doorway set into it. The ceiling was curved and that charmed you, reminding you of a picture you'd seen of an old-fashioned train.*

"What do you think?" you asked Eliza.

"I love it."

"I do, too."

"Do you know what this place is?" Eliza asked. She answered her own question. "It's Mole's house. From The Wind in the Willows.*"*

"Yes!" you said. You both loved that book. "Dulce domum."

"Sweet home," Eliza said, as if you hadn't already looked that up.

"It's even underground," you said.

"This could be our place. Nobody else will ever know about it."

The second time you visit, which is the following day, you bring with you a poster you have made, with the words "Dulce Domum" ornately inscribed, and decorated with pictures of autumn leaves, a mole, a rat, and a toad. You fix it to the inside wall of the bunker beside the door. Then you clean the surface of the desk and place your copy of The Wind in the Willows *upon it.*

19

Apart from Eliza, Dan was the only other person to know about the bunker, but I had never told him its precise location. Only Eliza and I knew that. We knew all the truths about one another.

I walked home from the shop, already regretting not bringing the few things I'd put in my basket, keeping to the inner edges of the sidewalk after I'd crossed the bridge, skirting the hedgerows and bushes. Every car that passed made me flinch. I kept thinking of the vehicle that had tailgated me on my way back from lunch with Max and Angela. I was afraid I was vulnerable to being driven at again.

At home, I found my laptop and tried to log on to Dan's email. I felt I *needed* to know why and what he was trying to find out about bunkers. I thought I knew his password, but it didn't work. He must have changed it. I tried to guess what he might have changed it to, but without success.

I was frustrated until something occurred to me: we had known Melanie so long ago that it was possible Dan had had to go to an old email account of ours to track down her email address. He and I had shared an account named "DanandLucy" in the days before my book deals meant I had to do things more professionally. I remembered the password to that.

I got in and found their email exchange easily. Dan hadn't said much in his initial inquiry, only asked if she knew where he could find information about local resistance bunkers, just as Melanie had described to me. Her reply was simple.

The person you need to speak to is Rupert Bailey. He's the *Bristol Post* archivist and all-round history buff.

She'd included his phone number, and I called it. The conversation fell into confusion immediately because Dan had apparently contacted Rupert already, after tracking him down by other means.

"Are you calling to cancel my meeting with Daniel?" Bailey asked. "Because I have things to show him. I've worked hard to pull the material together."

"No, no. We just got confused about the timing. Could you confirm for me?"

They were due to meet the next morning.

I was shaking by the time I hung up and told myself it might be because I hadn't eaten. Because I had failed to bring the shopping home, I got a tin of pineapple rings out of the kitchen cupboard and forked some of them out, then drank the juice straight from the tin.

I looked at the clock. It was midafternoon. Only a few hours before I expected Dan to be back. If he was coming back this time. I carried the tin of pineapple into the hall and ate another ring as I stared at the floor. Blood. No blood. Which was it?

Eliza had nothing to say.

A cloud passed over the light well.

The silence was hideous.

A noise shattered it, so loud that I jumped. Pineapple juice spilled down my front. It sounded like a chain saw, and it was close. I put the can down and covered my ears with my hands, but it didn't help much. The doorbell rang, cutting through the din. A man in a hard hat stood outside.

"Hello!" he mouthed. He gesticulated to the side of the house and made a thumbs-up. I could see a van with the words "Tree Surgeon" on the side of it.

"What are you doing?" I shouted, and he cupped his ear. I

repeated the question and he said, "Some work round the back. Starting with the hedges. We agreed it with your husband."

I didn't want them here, the noise was horrific, but I thought Dan might mock me if I sent them away, accuse me of not being able to handle overseeing something simple.

I retreated upstairs and opened his wardrobe. I started to go through his pockets, not sure what I was looking for. I found indigestion tablets and an energy-bar wrapper. The silky linings felt familiar, even though I hadn't done this for a long time. Not since I'd researched gaslighting for my last Eliza novel.

That had been a bad time. With every new piece of information that I read about it, suspicion had grown in my mind and invaded my thinking about my own relationship. I started to think Dan was gaslighting me. I second-guessed everything.

It was the first time he suggested I see a psychotherapist, or perhaps it had been a psychiatrist, I forget now, but I hadn't needed to in the end. My paranoia had ebbed once I'd moved on to the new book, which brought with it a different set of crimes and psychopathologies for me to study and absorb. Or be absorbed by. I was never quite sure which was the more accurate description.

The chain saw stopped abruptly. I heard a shout and a creak, followed by a mighty crash. It felt as if the house shook. I ran to my office and opened the shutters to see what had happened. The cedar tree had gone. Felled. The severed trunk bore a brutal wound.

And there was worse. Where the tree had stood, now there was an overwhelming amount to see: clouds gathered on the horizon, rimmed with gray menace, and between them and me, beneath the domed sky, was the canopy of the woods with just beyond it, from this angle, if you knew where to look and what you were looking for, a glimpse of the rooftops of Charlotte Close.

A sob escaped me.

I turned. Dan had positioned the desk and ordered the felling of the tree so that this would be my view, every single day. Had he planned it?

I walked to the window and put one hand on the glass, flattening my palm against its cool surface.

Was Dan trying to break me somehow, by exposing me to my past, like a dose of poison administered daily and increased incrementally?

"What do you want from me?" I thought, or perhaps I said it out loud. I wasn't sure if I was asking Dan or Eliza, or both of them.

My palm and my fingers separated from the glass. I felt as if I had no control over my own movements. My hand drew itself back and then hit the window so hard that a crack split the pane, a fragment of glass fell clear, and as it shattered on the patio far below, a thread of blood appeared along the tender edge of my hand, beneath my little finger.

The men in the garden looked up from the mess of severed tree limbs and sawdust. I stepped back, out of sight, out of the room, clutching my injured hand, the wound beginning to throb. On the splintered boards of the landing, I sank to my knees and broke down completely. I heard myself choking out words. "Eliza," I said. "You hurt me."

"Quid pro quo," she said.

I looked up to see her leaning against the banister at the top of the stairs. She had tied a scarf around her neck to hide the injuries. Her expression was resolute. I wasn't sure what it meant.

I kneeled there like a supplicant, looking up at her, both my hands bloody now, and in the next cold, still moments, when the house seemed almost to expand around us, as if to give us room, as if she and I were the point around which everything turned, nothing mattered except the question I knew I had to ask her: "Did you hurt Dan, too?"

20

Eliza disappeared. I knew what she was doing, she was playing the psychological games I'd taught her to use in the books. Dial up the pressure on someone, then retreat, disappear for a while. Let them sweat. It's very effective.

I got to my feet. The dimensions of the house seemed normal again. I dealt with my wounded left hand. It felt so sore. In the bathroom I washed it and bound it up as best I could.

The doorbell rang. My head jerked up. This house could never leave me in peace. Viewed in the bathroom mirror I looked terrible, drawn and frightened, my eyes puffy and my cheeks glazed with the crisp sheen of dried tears. I washed my face hastily, paying particular attention to a smear of blood on my cheek. The bell rang again. So insistent. Perhaps it was Dan. Though he would have keys. Perhaps it was the tree man. He knew I was here so I couldn't ignore it. From the landing, I saw a new car in the drive, one I didn't recognize.

I opened the door a crack. A man and a woman stood outside, both of them in police uniform. For a moment, I felt as if the falling cedar tree might have ripped through time and I was a child again, at home on Charlotte Close on the summer solstice, watching uniformed police officers arrive on our street in the hazy dawn. These officers wore the same grim expressions. They showed me their identification badges and I tried to look as if I was focusing on them with the careful concentration of a person for whom this was a new experience.

"May we come in?" the male officer said. Such kind eyes he

had, so warm. I felt vulnerable to kindness in that moment. I opened the door and they stepped in. His partner rubbernecked at the house as the radio on her shoulder chattered to itself at a friendly volume, until she pressed a button and quelled the noise. He asked if there was somewhere we could sit down.

I took them to the kitchen, where I sat with my scraped and injured hands out of sight under the table.

"Are you the owner of a vehicle with the license number WK17 EDY?"

"It sounds familiar. I'm afraid I don't remember the license number exactly." I knew I sounded vague, but it was true. How do you hold a license plate in the same head where you have to hold an entire series of novels?

"It's a white F-Type Jaguar."

Dan's baby. "Yes, that's ours. My husband owns the car, technically."

"Unfortunately, your vehicle has been found abandoned and, I'm sorry to say, burned out. Were you aware that it had been stolen?"

"No, I wasn't. My husband took it."

"Is he away?"

"Yes." My voice croaked. I felt a cold sweat break out. The ache in my hand seemed to spread up my arm and swell. Everything went black.

Time disappeared.

"You fainted," the female officer said when I opened my eyes. It took me a moment to locate the various parts of my body. I was sprawled on the floor, my head supported by something soft they'd bundled beneath it, and her hand was on my upper arm, fingers sinking humiliatingly into my pudgy flesh.

"Again," I thought. It was as if this house had the capacity to inflict blows that could fell me.

"What?" the officer said.

"Sorry," I said. I hadn't meant to say it out loud. I made an effort to lever myself up and pain slid sharply from one side of my head to the other.

"Stay where you are," the female officer said. "I've got you. You hit your head pretty hard when you went down. We need to get you checked over, and I think your hands need looking at, too."

I heard them making phone calls. The kettle boiled. They offered me sugary tea, then led me to their car. We were going to A&E. I slumped in the back seat and shut my eyes until we had reached the city. Arriving in the waiting area with a uniformed escort made heads turn. A mother pulled her young son a little closer to her. I would include that detail in a future novel, I thought.

I stood between the officers at the reception desk and Amy, the woman officer, said, "Head injury. She fainted and hit it on a tiled floor. She was unconscious for approximately thirty seconds. She also has some cuts and abrasions to her hands."

We sat in the waiting area. By now I felt fond of my kind officers. I shut my eyes and basked in the feeling of being looked after for a while. I decided I wanted to confide in them.

I said, "I have to tell you something. I think my husband is missing."

X

The first person to see you when you run out of the woods on the night your brother disappears is your mother, Carol, who has just discovered that neither of her children is in bed.

Carol Bewley has searched the entire house and flung the front door open to begin looking outside, only to see you standing at the end of the short driveway.

An office manager for an accounting firm, Carol is not prone to panic or to catastrophizing but had woken abruptly from a nightmare that night and on a whim, or perhaps it was a mother's instinct, she decided to check on her children. "It was something I used to do all the time when they were babies," she will tell the police, later, "but not so much now that Teddy is nearly four."

She looked in his room first and hurried from there to Lucy's when she found him gone. "He sometimes got in with Lucy in the night," she will say. "I thought that's where he would be." When she discovered her daughter's bed empty, too, her scream woke her husband, Martin, and they began to search the property.

"I used to look in on the kids a lot," Martin will tell the family liaison officer, who notes this down carefully while nodding in an encouraging way. "I'm a bit of an insomniac, but that night, I slept like a log."

When you are discovered at the end of the drive, you are disheveled, by all accounts, with bits of foliage in your hair, your legs filthy dirty and scratched from shin to thigh. You look wild. Shocked. Your father will later say you were crying silently. Your mother won't contradict him, but her memory is that you weren't crying at all.

21

The atmosphere between the police officers and me snapped instantly from relaxed to tense. I'd known that it would, but I didn't like it when it happened.

I watched them exchange a glance with which they acknowledged to one another that their day had just become a lot more interesting. These were the professional moments Eliza lived for and the two officers in front of me were clearly no different.

I was discharged from the hospital after a scan. I clutched a printout of concussion advice in the car on the way back home. I thought how ironic it would be if Dan were home when we got there but he wasn't.

They looked at the house in a different way this time. They didn't sneak surreptitious glances into the grand rooms or drink in the square footage with envy. Instead, they scanned the spaces with calculating eyes.

They asked me questions and took copious notes. I knew that they were trying to understand what had happened to Dan, to discover more about him and about his and my relationship so that they could construct a narrative about what had happened. My job and theirs weren't so dissimilar.

But it was hard to concentrate. I was thinking about the car on fire. Wondering how it looked. My mind froze on that image. The fearful beauty of it.

Detective Sergeant Lisa Bright arrived at the house soon after we did, summoned by her colleagues. A potential missing person was a matter for the Criminal Investigation Department, she explained as she showed me her badge, as if I wasn't already aware of that.

Age for age and size for size, she and I were a pretty good match. We could have raided each other's wardrobes, though I think she would have found richer pickings in mine than I would in hers. She wore a black business suit and a blue shirt. Dull but suitable. I also noted a modest engagement ring and a plain wedding band. Her nails were as bitten as Max's. She had gray eyes.

"When did you last see your husband?" She looked at me as if she had all the patience in the world, and I got the sense that there was nothing she wouldn't wait for, or keep in pursuit of, if she felt it necessary. I sat up a little straighter. That level gaze put me on my guard.

I'd already answered her question, when speaking to the other officers, but I understood that she wanted to observe me as I answered.

"Last night. Before bed. We had been at a drinks party with neighbors. I came home a bit early, and Dan followed soon afterwards. A man came by, a structural engineer. Dan talked to him. I got the impression it was a bit of an intense conversation, but I might have been wrong. The man didn't stay for long, only a few minutes. Dan came in afterwards and he and I had words and he drove off."

"Words?"

"An argument."

"And you haven't seen or heard from your husband since then?"

"That's correct."

"Is it out of character for him to disappear like this after an argument?"

"He's done it once before but that was years ago. It was more of a freedom thing."

"Can you explain what you mean by that?"

"We work closely together. Sometimes he needs space." I glanced at her ring finger. "You know, we all need space now and then."

"Does he help you write your books?"

I couldn't help laughing. As if. "No. He helps with everything else. Admin, money, social media, that kind of thing."

"What makes you think that Dan's disappearance on this occasion is different from before?" she asked.

"I didn't think it was until I was told about the car." My chin wobbled unexpectedly. I felt almost as if I had been playing a role in one of my own books up until this point, that nothing was quite real, but I was suddenly sickeningly aware that things actually looked horribly worrying for Dan. I was afraid for him. I blinked back tears.

She waited for me to compose myself before asking, even more gently than before, "What time did Dan leave last night?"

"I don't know exactly. It was probably around ten."

"Are you able to give me contact details for the structural engineer?"

"No. I'm sorry. I didn't even know he was coming. Dan deals with all that."

"Do you know what company he was from?"

I shook my head.

"Can you describe him?"

"He had white-blond hair. It was very distinctive, and he was probably medium build. I only glimpsed him through the window. It was dark."

"And you say their conversation was intense. What do you mean by that?"

"I'm not sure. There were no raised voices or anything like that, but it sounded tense, somehow."

"But you couldn't hear what they were saying?"

"No."

"And Dan didn't tell you what they talked about."

I tried to remember. "I think he said it was about some work he wanted to do in our basement, taking down a wall."

"Okay. And have you been in contact with Dan's friends or family?"

"No, because I wasn't worried until your officers came here, as I said. And I'd have felt ashamed to admit we'd had a row, if I'm honest."

She nodded, as if she understood. Something behind me caught her attention. I turned, but there was nothing to see. The tree men were long gone. They'd neatly trimmed the hedges after massacring the cedar tree.

"I saw a man out there the other morning," I said. "He was lurking in the bushes."

"Tell me about that."

She wrote it all down without displaying any emotion. I felt as if everything I was telling her made me seem stupid. I didn't know if my reactions had been right or wrong. I never knew.

"Can I ask what happened to your hands?" she asked. She was looking at my right hand, where the knuckles were half-raw, half-scabbed. My left hand had been dressed in the hospital.

"Don't tell her about the blood on the floor and the scrubbing," Eliza said.

I stiffened. *Of course I won't.* A small furrow appeared in DS Bright's brow as she watched me. It seemed as if she never blinked.

"I scraped my knuckles on a cheese grater," I said. "You know, one of those very sharp ones."

"Sure," she said. "They can be lethal."

I wasn't sure if she was being sarcastic. "It was such a stupid mistake," I said. "And I cut my other hand on a window. I was cleaning it. In some of the rooms we have old glass. It's very fragile."

"Here?"

I nodded.

"Can you show me?"

I had the worst feeling, as I took her upstairs, that the window would be intact. The feeling mounted so that by the time I showed her into my office I felt as if I could hardly breathe. But there was a jagged hole in one of the small panes of glass. She looked at it closely. "Do you mind if I take a photograph?" she asked.

I stood well back in the room, near the door, frightened of the view. She snapped a picture, checked it, and put her phone back in her pocket. She also took a good look around. "Beautiful," she said.

"It's my office. Dan renovated it for me."

"Very nice." She turned around. "The view is lovely, too."

"I'm very lucky," I said in a cracked voice.

She touched another pane in the window, near to the broken one, as if testing its resistance and considering how much force would be needed to break it. I watched mutely. She examined the bookshelves, where Dan had already shelved most of the English-language and translated editions of my books. I supposed they looked like quite an achievement. She inclined her head as she read the titles on the spines.

"Impressive," she said after a while. "You've been busy, haven't you?"

"I work hard."

She looked at another shelf. It was filled with books on forensic evidence, crime scene analysis, and similar. She ran her fingers over the spines. I felt uncomfortable.

"And do you do a lot of research?" she asked.

"Sure. When I need to."

"Would that include talking to professionals?"

"Yes."

"Interesting."

"It is."

As we went downstairs, she gave me reassurances about how they would do everything in their power to find Dan. She promised me that they took this sort of thing seriously even though he hadn't been gone for long. The car, she said, was a factor that worried her. She would keep in very close touch, she added, and my skin prickled.

I watched her drive away until her vehicle's taillights disappeared when she turned onto the lane. After that I double-locked the door and leaned back against it. Eliza was sitting on the stairs.

"DS Bright is an operator," she said. "Don't be fooled by her mild manner."

22

All night, I dreamed of the bunker, and Teddy, and a car in flames.

When I brushed my teeth in the morning, there was blood in my spat-out toothpaste and I wondered if I was getting gum disease. My hand throbbed and my head did, too.

Seen from my bedroom window, the sky was made from mother-of-pearl, bathing the house and the woods with delicate light, soft and sickly.

There was nothing in the fridge. I found a shopping list Dan had started and wrote "bread, milk, yogurt" on it. I thought for a moment and added "lunch" and "dinner" beneath it, but no specifics would come to mind.

I tried to phone Dan again. I nursed a tiny bit of hope that he might pick up, but he didn't. It went straight to voicemail.

I remembered that he had a meeting this morning with the man called Rupert about the bunker and decided to go in his place. I wondered if Dan and I would both turn up there at the same time. It was nice to imagine.

I took a cab into the city and time was tight. I ran up the path to St. Mary Redcliffe Church, raising a flock of pigeons. Rainwater dripped from the mouths of the gargoyles sitting on the roof of the porch. It was as if they were salivating. I wondered if Dan was watching me from somewhere as I stepped into his life.

A man rose from a bench in the shadows and approached me. White stubble covered his cheeks, darkening into the folds of his jowls. He wore a felt hat, a waxed jacket, and battered suede shoes.

"Mr. Bailey?"

"You're not Daniel."

"I'm Lucy. Dan wasn't able to come. He sends his apologies."

"Coffee in the crypt?"

We sat in a corner at a small table that wobbled. I got in the coffees and cakes. I couldn't remember when I'd last eaten. It was gloomy down there, and cold.

Rupert opened his bag and the worn leather top fell back with a slap. He extracted a cardboard folder and a fountain pen. He saw me eyeing the pen and held it up so I could take a closer look. It was very beautiful.

"Dan told me you're a writer."

"I am."

"So, do you think of the pen as a tool or a weapon?"

I was taken aback.

"I think it's my soul," I said reflexively. I was being flippant. I didn't have time for this, but he took me seriously. He sat back in his seat and studied me over his reading glasses.

"Your soul is your own, my dear, no matter what you say or do. You and it are answerable only to one another. It is both your conscience and your essence. No implement can get between you, even one as suffused with mythology as the pen."

Who are you? I wanted to ask, but I found I was lost for words.

Rupert bit into a custard slice. Pastry flakes dropped onto the tabletop. He wiped his lips. His cheek bulged. I could see into his mouth when he chewed. I felt barely there. It seemed like an age before he swallowed his mouthful.

"As I said on the phone, Daniel contacted me to ask if I had any cuttings relating to wartime resistance bunkers in Stoke Woods and the surrounding area." He pushed the folder toward me. "This is what I've managed to find. It's taken some putting together, but it's extremely interesting material, and somewhat underresearched because of the secrecy surrounding Britain's wartime plans for a possible invasion by Germany. I believe that if you met any members of the British resistance alive today, they probably still wouldn't admit to having worked for it, let alone the locations of these places. The vast majority of bunkers that have been discovered have been stumbled upon by chance."

I took the folder but didn't open it, though it looked as if Rupert expected me to. My heart was hammering at the thought of what might be inside it. He finished his custard slice. I didn't say anything, nor did he. There was an energy about him that got my hackles up. I had the feeling he was disappointed in me, as if he'd wanted this meeting so he could discuss his passion for history, or for some other reason that I wasn't aware of. I wondered if he was one of those men who don't like women. Or who want to dominate them.

"Your husband said you write crime fiction," he said after he'd drained his coffee.

"I do."

"Do I know your work?"

"You know my name, so you tell me."

That was rude, but it was a question I hated. I just wanted him to go, so I could look at what he had brought on my own.

He took the hint. As soon as he disappeared up the stairs to the outside world, I opened the folder and read the first clipping:

The bunker rumored to be situated in Stoke Woods near Bristol is one of a series built across the south of England for use by Winston Churchill's resistance force. The Auxiliary Units formed a secret army, made up of groups of 6–8 men, recruited mostly from local volunteers who had an intimate knowledge of a particular area. The purpose of the Auxiliary Units was to resist enemy incursion in the event of an invasion by German forces. This resistance would take the form of nighttime raids where explosives would be used to destroy enemy resources. During the day, the men would retreat to the bunker to rest and plan the next night's raid. Life expectancy for members of the Auxiliary Unit in the event of an invasion was approximately 12 days.

A typical bunker had a floor fashioned from railway sleepers or concrete, covered overhead by a prefabricated roof made out of elephant steel, an extremely resilient material. The bunker would probably have had two chambers, the outer one providing shelter for the men, with the inner chamber for storage of explosives and weaponry.

I stopped reading. Even this dry description had triggered powerful memories. I knew exactly what the bunker looked like and could recall in an instant its fusty smell, part damp earth, part the chemistry of manmade materials being reclaimed by nature. I knew what every surface inside that place felt like to the touch; how many footsteps it took me as a nine-year-old to get from one end of it to the other.

I shut the folder and pushed it away from me. It took a while for the memories to ebb and it was only once they had that I could move.

I looked around. A few other people had arrived and sat at tables just like mine beneath the low arches. It seemed extraordinary to me that we could occupy the same space, yet they could be unaware of the place I had just visited in my imagination, and of the power it held over me. Were they, too, half living in vivid alternate worlds? A woman at a table near mine blew her nose before turning a page of her newspaper. A young mother spooned food into her baby's mouth and smiled. I wasn't sure they were.

I gathered up my stuff and shoved the folder into my bag.

By the time I pushed through the heavy doors of the church and reemerged into the city center, I had come to the conclusion that Dan was hunting for my bunker.

Why didn't he ask me where it was? I wondered. Was it because he knew I wouldn't tell him? He'd asked me before, after all, and I hadn't told him then, but inquiring would surely have been worth another try before searching for it himself. My husband was not an outdoorsman. I couldn't imagine him spending hours hiking in the woods looking for it. Had he thought he was going to get an easy answer from old documents? And the question that frightened me most was this: Why would he be searching for it at all?

I didn't have any answers. Just a horrible sense that things hadn't changed just a little while I'd been writing my last book, but significantly and in ways that were frightening. I hadn't emerged from my writing den just to find an unfamiliar landscape; I'd walked straight into a web that had been woven around me and now I was at its center, disoriented, uncomprehending, and trapped.

XI

Detective Inspector Charles Cartwright is woken by a call to his landline. He answers quickly, listens carefully, confirms he'll be there as soon as he can, and dresses as dawn softens the sky from deep black to dark, velvety blue. DI Cartwright is always bad-tempered in the morning, but there's nobody sharing his home who might protest when he takes this call in the early hours, swears as he struggles into his trousers, or slams the door shut on his way out.

The sunrise lifts shadows as he drives across the city. He can feel the somewhat cool night air readying itself to warm into a humid fug. The city has been stinking of a heat wave for a week, with days that are pressure-cooker hot, that can squeeze the patience out of even the most stoic of Bristol's citizens. CID has been kept busy dealing with the fallout.

It's 5 A.M., a good time to travel. Not much sign of trouble on the streets, hardly any traffic. He listens to Puccini at high volume, the car windows down. Revenge on the drunks and their ilk who caroused down his street yelling at the tops of their voices last night. They should have more respect for the solstice. Everything is just an excuse to get wasted these days.

When he arrives on Charlotte Close the light is milky blue and he walks briskly down the length of the cul-de-sac, making sure to look about him as he does. It's useful to get a sense of a place before you have to start dealing with people's emotions. As he understands it, young Teddy Bewley disappeared sometime the night before. His sister had taken the little boy out to the woods in the middle of the night and had come home without him. Charlie's expression tightens at the thought of it. He has little patience when foolish behavior has predictable consequences, even where children are concerned. To him, protection of human life is paramount.

His impressions of Charlotte Close are straightforward: small community, safe 1960s architecture, modest-income family homes, a little pocket of suburbia dropped, almost as if by accident, into the woods. You'd never get planning permission nowadays.

He nods at the uniformed officer standing at the door to number 7 and enters the home. The family is in the kitchen. Karen, the family liaison officer, is there already. She nods a greeting to him.

He takes a good look at the family. Parents are in their thirties. Mum's expression distorted with shock and grief, Dad's face a taut mask of repression. The bag of emotions he is clamping shut will fall open soon, Charlie thinks. It always does.

The daughter refuses to make eye contact. Her hands rest on the table, chubby fingers in constant motion: clenching, slotting between one another, walking around and through each other. She watches the dance of her own digits as closely as if they are strange creatures displayed behind glass. Once or twice, she pauses, as if listening to something that nobody else can hear.

He frowns. She's not what he was expecting. Her body language oozes discomfort above anything else. His professional curiosity kicks in. She feels guilty, he thinks, and he wants to know how far that guilt goes. Is it because she has taken her brother out and lost him, or does she know more . . . has she done more?

"I'll talk to Lucy first," he tells the FLO sotto voce when they huddle in the hallway. "Let's see if we can do it without either parent in the room. Can you suggest that you sit in as the appropriate adult? Make it sound like that will give us the best chance of finding the boy?"

He believes it will, but Karen looks as if she might object, which irritates him. She's an excellent FLO, an astute observer, but she could do with staunching the bleeding heart sometimes.

"Thank you," he says, cutting off any reservations she might be about to express. "I'll do the interview in the sitting room."

23

The folder lay on the kitchen island, closed. I would have to work up the courage to look at it again.

I checked my emails. Over the past day Max and the publishers had sent encouraging messages saying they hoped the edits on the book were going well. On the Eliza fan fiction page, MrElizaGrey had posted again, a story about Eliza titled "Vigilante Queen." I was about to read it when DS Bright phoned.

"I'm sorry I haven't got any news," she said. "Just a question."

"Sure," I said.

"Would you mind coming out to take a look at your car in situ?" she asked. "Before it gets towed? I'd like you to cast an eye over it and tell me if you see anything that looks wrong, or odd, about it."

"Like what?"

"Like body damage, perhaps a dent that wasn't there before, or the remains of any objects that are unfamiliar."

They picked me up. We drove across the bridge and then down a road cut into the steep side of the gorge until we were at water level, on the city side of the river. It was high tide and the river ran thick, brown, and fast. In a turnout, just half a mile along, was the carcass of Dan's beloved car.

We pulled over and got out. I wrapped my coat around me.

The sky was bruised behind the shell of the car, as if the pall of noxious smoke sent up by the flames was lingering like a soul that didn't want to pass.

The wreckage stank. The car was all but obliterated. I don't know what they thought I might be able to see when all that was left was blackened and distorted. How beautiful it must have looked when it was burning, I thought. The flames, the water behind them. I loved the elemental. The simplicity of it. Its undeniability.

I got a kick out of DS Bright lifting the crime scene tape so I could duck beneath it, I won't pretend I didn't. I walked around the outside of the car and peered into the wreckage.

"See anything?" DS Bright asked.

I shook my head. "Nothing."

I wondered if Dan had watched the car burn, or if he had been far away. He must have been somewhere else. He wouldn't have been able to bear to watch his baby go up in flames, would he? It would have tormented him. I didn't want the car to be left out here like this any longer, on display for anyone driving past to see. It was so ugly, so horribly charred, exuding violence. I couldn't stand to look at it any longer.

"Can we go now?"

"Absolutely," DS Bright said. She wore a moss-colored beanie that made the color of her eyes shift from gray to green. She looked wholesome, somehow. In the car she rubbed her hands together to warm them up. "Do you remember you mentioned a structural engineer who came to your house on the evening you last saw Dan?"

"Yes."

"Right. It's just that we've been calling around local structural engineering firms and none of them have a record of any of their engineers visiting that day."

"I don't think it was an official visit. He called in because he was passing. They'd been trying and failing to get hold of each other to make an arrangement. Or that's what Dan said."

"Uh-huh."

"Maybe he wasn't an engineer," I added. "Maybe I remembered that wrong. He might have been a surveyor, or a builder.

He was something to do with the house, though. I'm sure of that, because Dan was, is, organizing the renovation."

"Right," she said. "It would be helpful if you could remember exactly."

"I know. I'm sorry but I don't. I'd had a few drinks."

"At your neighbors' party?"

"Yes."

She nodded. "We've begun interviews with your neighbors," she said.

I felt a throbbing in my head and a tightening around my chest. "Don't talk," Eliza said, but I couldn't stand the pressure of keeping everything to myself any longer. "Talk to me, not her, then," Eliza said, but I couldn't stop myself from blurting out what was on my mind:

"I think my husband might have been having an affair with my neighbor Sasha Morell. She lives in the first house on the lane." My words tumbled out. "I witnessed them having an intimate moment. At least I think I did."

I told DS Bright what I'd seen. It felt like a relief to say it. She made careful notes, her notepad angled away from me so I couldn't see what she was writing.

"We'll bear that in mind," she said.

When we'd gotten home and were alone, Eliza said, "You should never have told her that. It gives you motive."

"Motive for what?" I asked.

"What do you think?"

My blood ran cold.

"Why didn't you answer me, before? Where did you go?" I asked.

"I wanted to see what you would do without me."

She said it innocuously, but the sheer unprecedented nature of it made it feel like a threat.

"Eliza," I said. "For the second time: Did you do something to Dan?"

But she had gone again. It seemed as if she had decided she would only be around for the conversations she wanted to have. It tore at me. Was this betrayal or malice? Something else? Little shreds of anxiety fell around me, and also little pieces of my heart because I had loved Eliza for as long as I could remember. I'd loved her even before I'd loved Teddy.

24

Max called.

"Are you all right?" he asked. "Is there something you want to tell me?"

My insides flip-flopped.

"I've had a call from a tabloid journalist," he continued. "Is Dan missing?" His tone sounded incredulous but there was also an unmistakable and cold undertone of gravity.

"How did they know?" I whispered.

"Police departments are leaky sieves. I'm so sorry, Lucy."

Of course, I knew that an inquisitive journalist's best friend is a police officer with a mouth like a torn pocket. My family had felt the full, life-shattering repercussions of intense tabloid interest in us after Teddy disappeared and I had never gotten over my fear of being a target of it again one day.

"The tabloids?" I wanted to confirm. If they started to look into me, it was only a matter of time before they discovered who I'd been.

"I'm afraid so. Look, Angela is going to call you because she wants to offer you her PR people. We know how you feel about publicity, but I think you have to take her up on this. We need to try to manage it."

I took the call from Angela. My heart was thumping in my throat. She spoke urgently and clearly. I pictured her mouth enunciating the words, lipstick stretching and cracking.

"This is so awful for you. You're a private person, Lucy, we're very respectful of that, but please let us help you here."

I heard myself agree. Or perhaps it was Eliza. I didn't know how to handle this on my own.

"Please expect a call from my colleague Noah. He's going to take care of everything and will be in touch very soon. In the meantime, I think it's great that you've got the book to work on, to distract you," Angela said.

After we hung up, I laughed at her suggestion that the book would distract me, but it sounded like a horrible noise.

I felt vulnerable. It would only be a matter of time before the press came here. I would have to keep away from windows in the front and back of the house. I moved around, pulling blinds and curtains and closing shutters where I could find them.

From a front window, I saw Kate Delaney and her children at the end of our drive. They were dressed for a walk. An elderly chocolate Labrador walked determinedly alongside them on stiff limbs. Kate looked toward the house. I stepped back from the window so she couldn't see me. It was hard to take my eyes off her. Her children were clustered around her, but she wasn't paying them any attention. It was as if she was trying to decide whether to come and see me or not. The police must have visited her, and told her about Dan.

Her older boy carried a large stick. I saw the little boy ask for it. His brother gave it to him but as soon as he did, the little one swung it at his siblings, hitting the shins of both of them. His sister retaliated angrily, pushing him over, and he landed on his backside and began to cry. "Serves him right," Eliza snapped. But Kate didn't think so. She swung around and scooped up her youngest child, cuddling him close. The stick dangled from his hand. His expression was triumphant. Kate chastised the other children, oblivious to or disbelieving of their obvious outrage at the unfairness of it.

I considered going out there, to explain what had actually happened, it felt imperative that she know the truth, but just as I was about to, Ben appeared. He glanced down my drive, too, so I stayed in the shadows. It was only late afternoon so it was surprising to see him, and I realized it must be the school holidays and he must have time off. A great distance seemed to have opened up between me and real life, and it frightened me that I couldn't really remember the last time that hadn't been the case.

I watched as Ben Delaney was immediately drawn into the drama by his older children. They reached for him but he held his hands up out of their reach and smiled as if to say, *Come on, now, don't be petty*, and with a gentle hand on each of their backs he urged them on. The old dog wagged at his side. Ben Delaney took the little boy from Kate and hoisted him onto his shoulders. The child looked delighted. Delaney took Kate's free hand and the family walked on, out of sight, toward the woods at the end of the lane.

It hurt me to watch this scene. I shuddered.

The house seemed colder than usual, the sort of chill that seeps into your bones and makes you tremble from the inside out. I felt the radiators. They were frigid.

The boiler was in a dark corner of the basement, where the smell of damp was strong and the gaps in the stonework spilled crumbling plaster and dense cobwebs. The quarry-tiled floor was in bad shape and the boiler itself was a box-shaped behemoth, the pipes feeding it a primitive set of arteries covered in a thick layer of dust.

I found a complex control panel and peered at it, but nothing suggested itself as a sensible thing to do.

I called Dan. Straight to voicemail again. I hung up.

I started to fret about the press. How long would it take them to find me? I wondered if they would creep down our private lane or try to approach through the woods. I knew they would go as far as it took to make my story as salable as possible. My memory of them hounding us after Teddy disappeared was one of my most traumatic. How they watched us. What they wrote about us. My parents hadn't been able to shield me from everything. My classmates made sure I heard the worst of what they called me.

The doorbell startled me. It rang insistently, followed by robust knocking on the door.

I went and looked through the spyhole. It was Sasha. I took a deep, steadying breath before opening up.

"I just heard that Dan is missing!" she said. "The police came round!"

She clamped me in a hug that I didn't want. My skin prickled with animosity. She released me and studied my face intently. It seemed like she had more questions than DS Bright. When had I last seen Dan? Where? How had he seemed? Was I all right? Had he called at all?

I didn't want to tell her anything.

"The boiler is broken," I said, because I didn't know what else to say and I wanted to divert her attention, give her something to play Good Samaritan over.

"What? Oh, no. That's the last thing you need. I know a very good man. Would you like me to call him? I can get him out ASAP."

She was so eager to help. I didn't like it, but what could I do? "Yes, please," I said, and invited her in, out of the cold. She got on the phone and oozed charm into the ear of her plumber.

"He can come later tonight, or first thing tomorrow morning at the latest," she said once she'd hung up. I was sitting on the stairs. She rubbed her hands together. "It's absolutely freezing in here." Sasha wore a coat, so it seemed she'd felt the cold quickly. "You can't stay here tonight. Come to ours. I hate the thought of you being in the cold with everything that's happening."

It was the last thing I wanted to do, and I was about to make an excuse when Eliza said, "If you go, and get to know her better, you might have a sense of whether she and Dan are involved with one another. You've got to ask yourself why she has so many questions about him and why she seems so stressed."

It was a thought, and a surprisingly tempting one. It would be good to have confirmation of what I suspected. "That would be nice," I said. "Thank you."

"How about you give me a set of keys for the plumber? I've got a safe box he knows the code to so he could grab them from there and come and go without bothering you. He's very trust-worthy."

I wanted to say no. I didn't like the thought of other people being able to get in and out without me.

"Of course, you don't have to," Sasha said, and I felt she was judging me for my reticence.

"Sure," I said. I found her a set.

It was hard to hand them over and watch her slip them into her pocket. I had the uneasy feeling that I'd done something reckless.

XII

The missing child alert is issued at 7 A.M.

The description reads as follows: *Edward Bewley (known as Teddy) disappeared from Stoke Woods near Bristol. He is three years old and has dark-blond hair, long bangs, and brown eyes. Teddy was wearing a pair of cotton pajama bottoms with a Thomas the Tank Engine logo on the right thigh, a green T-shirt, and a pair of red sneakers. Teddy has a distinctive birthmark on his left upper arm. He may have a pale blue, fleecy, satin-edged blanket with him, approximately 60 x 80 cm in size.*

DI Cartwright has already established two important things that suggest to him that part of Lucy's story is true, at least. He believes that someone Teddy knew took him from the house. Carol Bewley has confirmed that he could not put on his shoes himself. Someone had to have helped him. This suggests that Teddy was awake when he left the property, was expected to have to walk, and was accompanied. It doesn't rule out a grab and bundle into a waiting vehicle, but it makes this far less likely in Cartwright's view. Carol and Martin Bewley both confirm that Teddy was overly attached to the blanket that has disappeared with him and would have been likely to cry loudly if he had had to leave the house without it. Taking it would have been an insurance policy for someone who knew the child and wanted to sneak him out.

As a result, DI Cartwright has the feeling that the first part of Lucy's story is true. It's the exact nature of what happened after the children left their home together that's beginning to gnaw at him.

25

Sasha showed me to one of her guest rooms. It was already made up and was as luxurious as any hotel I'd ever stayed in, more luxurious than most. I felt like an imposter.

"I'll leave you to settle in," she said, and she yawned in an economical way, like a cat. It made me think about how her jaw was hinged, the mechanics of it beneath her skin. I bet Dan never thought of her like that. He was a man who enjoyed surfaces, texture, who ran his hand over tooled furniture, a fine glaze, soft skin. He would like the curtains in here, so thickly lined that the hem filled my fist.

I threw my tote onto the bed. I'd packed in a hurry while Sasha waited downstairs. My things fell out. Strewn across the crisp bed linen were my tired plaid pajamas; my toothbrush, whose bristles resembled a well-used boot cleaner; a squeezed-flat tube of toothpaste; and the folder of documents about the bunker.

I was daunted by the thought of going downstairs and talking to Sasha and James. I washed my face and tugged at my clothing, smoothing it out and tucking it in where I could, but I still looked a mess. I took my time on the stairs and stood for a moment in the hall wondering where they were, too shy to call out.

I heard their voices coming from the living room. I was right behind the door, about to push it open, when James spoke loud enough for me to hear.

"Don't get involved," he said. "Why would you? Let her stay the night tonight, then send her home tomorrow. Help her make other arrangements if that makes you feel better, but she can't stay here indefinitely. This could go on for weeks before anyone knows what's happened."

"Don't you think she's reacting oddly?" Sasha said, and her voice dropped so low that I had to lean right against the door to hear. "I mean, not to mention before now that he'd disappeared, not even to come around and ask if we'd seen him?"

James didn't respond. I heard only silence, as if it wasn't just me holding my breath, but them, too. I imagined their eyes turned toward the door. I took a couple of paces back as quietly as possible and hurried upstairs again, where I shut myself loudly into the bathroom at the top of the stairs. I sat on the loo for a few minutes, then flushed it and washed my hands, in case they were listening.

When I came out, Sasha was in the hall, one hand on the banister, looking up.

"Hey, you," she said. "Come and join us by the fire."

Sasha was a good actress. She'd put on an expression that was a picture of sympathy. Her figure was silhouetted beneath a sheer black shirt that had the drape of expensive silk. I knew that if I wore the same outfit, the shirt's gauzy panels would not waft but sag and catch on the ledges formed by my collapsed flesh, which had a tendency to hang over my waistband like melted candle wax. I felt a small but insistent tug of jealousy.

James stood up when I entered the room. It was all very formal. I found myself nodding at him because I wasn't sure what else to do.

"How are you holding up?" he said. He, too, was doing a good job of feigning compassion.

I sat opposite him, at one end of a sofa, by the fire. I wedged myself against the armrest. On the coffee table between us was a stack of glossy art, design, and travel books; beside them a paperback copy of my most recently published Eliza novel, well-thumbed, looking like a dowdy gate-crasher at a glam party. It was Dan's favorite of my books.

"I'm okay," I said, "because I'm sure Dan will be home soon."

They exchanged a glance. Sasha got up. "Yes, quite," James said, though it seemed as if he had to fumble for that simple answer. "Of course." Then, "That's right."

On the fire, a log settled, and sparks rose before dying back down. I heard the clink of expensive glassware as Sasha placed a tumbler of something amber-colored on the table in front of me. She handed another drink to James, then got herself one before curling like a cat on a chair between us and cradling a glass between her palms. I noted her manicure was badly chipped, which gave me some pleasure. Schadenfreude, even small-scale, even at inappropriate moments, can be satisfying.

"Medicinal," she said, raising her glass somberly. I didn't mention that I don't drink spirits, that I consider it mannish. I sipped the whiskey and had to suppress a cough. I thought about Dan falling in love with Sasha and wondered if James knew or suspected anything. I glanced at him, but he was staring into the fire.

"What's that?" Sasha asked, breaking the silence, indicating the folder I'd tucked between my thigh and the arm of the sofa. I'd brought it down with me, hoping I might read it and avoid conversation. "Research for a book?"

"Sort of," I said.

"Your next?"

I nodded. I wasn't going to say what it actually was.

"Is it another Eliza book?" she asked.

Why would she ask that question and in that way? The way it was phrased was what I'd expect from someone who worked inside publishing, or was very close to it. Had Dan told her something? Was she using his words? Had he confided in her about me? It was such a humiliating thought.

"Of course," I said. I watched her carefully and she seemed to be doing the same in return.

"Are you all right? You're very pale," she asked.

"I feel a little nauseous." It was true, I did. It was a thick feeling at the back of my throat. My saliva tasted bitter. The heat from the fire was suddenly stifling.

I wondered how it was that Sasha had noticed I was unwell before I did. It was something Dan did to me, often, and it made me feel unbalanced, suggestible, and had been one of the things that had played into my paranoia that he was gaslighting me. But there had also been occasions, especially at times when I'd been working so hard that the rest of life had gone out of focus, when I'd liked it, and felt grateful that he was paying attention to me, that he cared.

"Actually," I said, "if you don't mind, I'll probably just go to bed."

"Don't you want something to eat?"

"No, thank you," I said, even though it was a lie.

James nodded. His face seemed more shadowy than before, craggy and impossible to read.

I took the folder with me.

I meant to read it before sleeping, but once I was in the downy embrace of the bed, I was unable to keep my eyes open. It was strange for me to feel comfortable so quickly in a new place. So strange that in the sinking moments before sleep I wondered if there had been something extra in the drink Sasha had given me.

26

I woke up in the middle of the night. It was the kind of awake where you know you won't be able to sleep again anytime soon. The bed was too soft.

I was afraid to put the light on in my room because I didn't want Sasha and James to know that I was awake. Overhearing her spinning my own behavior against me had been horrifying. And dangerous. I was wary of what she might tell the police.

I thought about DS Bright. She presented as relaxed, almost disheveled, but I agreed with Eliza that there was more to her beneath that demeanor. I thought of it as a feline watchfulness, a calmness, qualities that masked what she might really be feeling. I hadn't figured that out, yet, but Eliza was right: I should be wary of Detective Sergeant Lisa Bright. She should not be underestimated.

I was more awake than ever now. I reached for my phone and went online, to the Eliza Grey fan fiction page, my safe space. I thought I could pass the time there, hoped it might make me feel sleepy.

I saw straightaway that the site looked different. An administrator had pinned a message prominently on the home page.

BREAKING NEWS: Lucy Harper's husband, Daniel, whom some of you may know as her personal assistant or have interacted with on social media, is MISSING. We are sending thoughts and prayers to Lucy and Dan at this time. Updates will be posted here.

So, the news was out now. Someone had started a group chat about it. It was full of expressions of sympathy. I felt disconcerted but also touched when I read the nicer comments. One person had written, They need to get Eliza on the case. Another said, Eliza will make sure justice is done, whatever it takes! I noticed that MrElizaGrey had replied to both: Don't confuse reality and fiction. Just that. I couldn't take my eyes off the words. They bothered me because this was something Dan had said to me, many times, over the years. When there were things that I thought I'd remembered, for example, but he'd reassured me that I hadn't. Or when I'd forgotten something that he said he'd already told me. I stared at the words on my screen. They seemed to pulse. "Is that you?" I whispered. Had Dan written this for my eyes?

I clicked on MrElizaGrey's profile to see if he was online now, thinking I could message him live, but he wasn't. I read his bio. It was only one line. Married to Eliza Grey. I'd seen it in the past and laughed at it, but now I wondered, was it something more? Was this Dan? Playing with me? But I told myself not to be foolish. Why would he bother to impersonate someone else online?

I was curious how these people knew about him. Had the tabloids published the story already? I pulled up a search engine and entered Dan's name. The news had broken across most of the national sites, I discovered. I clicked on the first link. It was a press release issued by Avon and Somerset Police:

> **Multimillion-selling author Lucy Harper's husband, Daniel Harper, known as Dan, went missing on the night of Tuesday 10 April. The couple's car was found burned out in the city of Bristol. Police are asking anyone who might have seen or heard from Dan to get in contact immediately.**

I clicked on a video of DS Lisa Bright standing in front of a screen bearing a police logo. She gazed right into the camera as she appealed for help. "We have reason to be very concerned about Daniel Harper's welfare," she said. I felt as if she was looking right into my eyes. I clicked back to the home screen and put my phone facedown. The screen went black after a brief pause and the room fell completely dark again.

My breathing was shallow, my head light. I felt as if I might melt into the sumptuous bedding and be suffocated by it. My bladder was aching. I got up but as I did, I felt the back of my neck prickle. I moved very slowly, holding my breath as I turned toward the window.

Eliza wasn't there. I'd thought she would be, but I was wrong. I exhaled with relief and held my bandaged hand to my chest. It throbbed.

And my neck still prickled.

Something bright was glowing behind the crack in the curtains, the thread of light tempting me toward it, as if begging me to open them.

XIII

The detective doesn't speak to you the way other adults do. He doesn't act like you're just a stupid kid but talks to you as if you are a grown-up. Initially, this feels like a nice surprise.

"Right, Lucy," he says, the first time you sit together. "Let's hear this story of what happened last night. You're not in any trouble so I want you to tell me everything, and it's important that you tell me the truth, do you understand?"

You nod. You won't lie about anything, you'll just leave the bunker out of the story. Eliza insists and you don't disobey her.

"Anything you can remember is helpful," he says. "So, don't leave any detail out. I'd like to hear everything."

You will tell him everything else you can remember, in detail.

Meeting DI Cartwright-but-please-call-me-Charlie's eye is difficult at first, but it becomes easier as you start to talk, and he nods, encouraging you to keep going, to finish the story.

He asks you to repeat it three times.

By the third telling, your nerves have settled, and you've warmed up to the task. With your newfound confidence you find yourself elaborating on the story. Eliza reminds you of little details and you use them to embellish your narrative, describing in detail the fire, the woods, and the spirits, the way they flitted beneath the canopy, ducking and diving among the mesmerizing flashes of moonlight that, you say, looked like light glancing off a disco ball. You describe the sparklers as dancing fairies. You tell Charlie about the golden people and you mimic their chant as best you can, showing him how it got louder and louder until he says, "I get the picture," and then, *"Remind me exactly when you realized Teddy had dis-appeared."*

"When I was watching the fireworks," you say. *"I thought he was right beside me but when I looked, he wasn't. He was gone."*

"Did you see any other people on your side of the bonfire?" Charlie asks.

You shake your head.

"Did you look for Teddy?"

"I looked and looked."

"Did anybody help you?"

You shake your head.

"Why not?"

"I don't know."

"Did you tell them Teddy was gone?"

"No."

"Your brother disappears and you don't tell anybody, even though there are people close by who could help you look for him?"

"I told Mummy."

"I know that," he says. *"I'm just wondering why you didn't tell any of the people who were there in the woods with you and could have helped you look for Teddy straightaway. In the time it took you to run home, how far away do you think he could have got?"*

"I don't know."

"You can guess, you're a clever girl."

"I don't know."

"I think you know more than you're saying, young lady."

27

I approached the window, feeling as if I was on the end of a thread, being reeled in, and parted the curtains. Colder air spilled into the room from behind them, and moonlight, too. Outside, the brightest of full moons shone.

It was strange to see the woods from this new angle. From between the bare branches and the lower-growing evergreens, the moonlight picked out a small copse of trees that stood taller than the rest. I knew those trees. They were redwoods. Imported here. Non-native. Intruders. They were beautiful and to me they were also special. As a child I had lodged my fingertips in their soft bark gullies while looking around me, down the public pathway, first in one direction and then the other, to check no one was watching, before I stepped off it and disappeared into the undergrowth. The redwoods were a secret signpost, just for me. They marked the way to the bunker.

For the first time since moving here I felt a pull from the woods, an urge to go out there and try to find the bunker again, to see what was left of it, if anything, after all these years.

"No," Eliza said. "You mustn't."

She was back. I felt relieved, but angry, too, because she'd gone at all, so I ignored her. I wasn't going to listen just because she'd decided to reappear when it suited her.

"Dan is looking for you," I whispered to the bunker. *If he wanted to find it*, I thought, *perhaps I should, too.* It might be why I had felt drawn to the window. Maybe the bunker would have something new to tell me. I even had an idea that Dan might be there, waiting for me, but I dismissed it as quickly as I'd thought it, because it felt silly and also unsettling.

I pictured the bunker as I had left it, on the summer solstice night, and wondered if I were to set foot in it now, would it be an underground *Mary Celeste* where everything had lain untouched since then? Was my tea set still on the desk? What was on the floor where Teddy had been?

It would be the bravest thing I'd ever done, to return there. It made me sick with nerves, but I couldn't imagine not doing it, now.

I hadn't been back there since Teddy went missing because I hadn't dared, and Eliza had forbidden it. But now, I thought that if it would get me closer to Dan, to understanding what was going on in his head, perhaps even to finding him, I would do it.

I realized I had to go soon, though. If media interest in Dan's disappearance was burgeoning, there was a limited amount of time before my every movement would be scrutinized. And I couldn't ask the police to check out the bunker. I would have to explain why it was significant, if I did. I was afraid to do that, afraid to see DS Bright's expression take on a predatory look, the look that told me she had decided who I was. What I was. Because when two people close to you have gone missing, all eyes will turn to you. I knew what that felt like already. I also knew it was probably inevitable that they would find out about my past, but I wasn't going to volunteer it. Who would do that to themselves?

If I wanted to find the bunker, I decided, I had to go this morning. I waited, jittery and tense, until the first hint of dawn. I was anxious about whether I would remember the route there at all, but I had a gut feeling that once I was in the woods, I would know it. The woods themselves would lead me, just the way they did the first time and all the times after that.

James was in the kitchen, dressed for work in a pressed suit, shirt, and tie. "Morning," he said. "How did you sleep?"

I found it disconcerting how attractive he looked. His shoes were freshly shined and clip-clopped across the floor tiles as he came to hand me an espresso. He smelled of the kind of scent that you can't help inhaling deeply and finding unfathomably pleasant.

"Fine, thank you," I said.

"Well, you're welcome to stay as long as you like. Sasha left a spare set of keys out for you so that you can come and go as you wish. She's a bit of an insomniac and might sleep late." He indicated a set of keys on the end of the table.

"Thank you," I said.

"Though I'm sure you'll want to get home," he added.

Wouldn't you like that? I thought, even though he was right. I smiled at him. "I'll be out of your hair this morning. I don't want to impose."

I felt like grabbing my stuff there and then and going home, but I wanted to get into the woods the moment it was light enough and didn't want to have to schlep my bag with me.

James let himself out and I wondered whether he would run into journalists outside, if they were already gathering or if that was my paranoia. I thought I should probably have warned him they might be there, but it was too late now. When his car was out of sight, I pulled on my shoes, grabbed my coat, slipped out of the house, and walked cautiously toward the end of the drive.

Members of the press were there. Only a couple of them, so far, and they were at the top of the lane, but that was more than I was comfortable with. They had cameras. I backed away and for the first time felt thankful that the lane was private, but I would have to find another way into the woods if I didn't want them to see me.

I went back down Sasha and James's drive and followed their boundary wall toward the end of the large garden. The wall and I were shielded from the house by a screen of trees and bushes. I was grateful for that. The last thing I wanted was for Sasha to see me. Even so, I glanced back at the house a few times, think-ing I could feel eyes on me, but nothing changed; there was no twitching curtain or silhouette behind the glass. I did notice that Sasha and James had built a fancy garden shed and done some landscaping around it. It all looked new and expensive.

The wall I was following was almost head height and curved to follow the road. As soon as I felt I'd gone far enough to be out of sight of the journalists if I scaled it, I began to look for a suitable place, but Sasha and James had maintained it too well. It wasn't until I reached the end of their plot, where there was a small orchard, that I found a short stepladder and leaned it against the wall. I landed with a thump on the sidewalk on the other side. Cars whizzed past. The journalists were out of sight.

The woods' car park was a short walk away. It was mostly empty, just one or two vehicles there that probably belonged to early dog walkers.

Stepping into the woods, everything felt familiar to me. I paused for a moment and inhaled. It was early enough in the year that the undergrowth was sparse, letting the long-settled winter leaves release their sweet, earthy smell of decay all around me, coaxing images of moving things from my imagination: crawling earthworms, insects, millipedes, ancient ferns and tight buds uncoiling and unfurling. I had always thought of the woods like this: beautiful and terrifying.

I followed the path until I found the redwood copse. It was as stately and beautiful as I remembered it. I looked to see if the path was clear in either direction. Old habits die hard. There was nobody there. I cut into undergrowth. Within minutes, brambles ripped my pajama pants. I was surprised to see I was still wearing them and realized I should have changed into more suitable clothing, but it was too late to go back now. I pushed on, determined, and it felt like seeing an old friend when I came to the oak whose trunk was distinctively split. I pressed on past it, excitement and apprehension building, but also a sense that I had to finish this, that I could not turn away now, no matter what might be waiting for me.

The land began to fall away, gently at first, then more steeply. The incline hadn't felt this pronounced when I was younger and had a lower center of gravity. I struggled to keep my balance and grabbed at low branches that I hoped would bear my weight. Some didn't. I slipped and slid and lost my bearings once, but not for long. I realized I remembered this landscape as well as the feel of my brother's hand in mine.

Moving on, I felt an increasing sense of urgency. I tore at the foliage in my path. Boughs snapped. It felt as if I would never get to where I needed to be until, suddenly, I stumbled down one final incline and knew I was there. I stopped dead and breathed in the air. I was in a dip in the landscape. I knew its contours.

I looked around, drinking in everything, my senses over-whelmed by the collision of now and then. Slowly, I became aware of the sound of my own breathing. It was a small, shud-dering detail among the movement all around me. I startled at the unexpectedly loud flapping of a bird taking flight from a tree near me. It brought me back to myself.

On the far side of the incline there was a curtain of ivy that looked as if it was covering a rock face. I approached it as if in a dream and found that it parted easily. Spooked, even though that was what I had expected, I pulled my hand back out and saw that it was a child's hand. My own. I shut my eyes and forced myself to reach back through the fronds, farther this time, until I felt cold, rough metal against my fingertips. It was the bunker.

"Lucy," Eliza said. "No. Leave now. You will not get over this."

Her words sapped my courage and I snatched my hand back out again. I felt cold and scared and was wet and scratched, covered in mud, but also afraid of crashing back through the woods, toward a life I barely recognized, no longer understood, and whose newest incarnation frightened me as much as this did.

You've come this far, I told myself. *Don't fail now. You're here for a reason.*

I needed to clear the foliage if I wanted to access the bunker because the door opened outward. I began to do that, but as I did I started to suspect that it had been accessed recently. The signs were small but visible: a freshly snapped branch, the undergrowth trodden down in places where I hadn't been. I pulled the last bits of ivy back and here was certainty: there were scratches around the door handle, and a thick padlock.

It shouldn't have been a surprise that someone else would find this place, it was on public land after all, even if it was exceptionally well hidden, but I hadn't expected it. In my head, the bunker was still mine alone. Lost to the rest of the world.

I examined the padlock. It was large, and shiny. I knew I would probably need tools to break it, but even so I pushed and pulled at the door, kicked it, though it wouldn't budge. I scrambled up the slippery side of the incline beneath which the bunker was buried and once I was on top, I looked for the old ventilation shaft and the cracks that used to admit a cylinder of light into the space below, but I couldn't find any trace. Everything was solid beneath me.

Something glinted. It was half buried in the leaf mold beneath my feet. I reached for it, and as I did, it took on the shape of something so familiar that I bent over and disgorged the contents of my stomach, dumping a gross splatter onto the woodland floor while clamminess spread over my skin.

I straightened up and examined the object in my hand. Dan's watch was chunky, metallic and heavy, an object of beauty in his eyes. I'd bought it for him, at his request, and taken pleasure in how much he treasured it.

I didn't like that it was dirty, and I didn't like that it was here. I wiped it with my thumb. Dan had told me about the watch's mechanical action what seemed like a million times. It needed to have been worn recently to work, within the last thirty to forty hours, or something like that. Once the glass was clean, I saw that the second hand was still.

This was Friday, the third day since Dan had gone missing. If the second hand had been moving it might have suggested Dan had been here since his disappearance. But it wasn't. And it didn't give me any answers as to when he'd been here, and why.

I pressed the face of the watch against my cheek. It felt as gorgeously smooth as human touch but I only lost myself in that feeling for a moment because I was overcome by a sense that someone else was there with me, watching me, and I didn't think it was Eliza.

"Dan?" I called, but the woods stood silent. "Hello?" I heard the sound of a branch snapping in the distance.

"Teddy?" I whispered and the skin on the back of my neck crawled.

I ran. Brambles caught me in their brittle arms, trying to drag me backward, but I fought through them and didn't stop until I was back at the split oak, then the redwoods, and when I broke out onto the path I startled a walker, and her dog chased me for a while, nipping at my ankles, mistaking fear for fun. I kept running until I found myself back in the car park, where I stopped, gasping for breath, bent double, sweating, torn, wet, muddy, under the gaze of a group of walkers, sharp-eyed and uncomplicated in their outdoor gear.

I straightened up slowly and put the watch in my pocket, wrapped my coat around me, and tried to walk past them as if I wasn't fleeing something.

"Morning," one of them said. She nodded economically.

"Morning." I moved on quickly, avoiding meeting their eyes, which I knew would tell me unequivocally that I was a sight they would remember.

It wasn't until I was nearly back at the main road that I realized I hadn't considered how I would get back to Sasha's house, or mine, without running into journalists.

28

As I walked, I hugged the wall, scanning for footholds or anything that might help me get back over it. Vehicles rushed past. I kept my head down when they did, aware of how crazy I looked in my pajama pants, not wanting to be recognized by anyone. I kept thinking, *If someone tries to hit me with their car now, I have nowhere to escape to.*

I heard a car slow down beside me. I walked faster but didn't look up. Its wheels churned the dirty water pooled beside the curb. It decelerated until it was keeping pace with me. My heart hammered. The wheels bumped up onto the curb. I pivoted. The car would have to reverse to keep up with me. I tried to move as fast as I could, but after running through the woods, my legs were leaden. I was too spent to move faster than a slow jog and after only a few paces I couldn't even do that anymore. My body gave up.

"Keep going," Eliza said, "come on!" Everything was hurting. "Come on!" she shouted, but I sank into a crouch.

I heard someone shout my name. I looked up, resigned to whatever this was, expecting at best a journalist and the humiliating photograph that would result. At worst, I wasn't sure what, but I knew in my bones there was a worse scenario.

Vi was leaning out of her car window. "It is you!" she said. "Are you all right?" I didn't waste time but launched myself toward the car, got in beside her, and started to cry in great heaving, messy sobs.

"Oh, my dear," she said. "We heard from the police about

Daniel. We're so sorry. You haven't been out looking for him, have you?" Her expression was aghast.

"Can you take me home?" I asked.

"Of course! Get in the back. Cover yourself with that rug."

I did as she told me. The rug was woolen, fusty and scratchy. I felt claustrophobic. When she restarted the car, I had a paranoid thought. *What if she doesn't take me home?* But after a few seconds I heard her indicator light blinking and the car slowed before creeping around the turn into our lane, where she swore at the journalists.

I asked her to drive onto Sasha's property.

"Barry and I are here for you as well," Vi said when I climbed out. "Don't hesitate to ask for help if you need it."

I let myself in with the keys Sasha had left for me and called out a tentative "Hello?" but not too loudly in case she was still asleep. I hoped she was. There was no answer. I went upstairs. Once I was in the guest room all I wanted was to get home. I took off my pajamas, pulled on my clothes, and threw the rest of the stuff into my bag, but couldn't find the folder.

I felt certain I had left it in the bedroom, on the bedside table, but it wasn't there. I crept downstairs and looked in the sitting room, running a hand between and behind the perfectly plumped sofa cushions. I also checked the kitchen. No sign of it there, either.

I was standing in the hallway, feeling uncertain, when something caught my attention. If there's one sound I recognize it's a printer mechanism at work. I followed the noise, pausing outside a door at the end that stood ajar. The sound of the printer was coming from within, repetitive but not quite rhythmic. I peered in and glimpsed Sasha, her back to the door, my folder open on a desk beside her. She was scanning and printing its pages.

I backed away, afraid to confront her. I crept down the corridor to the front door, opened then shut it with a bang, and hollered this time: "Hello!"

Sasha appeared from the room at the end. She wasn't carrying my folder. "Hey, you," she said. "Any news?"

"Not yet. But there are people from the media camped out at the end of the lane. I heard them so I went out to see how bad it is." I hoped she'd buy that as an excuse.

"Yeah, James texted to say there were one or two out there when he left for work this morning. They tried to talk to him but he said nothing, of course."

"That's good of him."

"Of course! We're all worried about you."

"It's very kind of you, but I should get home this morning."

"You're welcome to stay longer if you like. I can't bear the thought of you going back to that house all alone. I don't even know if the plumber's been. I'll text him."

"It's fine. I'm heading over there now."

"Will you at least have a coffee with me before you go?"

She linked her arm with mine and walked us both toward the kitchen, holding me a little closer to her and walking a little faster than I would have liked. It was the first sign that she was afraid she might be caught in the act of copying the contents of the folder and was panicking over how she would get it back to me. I went with it.

We didn't talk while she made coffee. She ground beans, filled a fancy stovetop pot that looked remarkably like one Dan had recently purchased for us, heated and frothed milk with unhurried movements, just as her husband had done earlier. Now and then she threw a smile at me.

"She's trying to figure out how to get that folder back to you," Eliza said.

Yep, she is, I thought.

Sasha excused herself, saying, "I'll be right back!" as soon as she'd poured our drinks. I sat very still and listened carefully for the creak of her footfall on the stairs. I thought I heard her go up, then down again. I smiled at her when she came back in. We made conversation but it was banal and flat, as if we had both just remembered how little we really knew one another.

The folder was by the bed when I returned upstairs, tucked under the glass of water on the bedside table, which, I guess, was exactly where she'd found it. She'd even aligned my drinking glass with a dried watermark that had puckered the cardboard.

I looked at it for a while before picking it up. It was obvious she cared very much that I didn't know what she'd done.

XIV

Carol Bewley notices the extent of your bruises when she takes you upstairs for a shower in the hours after the police have arrived and the search for Teddy is under way.

"Can you hand her clothes out to me?" you hear Karen, the family liaison officer, say from the landing as you're getting undressed.

"Why?" Carol's voice is a bark. One of her children is missing, and at this stage she is protecting the other with the ferocity of a wild animal.

"It's a request from DI Cartwright but nothing to worry about. Just routine procedure."

Carol stares at the back of the bathroom door, uncertainty flickering across her expression. She picks up your clothes and opens the door a fraction.

"Lovely," Karen says. "If you could just pop them straight in this bag for me . . . That's grand."

Carol shuts the door and turns on the shower. "Jump in, love," she says. She's said these words to you countless times before, but her voice is thicker than usual today, as if she might be about to be sick. She takes a towel from the rail and sits on the closed toilet seat, bent double over it. "Get in, Lucy," she repeats, because you haven't moved. She drags her head up to look at you, but her gaze stays level with your thighs. "What happened to your legs?" she asks. "Where did you get those bruises?"

Your thighs are mottled with red marks. You remember carrying Teddy to the den, the pendulum slap of his shoes against you.

"Don't breathe a word about that," Eliza instructs.

"I don't know," you say. Carol opens her mouth to reply and you wait, terrified, because you're not sure if you can hold the truth in, but she closes it again, then pulls the towel up over her face and sobs into it, and it feels like a shutter has come down.

You get into the shower and close the door.

The water runs. The bathroom window is wide open to the back garden. On the parched lawn your dad paces and DI Charlie Cartwright leans his tall frame against the wall of the house, in the shade, and speaks to your dad in a low voice about what's being done already and what will be done.

Both men look up as a helicopter appears overhead, drowning out their conversation. To Carol, sitting just beneath the window, her face still buried, it feels as if the blades are inside her head, dicing up normality so small it can never be pieced back together.

To you, in the shower, feeling and hearing the water beat down on you, sluicing the smell of the bonfire away, the helicopter blades add an extra layer of noise, creating a cacophony that surrounds and overwhelms you. You squat and cover your ears until it ebbs away.

You're not sure how long afterward it is when your mum opens the shower door and reaches in to turn the water off, but it feels like an eternity and by then you're trembling all over like a forest leaf in a brisk breeze.

29

See that gap in our hedge to the right of the pergola?" Sasha said. She pointed to a spot in her garden. "It's bigger than it looks. If you duck through it, you'll find yourself in Barry and Vi's garden. Cut straight past their vegetable patch into Ben and Kate's, then go diagonally across their front lawn and you should be able to squeeze through the hedge into yours and the journalists won't be able to see you at all."

I looked at her.

"We visit each other that way sometimes," she said. "If we're having a barbecue or something. It's easier than walking up and down the drives." She shrugged. "I'll text Vi and Kate to let them know you're coming, so nobody calls the police."

I pushed through the gap just the way she'd told me.

Vi and Barry's garden was much less manicured than James and Sasha's. I found myself standing beside four raised vegetable beds that were divided from the rest of the garden by pleached fruit trees. The beds were built from old railway sleepers and surrounded by gravel that crunched underfoot. Grass cuttings were heaped in a corner in a makeshift compost bin constructed from old pallets. Their greenhouse was barely standing, though somebody obviously still worked in there because seed trays were neatly lined up on the benches.

The rest of the garden was laid to lawn punctuated with several blossom-laden trees. The grass hadn't been cut yet this season. My feet sank ankle-deep into it. I saw Vi in one of the downstairs windows and she gave me a thumbs-up. I guessed she'd seen the text from Sasha.

Ben and Kate's garden was much smaller and wrapped around their home. Their parking area was empty. Kids' stuff was strewn over a scuffed lawn bookended with football goal-posts and a playhouse. Beside a tatty trampoline, I found a space where it was possible to push myself through the boundary hedge and was at last in my own garden, opposite the kitchen window. *This is very close to where I thought I saw the shadowy man*, I thought, and hurried around the side of the house.

DS Bright's car was parked in the drive. She sat in the driver's seat, facing me. We stared at each other. I felt guilty, as if I'd been caught out in some way. As I approached, she opened the car door and her booted feet crunched the gravel, one after the other.

"I stayed at my neighbor's house last night," I said. "I didn't want the journalists to see me coming home." I felt I had to explain.

"Understandable," she said.

"Do you have any news?" I asked, and thought that should probably have been the first thing to come out of my mouth.

"I'm afraid I still don't have anything to update you on as yet, but I'd like to ask you about something. Do you mind if I come in for a quick chat?"

She followed me to the porch. There were boxes stacked just inside it. They were addressed to me. Two had publishers' stickers on them so I knew they were probably editions of my books. I dragged them inside. The others were unmarked. I didn't want to touch them. I thought they might be from Eliza's fan.

"Something wrong?" DS Bright asked, watching me.

"No," I said.

"Do you want these boxes in, too?"

I didn't, but I was afraid of looking even more paranoid.

"Sure," I said. "Thank you." At least I didn't have to touch them myself. "Heavy!" she said as she picked one of them up. When she had put both down on the hall floor, I imagined blood seeping from the seams of the boxes and pooling beneath them. I hurried into the kitchen and put the kettle on.

DS Bright sat at the table. I gave her tea in Dan's mug, black because there was no milk, and sat opposite her. I noticed my hands were clenched, so I unclenched them and cradled my mug and beneath the scabs, the knuckles on my unbandaged hand turned from white to pink. The hospital bandage on the other was looking dirty after my trip to the woods.

"We are making a start on accessing your husband's phone records and social media accounts," DS Bright said, and I nodded even though I already knew what they'd be doing, because Eliza followed correct police procedure in all my books. I was a bit of an amateur expert on it, in fact. I thought it best not to point that out, though.

"Good call," Eliza muttered. "Detectives always think they're the smartest person in the room."

I tried hard not to let a little smile play across my lips and focused on the locket DS Bright wore on a chain around her neck, so that she wouldn't read any amusement in my eyes.

"That's good," I said.

"The thing I'm wondering about," she said, "is why you didn't tell my officers right away that your husband was missing."

"I did."

"Well, you didn't, actually. They spent some time in your home with you and you said nothing."

"Well, he hadn't been gone very long. And I fainted when they told me about the car. You can't tell people something when you're unconscious."

"But after you regained consciousness, you were with them for around an hour, both in their car and in the hospital, before you told them that you believed Dan had disappeared. I just wondered why the delay, given that you knew by then the car had been discovered burned out and that, according to your statement, you believed your husband had taken it when he left."

"I was concussed. I wasn't thinking straight."

She blinked and nodded lightly. Her expression didn't change otherwise. She was waiting for me to say more, but I knew better than to fill a silence just because it was there. That was the oldest trick in the detective's playbook. Eliza had used it plenty of times.

DS Bright sipped her tea, and I sipped mine, mirroring her. When she put the mug down, she said, "This is nice tea. Thank you. Now, is there any other reason you might have withheld that information, do you think?"

I didn't know what to say. No words would come. Eliza stepped in and spoke for me. "Look," she told DS Bright, "I'm someone people watch. I have a profile. I'm cautious about saying things that might generate headlines before facts are established."

"I would have thought that weaponizing your profile to help us find Daniel might be very useful."

"It will be. I'm sure you drove past journalists when you arrived here."

"I did indeed."

"And we both know they can be both a help and a hindrance." I wanted Eliza to stop talking. She sounded too feisty. She was protecting me, I knew that, but I was afraid she'd go too far.

DS Bright smiled carefully. "I take your point." She'd noted the difference in my tone, I could see that.

"So, I was thinking," she added. "You said the other day that you thought Dan might have disappeared just to get you worried."

I nodded. "A sort of game between us," I said. "If you see what I mean."

"Here's the thing: disappearing strikes me as quite an extreme thing to do, for a game."

I felt embarrassed. I wasn't always sure what was extreme

and what was normal. I'd only ever been with Dan. I tried to make light of it. "You know how couples are."

Her head pivoted from side to side as if she was weighing this up and finding herself unconvinced. "Any other games you played?" she asked. "That you can tell me about?"

I thought of the time Dan made me believe I'd forgotten a lunch. I'd been working when he called, lost in a draft of one of the earlier Eliza books.

"I'm at the restaurant!" he said. "Where the hell are you?"

"I thought it was tomorrow!" I said.

He had arranged it so we could celebrate a foreign book deal. We were going out to eat French food because a French publishing house had bought another Eliza novel. I rushed to the restaurant and arrived hot, bothered, and guilty that I'd forgotten.

"Can't you keep track of anything?" he'd said.

"It was tomorrow," I said. "I'm sure it was."

"Maybe it was," he said. "It's your book deal we're celebrating, so I guess you know best."

Back at home, I'd checked the diary. Something was scribbled out for the day after, and I knew I hadn't done it, but it was impossible to read what it was. It could have been proof that I'd been right, and Dan had been messing me around, but I'd never know. And if he had done it, was that a game? Certainly, it had felt as if I was being played. Some might call it gaslighting.

DS Bright cleared her throat. She was waiting for an answer. Eliza spoke for me.

"No," she said. "There were no more games. Unless you count Scrabble."

When DS Bright had gone, I opened one of the boxes in the hall. I didn't want to, but opening it felt better than picking it up without knowing what was in it. I held my breath as I slit open the tape with a knife. The first box contained a sumptuous bunch of flowers in a vase. Their scent was strong and cloying. There was no note. The other box contained a hamper of edible goodies. A small envelope was lodged among them. I opened it. My hands were shaking.

Dear Lucy. Some treats to help you along with your edits and welcome Eliza back to the book! We CANNOT WAIT to read it. Angela and the rest of Team Lucy xxxx

They must have sent this before they found out that Dan was missing. In the absence of a note I assumed the flowers were from them, too.

My phone buzzed with my publisher's number. I answered.

"Lucy, hi, this is Noah Cole. I'm the director of PR at MunhallShone. Angela asked me to give you a call."

He sounded warm and said some nice things about me and my books before getting to the point.

"We've had a meeting about how to proceed and we're all in agreement that the best course of action would be for you to give an interview to a carefully selected broadcaster, where you'll make a short statement about Dan's disappearance and answer one or two questions that we will pre-agree with them. Because of your profile, we should have our pick of interviewers, so it will be someone you're comfortable with. And ideally, we should do this as soon as possible. How does that sound?"

He heard my hesitation. I felt as if actively engaging with the outside world was tantamount to launching myself into a snake pit, but I didn't believe any other option would be better. I knew I probably owed him full disclosure about what the media might find out if they dug into my background, but that wasn't going to happen.

"I want to reassure you that we feel certain this is the best way to calm things down as much as possible and to get your message out there, in your own words. We will help you prepare for the interview. We'll script your statement and your answers.

Everything we can control, we will control. It could help to find Dan. Are you aware that there are hashtags popping up on social media?"

"No," I said. The thought sickened me. "What are they?"

"#WheresDanHarper has been trending. We also have quite a lot of mentions of Dan using the hashtag #internetsleuth. It's why we think an interview is the best course of action. It means the message is ours. Yours."

"Okay," I said, though I felt riven by nerves. "I'll do it."

"How is the situation on your end? Any reporters at your door, or calling?"

"There are some at the end of my lane."

"Okay. They're probably local press at this stage, maybe tabloids. Don't engage with them. We'll get this organized as quickly as possible. I'll be in touch as soon as I have more to report."

The phone call left me uneasy, queasy. I understood that we were trying to control the situation but being handled produced the usual miserable feeling of powerlessness in me.

I took the hamper into the kitchen and tore open a packet of chocolate biscuits. They were delicious. There was enough stuff in there for me to eat for several days, I thought, so I could avoid going out.

I picked up my coat from where I had cast it onto a kitchen chair. Dan's watch fell out of the pocket and onto the floor. I picked it up and saw the face had cracked. "I'm sorry," I said. Dan would be very upset when he saw this. A tear fell onto the glass and shuddered there for a moment before I wiped it away.

"Take it outside," Eliza said, "and bury it."

I pulled on a big coat and put up the hood before going out. It was blustery. I could only think of how photographers could be lurking anywhere. The most private place in the garden, out of sight of the wood and the end of the driveway, was by the side of the house, near the kitchen doors.

I chose a spot in a muddy flowerbed, digging a hole with my

hands. The earth got beneath my fingernails and muddied my cuffs and the bandage. I put the watch in the hole and watched as the earth closed back over it, both sides coming together as if they were a viscous liquid. I finished the job, piling more handfuls of earth on top, and did my best to make it look undisturbed.

Inside, I took off the bandage and threw it away. I washed my hands over and over again until they were red and sore, and the scabs threatened to break off and the cut seemed likely to reopen, and then I stopped.

30

The house was warm now. Almost too hot. I brought the bunch of flowers into the kitchen and pulled off some of the packaging, but not all of it. It defeated me.

I assumed the plumber must have fixed the boiler, although there was no note from him, or invoice. Perhaps Sasha would forward that. I would have to get my keys back.

I fetched the folder, wanting to know what was in there that she could be so interested in, and emptied it onto the table. One page contained a diagram and my heart skipped a beat, because I recognized instantly that it showed the inside of the bunker.

To anyone else, the piece of paper I held in my hand might seem innocuous, containing just a few straight lines, neatly drawn, carefully labeled, but to me it was such a powerful reminder of a specific place that it almost felt like an assault.

Sensory recollections flooded my brain. I saw the exact spot I had left Teddy. I felt the bitter prickle of wood smoke in my nostrils. I heard him cry, but not when we were in the bunker; this was earlier, while we were walking through the woods. Moonlight flickered among the trees. The golden glow of the fire grew incredibly intense.

I shut my eyes and reminded myself to breathe and stayed that way until it all subsided. "Good," Eliza said. "Well done."

When I was calm, I looked at the plan again. I began to notice differences between what I remembered and what was there on the paper. The diagram wasn't quite right. That was natural, I supposed, my memory being hazy at the best of times, but I wasn't convinced the mistake was mine. If there was one thing I had known well, it was every inch of that bunker.

I examined the diagram more closely and saw a couple of lines of text at the top of the page.

Diagram is only a typical example of one of these bunkers. The interior of the rumored bunker in Stoke Woods has not been examined because its exact location has been difficult to establish. Local historians speculate that it may have collapsed naturally or been damaged by quarrying activity.

So, this wasn't an exact drawing. That explained the discrepancies. I felt relieved. Whoever drew this hadn't been there. But Dan had.

"His watch has. You don't know that he has," Eliza said. She never inferred things, but interpreted evidence literally. It was one of the big differences between us.

But I thought I knew Dan had been there. I'd felt his presence. And it didn't surprise me. He had long had an obsession with Teddy's disappearance.

I first told Dan about my brother when I was drunk. Heady days, dizzy days. We were still dating at the time, though things had progressed to the point where we had begun to swap personal anecdotes, offering morsels of private information to one another as if they were carefully chosen little tributes. Which, in a way, I suppose, they were. Quid pro quo.

Dan and I had gotten drunk in his flat. He had been talking about his writing, about his experiments, past and planned, with narrative voices and styles. We lay side by side on the couch and I put my hand on his ribs and felt his heart beating as he enthused about his experiments with first person, second person, third person, omniscient narrator, magical realism, and bildungsroman, and also a stream-of-consciousness novel that he was working on at the time. He spoke in long paragraphs strewn with references to writers whose names I did not recognize but I understood that I probably should have.

I was in awe of his passion then, and his self-professed love of the craft. I wanted to impress him in return. I had had a lot to drink. My inebriated imagination suggested that I tell him about Teddy.

"Don't," Eliza said. "Do. Not."

But I began to whisper my story to him, and I felt his heartbeat quicken as I did, even though he lay still as a board. He sat up once I'd finished. I felt abruptly cold where his body had been pressed against mine just moments before.

"God," he said, "I've got so many questions. This is incredible." The light in his eyes was hungry.

"You can't tell anyone," I said.

"No. Of course not. But . . . wow."

I had a sinking feeling that my story titillated him like a cheap read in a tabloid. This disconcerted me. I had expected more intimacy to result from my revelation. I tried to snuggle, to hold back the feelings of sobriety and disappointment that were creeping over me, but Dan was already in another place.

"What did you expect?" Eliza said. I could hear the disappointment in her voice.

It was years later, in the aftermath of another drunken night, one where we had met Max to celebrate my first big book deal, that I woke to find Dan standing in the bedroom doorway, shirtless and holding a breakfast tray. He was staring at me. Milky morning light paled his narrow, sloped shoulders. I busied myself sitting up in the bed, covering my breasts, which always seemed vast and almost obscenely buoyant by comparison to his tall, rangy frame.

He had made coffee and toast for me. That was a first. He put the tray on my bedside table and climbed back into bed with me. I bit into the toast. White bread, the middle of each slice soaked in warm butter, the yeasty tang of Marmite biting my tongue, the crisp crust. Bliss and rapture unconfined. He watched me eat. I littered the bed with crumbs. He sipped from a cup of black coffee.

"You should write about Teddy," he said.

"Never."

"No, I mean it. You really should. It's incredible material. And now that you've got a platform it would attract a lot of attention."

He reached for me, his fingers grazing my jaw. I wasn't expecting him to touch me and I batted his hand away more violently than I should have and scrambled from the bed, clutching the duvet around me, the tray of toast and coffee dislodged from the bedside table and tipped everywhere. Dark liquid spilled. What crime writer, even a fledging one as I was then, doesn't, if only for a moment, see that as blood?

"Whoa!" Dan said. He raised his hands in a gesture of surrender.

"Teddy being in the bunker is a secret, and whatever happens, it stays a secret," I said.

"Hey, relax." He shifted across the bed toward me. I backed away.

"Don't touch me."

"I'm not going to."

I threw up the toast in the bathroom. He held my hair back from my face as I bent over the toilet bowl. I think he did, anyhow. That could have been another time.

I looked again at the diagram and imagined Dan studying it. I searched through the other papers but found nothing that stood out. It was all dry historical fact. Except for the one line about the expected mortality rate for the men who might have used the place. That wasn't dry at all. Approximately twelve days they were expected to live.

"Put it away," Eliza said. She sounded fatigued.

"Is Dan playing games with me?" I asked her. "Why is he interested in this stuff?"

"Honestly, you should stop tormenting yourself," she said. "Rest. Try to calm down. You're not doing yourself any favors."

My phone rang. It was DS Bright again. It felt as if she was hounding me.

"I won't keep you," she said, "just another quick query, if you don't mind."

"Okay."

"Who are the professionals you consult when you're researching your novels?"

I reeled them off. The retired detective inspector, the two forensic scientists, the judge, the prison officer, the martial arts expert, the professor of pharmacology, and the crime-scene cleanup outfit. There was no point in omitting any of them. They were all thanked by name in the back of my books.

"There was no point in lying about it," I said to Eliza, afterward.

"I agree," she said. Neither of us mentioned how my borrowed expertise might make me look more suspicious in the eyes of the police. That was a given.

"I hope she doesn't look at my internet search history." I laughed. It's a crime writer's joke. But Eliza made no comment. She had gone again. And I didn't know which was worse—her or Dan, playing with me.

XV

Who is Eliza?" Charlie asks, for the second time. The French doors are open to the garden but there's no breeze. Everything is hot and still. You've gotten used to the sound of barking dogs coming from the woods. They're looking for Teddy.

"Shouldn't she have a break?" Karen asks. She sits in the corner, fanning her face with an envelope. Her cheeks are red.

Charlie ignores her. You're tired of talking to him. It's so hard to make him happy. He wants stories, but you never seem to be able to tell him the right one.

"Where do you think Teddy is?" he asks. Another question he's asked before. You think you hate him.

You slump. If your dad were in the room, he would tell you to sit up straight. You have given it your all with Charlie so far, trying to be as helpful as you can, telling him everything Eliza has said you're allowed to share with him. You don't know what else you can add.

"Tell him about the spirits again, maybe?" Eliza suggests.

There's a fan in the corner of the room. It moves slowly. It's noisy. You're staring at it. You yawn.

"Come on," Eliza adds. "Tell him, then he'll let you go."

"I think I do know where Teddy is," you say, dragging your gaze away from the oscillating fan and back to Charlie's face. He looks as hot and tired as you feel.

"Uh-huh?" Charlie nods. He has a way of looking at you that makes you feel like you're being examined under a microscope. He hardly blinks, like a crocodile. His eyes are skewering you, seeing right through you. All you want is to go to your room, lie on your bed with a book, and lose yourself in another world.

"The spirit king has taken him!" you say. This is obvious to you and Eliza. You've discussed it at length. If it's the summer solstice, then the spirits were out to play, crossing from their world to ours and back again. They must have taken Teddy with them.

Charlie removes his spectacles and scratches his forehead with the end of one of the arms before replacing them. He looks over at Karen.

"I think we're done here for now," he says.

"The spirit world is very beautiful," you say. Flecks of moonlight glimmer at the edge of your vision.

He exhales, as if he feels sick, and leaves the room without looking at you.

You feel ashamed. Again.

31

The television interview took place in my kitchen on Sunday morning. It was overwhelming. They only gave me notice of it the night before.

Noah arrived first, with a script for me to learn—a short statement about Dan's disappearance—and I rehearsed it with him, but it was hard to concentrate. I kept messing it up. The words tumbled over themselves and I couldn't commit them to memory. I was distracted by the arrival of the crew.

"You're doing great," Noah kept saying, but I thought he seemed nervous, and when they suggested I change my outfit— "We want to make sure you're relatable"—I found myself in my bedroom in front of the open wardrobe, unable to focus on anything, let alone choose an outfit.

"The trouser suit," Eliza said.

"Not a dress?"

"Not the one you're thinking of, no. Absolutely not."

I dressed according to her instructions. When I got downstairs, Noah and his assistant said they approved.

The interviewer was in place, a woman I recognized from the television, here in my house. Her name was Cathy Coates. It didn't seem real. "We pulled strings to get her," Noah had told me. "She's perfect for this."

Cathy and I shook hands. She had a beautiful manicure. Noah advised me to keep my hands folded in my lap. He demonstrated how to do it so that my injuries didn't show. By then, the confidence he'd projected when he arrived had lost some of its luster. I felt as if I was draining it from him and I didn't know how to make it stop.

"I'm so sorry about your husband," Cathy Coates said. "And I love your books." I almost said "I love you," as a reflexive response, but stopped myself. I sat opposite her. The lighting was horribly bright, and I was disoriented by the number of people in the room and the dark eye of the camera in which I could see a distorted version of myself and Cathy. I could hear my breathing. It was shallow and too fast. They clipped a small microphone onto me, and I worried the sound engineer could hear my rapid breaths, too. Noah smiled in encouragement from behind the camera, but he looked more worried than ever, and so did his assistant. My mouth felt parched. People kept reassuring me that I was brave and that I was going to do great, but I felt panic swelling inside me. It was hard to keep my hands still like I was supposed to.

People worked around us, so many of them, making so many little adjustments that I didn't know where to look, and couldn't concentrate on mentally rehearsing what I had to say and I knew, suddenly, that I couldn't do this. I would have to put a stop to it. I reached for my microphone, I wanted to rip it off, but someone said "Action" and Cathy's whole demeanor changed for the camera and Eliza took over.

She recited our speech flawlessly, projecting pitch-perfect levels of spousal concern.

"What would you like to say to Dan, if he's listening now?" Cathy Coates asked. She looked at me so intently, so warmly.

"Dan, if you're listening, please come home or get in touch to let me know that you're okay," Eliza replied. "I'm worried about you. I miss you. I love you."

She answered Cathy Coates's other questions smoothly, and by the end Cathy had a tear in her eye. "Thank you for letting us share this difficult time," she said as she removed her microphone. "I hope this does some good."

The studio lights were switched off. Noah gave me two thumbs up.

Once it was over, gear was packed up and people disappeared as quickly as they'd appeared, and I was alone. Without anyone there to ground me, the house's empty spaces seemed to gape around me.

"Thank you," I said to Eliza.

"We dodged a bullet. You were in no state to do it yourself," she said. "And I'm always here for you. You know that."

I wanted so much to believe that unreservedly, the way I used to.

32

For the rest of Sunday, I didn't know what else to do. I turned on the television but avoided the news, just in case. I binged episodes of an interior design competition where the contestants tore each other's work to shreds and took offense when it was their turn to be on the receiving end of it. How towering the self-confidence of the creator, the maker of worlds, I thought. I turned it off because it made me think about Dan.

I knew better than to go online, but I did it anyway. I was desperate for distraction. I avoided social media but couldn't resist the Eliza fan page. It was heaving with comments. The armchair detectives had swarmed out of the woodwork.

Look to the books, one of them had written. The clues to what's happened to him must be in there. Truth feeding off fiction?

Bit of a coincidence! another wrote. Crime writer's husband goes missing!!

Is this a case of "write what you know" or "do what you write"?

I wonder if she'll still be able to write when she's in prison? Where imagination meets reality, MrElizaGrey had written. For most people, this might have been cryptic on first reading, but not to me, because "where imagination meets reality" was a phrase that Dan used over and over again when he was talking about writing. I stared at the words on the screen. I had dismissed my suspicions about a link between Dan and MrElizaGrey as a coincidence the first time I'd made the connection but now I wasn't too sure. Was Dan posting online as MrElizaGrey? Was he trying to communicate with me, knowing I couldn't keep away from this page?

This time, I felt the answer in my bones: MrElizaGrey was Dan.

"You going to answer that?" Eliza asked.

"Answer what?" But I heard it as I spoke, the banging on the door.

When I opened the door, the moon was visible behind them, a scrap of cloud in front of it, delicately silvered, unbelievably fragile. No. It was a reminder that perfection can be marred. Hell, no. It was moving swiftly. That'll do.

When I opened the door, the moon was visible behind them, a scrap of cloud in front of it, delicately silvered, moving swiftly.

"Can we come in?" DS Bright asked. She wasn't smiling and I felt afraid. It was too late for a routine call.

We sat around the kitchen island and I felt as if someone had poured water into the room, filling it to the brim, submerging us. Our movements slowed, our communications were garbled, I wouldn't have been surprised to see bubbles rising from our mouths, but I still couldn't escape hearing what they had come to tell me, though I heard it only in fragments.

A body found.

Forensic examination.

Suspected identity is that of.

Your husband.

We wanted to warn you.

We're so very sorry.

We believe your husband may have been murdered.

"Where did you find him?"

"In the countryside, but not very far from the motorway junction at Easton-in-Gordano, so only a few miles from here. He'd been buried in a shallow grave by a hedgerow which borders a patch of woodland that's out there. A dog walker came across him after her dog strayed."

What a horrific image that was. A dog. Tongue and fur and the slowing of its beating tail as it got serious about what it was smelling. Its heart pounding, olfactory receptors screaming: "Death!" Did it lick Dan? The thought was unbearable.

"Can I see him?"

"We would appreciate it if you could identify him formally in person, but only if you're willing. We can do it with a photograph if you prefer."

"I want to see him," I said. I didn't think I would believe it was real, otherwise.

XVI

Karen comes up to your bedroom.

"What are you reading?" she asks.

You show her the book cover.

"Hmm," she says. Her drawn-on eyebrows rise. "Is it any good?"

You nod.

"What's it about?"

"Nothing, really."

You like Karen, but you don't feel like talking. All they want you to do is talk, but you never seem to be able to say what they want to hear. People have been getting cross with you. She sits on the end of your bed. You pull your feet closer in.

"Charlie and I were wondering," she says, "if Eliza knows what happened to Teddy. Do you think she does?"

This is not right. It's not up to other people to say things about Eliza. She is your special friend. No one else can even see her.

"She doesn't," you say.

"Does she talk to you a lot?"

You shake your head. You know by now that admitting that Eliza talks to you constantly makes other people think you're wrong in the head.

"How often, would you say?"

You shrug. "Only sometimes."

"Does she ever tell you to do things that you don't want to do?"

You bite your lips. The feeling of your teeth mashing into the shiny soft flesh is a good distraction.

"Lucy?" Karen says. The longer Teddy is missing, the more impatient everybody is getting.

"No," you reply.

"Your mum told me that sometimes Eliza does naughty things. She said Eliza broke some of Teddy's new toys when he was a baby. Do you remember that?"

"Eliza isn't naughty now."

"No?"

You shake your head.

"Not at all?"

You have learned that there are only two things that get you out of these talks. Either the adults get cross and walk away, or you get sad about Teddy.

It's easy to cry when you think about him and how much he loved you.

"Oh, Lucy," Karen says. She reaches over to hug you. You stiffen, but you don't push her away. Last time you did that, she stared at you as if you had just told her something shocking.

"I miss Teddy," you say, and you cry the way you have heard your mother crying, a wail that scrapes out everybody's insides.

33

Monday morning. Almost a week since Dan disappeared. I had been to a morgue before for research purposes, but this was different. This visit, I wasn't part of the professional gang, I was on the other side, being handled.

It was horrible.

I let Eliza take the lead.

They escorted me into the building via the relatives' route, and took me to an airless room, barely expanded from the size of a corridor, where an exuberant silk poinsettia set the wrong tone. Leaflets fanned across every flat surface.

"Are you ready?" DS Bright said, her hand poised on the door handle to the next room.

"Yes." Though it was hard for me to walk steadily.

Dan's body was on a table, beneath a sheet. I wondered if it was possible that he was alive, beneath there, if they could have made a mistake.

"There's some bruising on his face," they said, "and a cut."

I heard Eliza say, "Okay."

They pulled the sheet back from his face. The movement was executed with skilled, careful fingers. They made a crisp fold in the fabric and laid it smoothly across his shoulders. Such calibration of touch. So different from Dan himself: the clumsiness of him, the mess he made when cooking, his innate laziness, his urge to cut corners, to leave a job incomplete, his sloppy affection for me, his exuberant confidence in his writing. He was a puppy dog at times, and who doesn't love one of those?

I leaned over, my face parallel to his, breathing the same air, except that only I was breathing, and I saw that this was him, and yet not him, because he was gone. Within myself, I felt the strongest sensation of crumbling because, however I felt about him, I didn't think I knew how to exist without him.

I traced the outline of the bruise on his temple. He felt so cold. He looked so pale. My tears wetted his forehead. The texture of his skin had lost all its vitality. I blotted my tears from the dip of his eye socket with the cuff of my coat.

The cut on his forehead was grotesque, the edges of the skin not reaching one another, the wound disappearing under his hairline. His hair had been cleaned and combed.

What was more unsettling, though, was the way his head lay. It was almost straight, but not quite, and I thought it was slightly more sunken onto the trolley on his left side, which was at odds with the care that had been taken over his presentation in every other respect. It dawned on me, sickeningly, that the reason for it might be that the back of his skull was partially caved in.

Eliza muttered, "I think you're right."

The chemical smell hit me then, faint enough but leaching unrelentingly from Dan's body, rising, choking up my airways. I retched. Looked at him again, to be sure. He was an effigy of himself. Collapsed somehow. It felt wrong that he wasn't wearing his glasses, because he couldn't see a thing without them. I wondered where they were and whether his missing watch had left a pale imprint on his left wrist.

I didn't know how to say goodbye to him. I didn't want to. It was also too public. Eyes were on me. DS Bright observed silently. And many more people would be watching when this news got out. The thought was terrifying.

But I knew I had to do this right or I would be judged. I said, "Goodbye, darling," and lowered my mouth to Dan's forehead. This time, the contact made me shudder.

Eliza spoke. "How did he die?" She wasn't asking me. She wanted DS Bright to confirm whether we had guessed correctly.

"We'll let you know as soon as we get the postmortem results," DS Bright said.

"Can we hold a funeral?" I found my voice again.

"We'll let you know when."

For hours afterward, even once I was home, I couldn't stop touching my lips. I rinsed out my mouth repeatedly and when I looked in the bathroom mirror, I saw darkness nestled beneath my eyes and I mouthed the word "widow" and paused to see how it fit.

I felt completely and utterly alone in the world. I had no family left.

Only Eliza.

When I slept, I saw Teddy on the metal table, not Dan. I woke a lot that night and every time I did, I found my cheeks and pillow were wet with tears and I was confused as to which of them I'd said goodbye to forever. In one fevered hour of dreaming, I saw myself there, lying on the table in the morgue beside both of them.

34

DS Bright arrived early on Tuesday. I was in my dressing gown when I let her in, and got hurriedly dressed while she waited in the kitchen.

She wanted to know more about Dan and Sasha. Her focus on me had dialed up a notch and I thought I also saw pity in her expression, which I hated.

"What did you see happen between Dan and your neighbor?"

"Little things. They got in each other's space in a way you only do when you're intimate with someone. He got sort of excitable around her, blushing . . . that sort of thing. He seemed smitten by her."

"Did you see them touching?"

"No."

"Did you witness anything that was proof of this alleged affair?"

"A wife knows."

"So, that's a no?"

"Yes. It's a no. But I know what I saw. Did you ask her about it?"

"We're still conducting inquiries."

"So, is that a no?"

DS Bright smiled thinly. "We'd like to offer you the support of a family liaison officer. I have someone in mind who is very good at working with victims' families."

"Refuse it," Eliza said. "They spy on you." As if I didn't know what an FLO did.

"I'm fine," I said. "Thank you, but there's no need." DS Bright looked disappointed. I wasn't surprised. "It would be easy for my neighbor to have an affair, by the way. Her husband works in London part of the week."

It felt good to say it, like opening a wound to fresh air. Or turning the crosshairs of a gun onto someone else.

"Lucy?" DS Bright was looking at me in a way that reminded me of another day, another interview a long time ago. Eyes on me. I got the feeling she'd been saying my name for a while.

"Yes?" I said.

"We'd like permission to search the house."

"You have it," I said. I wanted to refuse, but it would look bad, and besides, I knew they'd just get a warrant if I didn't agree.

"It will include some forensic testing."

"Of course," I said.

But in the chair beside DS Bright, Eliza appeared. I couldn't keep my eyes off her. She had turned absolutely white.

I blinked and she was gone. I looked back at DS Bright. She was studying me closely again.

"Have you found the structural engineer yet?" I asked.

"Not yet."

"Do you think he could have followed Dan and done something to him? He was here right before Dan left." My mind began to race. "Perhaps he wasn't who he said he was? Or who Dan said he was?"

"We'll find him," DS Bright said. "If he exists."

XVII

Charlie comes to the house with Karen. You watch them arrive from the window on the upstairs landing. You stand back so they can't see you.

They talk to your parents for a while, after which your dad calls up and says they want to talk to you. You drag your feet on the way downstairs.

"Your mum says you had some bruises on your thighs the day after Teddy went missing," Charlie says. "Can you tell me where you got those?"

"I don't remember."

"Are they still there?" he says.

You shake your head.

"Do you mind showing Karen where they were?"

"Don't," Eliza warns you. "They'll know you carried Teddy."

You shake your head again.

"What was that?" Charlie asks.

"What?"

"It was like you were listening to something."

You don't respond.

"Was it Eliza?"

"It wasn't anybody."

"Is that true, Lucy, or is Eliza telling you not to help us?"

"It's true."

"Where did you get those bruises that were on the front of your thighs? Did Teddy hit you?"

"No."

"Did he fight you when you were out in the woods? Were you trying to make him do something he didn't want to do? Was there an accident?"

A vein is bulging on the side of Charlie's forehead.

"Because you can also get bruises like that from carrying a little one. Their feet bang into your legs. Is that what happened? You told us you didn't carry your brother, that he came everywhere with you willingly. So, you're telling me one set of stories but I'm seeing evidence of another."

"Don't tell him you carried Teddy," Eliza says.

"I didn't carry him. I don't know how I got the bruises. Maybe it was when I climbed a tree to see the bonfire."

"You climbed a tree? You didn't mention that before."

Charlie looks very tired, almost as tired as my parents.

"I climbed a big tree," I say, and when I consider it, I think maybe I did climb a tree because it would have been an amazing way to see the bonfire and I can imagine what it looks like from high up, so I describe it to Charlie and he writes it all down in his notebook, just like everything else I tell him, and I like seeing him do that because it means that Charlie thinks I'm helping.

35

Luminol" was a word I'd loved, its syllables so rounded they practically constituted a mouthful. If it were a food, I'd say it would be a dark chocolate mousse. It used to give me pleasure to use the word in my books. My feelings about it changed when I learned they would be using luminol in my own home, to look for traces of blood there that might be invisible to the naked eye.

Cars arrived in my drive, each one disgorging people who would process a potential crime scene. I recognized them from my novels.

DS Bright was anxious to get rid of me. "You can stay here but you might find it very disruptive. Do you have friends or family you can stay with? Can we drive you somewhere?"

I wasn't surprised she asked that. Eliza would tell you that if you're undertaking a police search of a property, the last thing you want is the homeowner to be there. You want to get on with your job and speak freely while you're doing so.

I had been at the heart of many fictional house searches, and now I was to be excluded from a real one, in my own home. The only safe haven I could think of was Vi's house.

I was disappointed when Barry opened the door.

No smile. Instead he observed me warily, peering over his reading glasses, his chin raised. "Hello," he said, but it didn't sound like a welcome. The lenses of his glasses were reflective. I saw myself in them, a dark silhouette.

Barry wore what I thought of as the retiree's uniform: a soft sweater over a shirt and corduroy trousers. His hair, such as it was, was combed neatly around a bald patch that had seen some sun. He presented sartorially as a man who spent time reading, gardening, or perhaps doing the crossword, but he exuded a tight, uncomfortable energy that was at odds with his appearance, as if this was a man who was ready and willing to be difficult.

He held the door partially open but didn't seem inclined to widen the gap to a more welcoming angle.

I was about to make an excuse and leave, thinking maybe I should try to find a hotel instead, or go to Kate and Ben, when Vi called from behind him, "Who is it?" and irritation flashed across his expression before he opened the door wider.

Vi tumbled out and took me in her arms. Over her shoulder I watched Barry melt away, into the shadows at the end of the hallway, and had to work hard to quell my flight instinct and relax into Vi's embrace.

She installed me in their sitting room, fussing about me like a mother hen. She brought me hot tea and sweet things and wrapped a blanket around me. Its texture resembled velvet, so soft that I shuddered.

"You're in shock," she said. "We all are."

"They're searching our house."

She was beside me on the sofa, her body angled toward mine. "Oh, my dear," she said. "What a time you're having of it. You're welcome to stay here as long as you like."

We were both disturbed by a sound from the corridor.

Vi turned sharply.

"Barry?" she called, but there was no reply.

"I'll be back in a moment," she said. She patted my knee, but her attention was caught by the noise. She hurried toward it. I heard footsteps in the hallway. Two sets. Barry had been lurking.

I tried to take in my surroundings. The upholstery was rich and faded, inviting touch. I pulled a cushion onto my lap and ran my fingers over its tapestry cover. The walls were lined with bookshelves, stuffed just as haphazardly as my own, each row of books bearing the weight of others lying upon them horizontally, as if they were pallbearers carrying coffins. Ornate vases stood proud on the mantelpiece, behind them a large oil painting. The paint had the patina of age. It depicted a young man's face, emerging from the blackest of backgrounds, something knowing in his eyes and something sensuous in the fullness of his lips. Between his fingertips he held a delicate flower by the stem while he looked right at me. I found the effect repulsive and deeply unsettling.

My impression was that this was not a house where things were displayed to seduce, soothe, or necessarily impress guests; it was a house where visitors were invited to make of it whatever they liked, and the owners would not care either way. It was also a house that had the settled, heavy feeling of having been occupied by the same people for a very long time.

Through the window, I had a good view of their cherry trees. Some of the blossoms had fallen and scattered the lawn.

I remembered a similar tree in our front garden in Charlotte Close. I hadn't thought about it for years. Teddy and I stood beneath it once as the blossoms were whipped into falling whorls by the wind and we shouted, "Blossom storm!" at the tops of our voices until somebody shushed us.

I wondered, were Barry and Vi living here then?

Time passed, the seconds counted by the ticking clock on the mantelpiece.

Outside, Barry walked beneath the trees, carrying a spade, and disappeared into the back of their garden. Vi didn't return.

I felt a compulsion to check my phone but was afraid of what I would see.

It had been years since I'd sowed a pretty lawn over the muck of my past and I'd cultivated it carefully since then. I imagined the tabloids plowing it up. Had they discovered my maiden name yet? Had they discovered that it wasn't my birth name? How long would that take them?

I let those questions ricochet around my mind as I avoided the one that was plaguing me the most: What had happened to Dan? It was too painful to dwell on.

I expected Eliza to talk to me, but she was silent. I was untethered again.

I didn't resist the phone for long.

I searched Dan's name but the first image to appear was one of me, on the roadside, in my coat and filthy pajama bottoms. They had photographed me after I emerged from the woods and before I got into Vi's car. My attempts to evade them had been pointless.

SOMETHING TO HIDE? ran the headline.

I heard myself begin to sob. I couldn't stop. I wept into the tapestry cushion, as quietly as I could, trying to mute my sorrow, and to hide it. I didn't want to be this vulnerable in front of my neighbors. When I eventually looked up I stifled a scream. Barry was outside the window, looking in at me with an expression of undisguised revulsion. I stood up and backed away, toward the door, and as I did, Vi appeared. We bumped into each other and I yelped again.

"What on earth is it?" she said. She reached out to steady me, one hand on my forearm. "What's happened?"

I turned back to the window and pointed, but Barry was gone and when I opened my mouth to explain, not a single word would come out for a while until eventually I said, "Can I sit with you, please?"

Her brow crinkled in consternation but she said, "Of course," and led me away from Barry and the creepy gaze of the painting.

The radio was on in the kitchen. Vi put a box of tissues in front of me and brought another cup of tea. It was a homey room with a partial view of Kate and Ben's house and their front lawn. The youngest boy was on the trampoline. I could hear its squeak as he bounced. His hair flew up and down as he ascended and descended. The dog lay on the lawn and chewed on a toy. The older brother kicked a ball into a ragged net. The scene had a sepia quality. I felt as if I was watching an old film. I couldn't tear my eyes away.

Vi asked me to chop salad for supper. I hadn't even realized it was getting late. The knife was sharp and once or twice it slipped as I tackled a batch of soft tomatoes. My heart thumped every time. Vi rolled ham slices into cylinders and heated up soup. It was cream-colored and watery. I didn't think I could stomach it.

She called Barry in from the garden and a sense of the outside hung around him, a cold aura, the mildest whiff of vegetation. He hardly looked at me and I said nothing about him startling me before. I didn't know what I would say.

He took forever to wash his hands in the sink before pouring each of us a large glass of wine, though neither Vi nor I had asked for one. The table in their kitchen was small and round, like the one we used to have in Charlotte Close. It was an intimate setup, yet Barry continued to avoid looking directly at me.

Vi talked in a bright voice. Apparently, texts had been flying between the neighbors, concerning the media. James Morell had suggested that they erect a barrier at the end of the lane, but Ben Delaney had objected on grounds of cost.

Barry snapped a cracker and raised his eyebrows. "Ben Delaney would object to an ambulance being called to save one of his children unless it had been his idea to call it," he said.

"To be fair to Ben," Vi said, "I think James and Sasha are using the situation to try to make this a gated lane. He wants the whole works: security system, video entry. But we don't want that. I'd feel as if I was living in a prison."

"He wants to know who visits his wife," Barry muttered.

"Barry!" Vi said, and glanced at me.

"Well . . ." He let the sentence tail off under her gaze, but didn't keep his mouth shut for long. "And let's not forget, Ben Delaney is scared the clients he let down are going to come after him. And there are probably quite a few of those. Incompetent little—"

"Sorry about my husband." Vi cut him off. "He has strong views and doesn't know when to keep them to himself." She put her hand on my arm again, and as she squeezed it I felt a little suffocated. "Lucy, there's a lovely poem about grief that might be a comfort to you," she said. "It's beautifully written, you might appreciate it. After supper, I'll find a copy of it for you."

It was too much. I didn't want to cry again, not in front of them. I excused myself and went upstairs. I badly wanted to get out of there and go back to my house, but DS Bright had left me a message to say they would be continuing to search late into the evening and I shouldn't return until the following day. I was stuck there for the night.

Vi had given me a room at the front of the house. Just down the corridor was a small, spartan bathroom, almost as old and dated as the ones in my house.

I was looking in the mirror when I overheard them talking in the kitchen below. Their voices were so clear it was as if they were in the room with me.

"I was so stupid to mention that poem. It was too much for her to hear tonight," Vi said. "I thought it might make her feel a bit better, but it's too soon. I think she's still in shock."

"You're assuming she's got nothing to do with it," Barry said. "Which is only fair."

"If she was anyone else, you'd ask yourself why she isn't staying with family," he said, "but then you remember who she is."

"If she was anyone else, you might be behaving in a more charitable way. Please make more of an effort."

"For her? I can't. And she can't stay here past tomorrow. Having her here is likely to attract some very unwelcome attention."

Barry's voice rose. As he finished speaking, I heard a noise like a slap, as if he'd hit the table with the flat of his hand, and I jumped.

Vi shushed him and all was quiet.

My reflection stared at me from the mirror. Startled, drawn, pale, frightened. I felt cold porcelain against each palm as I gripped the sides of the handbasin. They knew who I was. They understood that I was little Lucy Bewley from Charlotte Close, who'd grown up on the other side of the woods from their home, whose brother had gone missing, and who had been accused of harming him.

And they hadn't said a word to me about it.

"Liars," I whispered to myself. I felt deceived by them. An impulse swelled in me. I wanted to go downstairs and confront them, do some damage to their home, slash through that horrible oil painting.

But here was Eliza. Finally. To calm me down and tell me what to do.

"Relax," she said. "It's okay. Don't do that. Don't be rash. You'll regret it. And they're bound to tell the police if you do. You don't want that."

"They'll tell the police who I am anyway, and then I'll be under even more scrutiny."

"The police will know soon enough. You can't hide it now. The only thing you need to remember is: don't mention the bunker. Just like before."

"Just like before," I repeated. I watched my reflection as tears ran down my cheeks. So much sorrow on display. But inside, I felt nothing but exhaustion.

I crept down the landing to my room and lay in Barry and Vi's spare bed, swaddled in a mismatch of bed linens, some scratchy, some too soft from years of washing. It was impossible to get comfortable. I was afraid to sleep; afraid the cracks in the ceiling would peel apart and show me a void I didn't want to peer into.

After a while, something occurred to me.

"Eliza?" I whispered. "Why haven't Barry and Vi told the police who I am already?"

"I don't know," she said. "And I'm also wondering *how* they know."

"It's because they were living here," I said. "At the time. They see little Lucy Bewley in me."

The thought chilled me, and for the rest of the night I couldn't get warm, and I could barely sleep.

36

I sat in DS Bright's car the next morning, beneath a sky so flatly gray it seemed artificial.

"We discovered blood," she said, and passed me a photograph. I shut my eyes before looking at it, bracing myself.

When I opened them, I saw my hallway.

It was so dimly lit as to be almost unrecognizable, but I saw my staircase emerge from the blackness and I could make out the geometry of the limestone tiles. Appearing in startling contrast was a smattering of blue phosphorescence, dazzlingly bright by comparison, and beautiful in its way. What it revealed was unmistakable. Smears of blood. A small pool near the basement stairs. A scatter of droplets.

I retched a little and covered my mouth. DS Bright turned the photograph over. I swallowed bile.

"Do you know where this blood might have come from?" she asked.

It was hard to reply. I couldn't stop swallowing. It was compulsive.

"Tell her you were cleaning the floor and didn't realize you had cut your hand. It bled on the tiles and you cleaned it up," Eliza said.

I repeated her words, adding, "This is my blood."

I held up my hands and rotated them to remind her of my scabbed knuckles and the cut.

DS Bright nodded slowly. She ran her tongue over the front of her teeth as if she had a nasty taste in her mouth that she was trying to get rid of. "Well," she said, "we can be sure of that once we've had it tested."

She showed me another photograph. The top of the steps down to my basement. A small pool of blood was visible there. Possibly more blood than might have resulted from my injuries.

"That could be from a previous owner," Eliza said.

I repeated her words to DS Bright. "You should speak to the estate agent to find out who lived here before. The place was empty when we bought it. Anyone could have snuck in. Anything could have happened here."

"We'll assess the possibilities once we've heard back from the lab." She slipped the photographs into a folder. "We've also analyzed the activity on Dan's phone," she said. "It last pinged a cell tower that would place him here at around ten on the night he died."

"He didn't use it after that?"

"No, and there's one more thing," she said. From her handbag she produced a baby's disposable diaper and slotted it back in before extracting one of my novels. She opened the book at a page that had been marked with a note.

"Do you mind if I read a short excerpt?" she said.

"Sure," I replied. "Go ahead." I had no idea what it would be. After five novels my recollections of the specifics, and even the broad strokes of plot and minor characters in each, were challenged, to say the least.

She began to read aloud: "'Diana stood in the blood. She removed her shoes, one by one, careful to step out of the pool of blood as she did and onto the unsullied areas of the floor in her stockinged feet. She might have swung the hammer at him in a fit of anger, but she had also known just where to hit, and she was prepared enough and smart enough not to leave bloody footprints at the scene.

"'She placed each shoe into a plastic bag that she pulled from her handbag. She removed her trousers and put them in a bag, too. The tiles felt cold and her bare legs were covered in goose pimples. She shivered. She had done her research and knew she had to work fast before shock kicked in to the point where it would disable her.

"'She fetched a tarpaulin from the basement. It was stored beside his gym equipment, specifically the dumbbells, one of which he'd used to threaten her with before, feinting a strike to her head, laughing when she ducked and cried out. Enjoying watching her cower.

"'She rolled his body onto the tarp and wrapped it snugly around him, securing it with one of the ties he used to secure the Christmas tree to the roof rack. She grabbed another tarp and heaved the wrapped body onto that and dragged him out. She was pleased with how little blood she'd spread while doing it. Pulling him across the floor was not easy. Things snagged. Putting him in the back of the car wasn't easy, either, but she did it. Diana had worked very hard to get stronger recently. Very hard indeed. And adrenaline helped.'"

The detective stopped reading. "I suppose you know how that goes on," she said.

I nodded tightly, I remembered it now, but she returned to the text anyway, and read on. "'There was less blood on the floor than she'd anticipated. Diana scrubbed until it was gone, until her hands bled. She washed every item of clothing she'd been wearing and then burned them, along with the shoes. Then, she drove him away. On her return, she would bury the outfit she wore to do that, too.'"

Eliza spoke through me.

"Detective," she said, "do you know how tall my husband was?"

"Um," she said.

"He was six foot three. And do you know how tall I am?"

A faint blush crept up her neck. It was the first crack that I'd seen in her imperturbability.

I answered my own question. "I'm five foot one. Let me ask

you, how do you think I managed to strike my husband on the back of his head? Did I stand on a chair and ask him to get into position?"

"In the book, the protagonist was standing on the stairs when she struck her husband," DS Bright said. "And may I ask, how did you know your husband was hit on the back of the head?"

"Because I saw him in the morgue," I snapped. "His head didn't look right. I'm not stupid. And I cannot believe you would compare this situation to my fiction. Even if I did do what you're suggesting, how would I have gotten his body into the car? There would be much more blood in the hall. Are you actually implying that I've murdered Dan and attempted to cover it up in a copycat crime based on something I wrote in one of my own novels? It's honestly laughable."

DS Bright was having to work to maintain her placid demeanor, but she wasn't giving up.

"I'm just making you aware of the uncanny similarities between this description and the luminol evidence I showed you. And there's something else. It's a little bit sensitive, but I hope you understand I'm obliged to ask some difficult questions sometimes—"

As if she hadn't just accused me of murder. I almost laughed. "What do you want to know?"

"I've noticed myself—and some of my colleagues have also remarked—that you haven't seemed to be very upset by your husband's disappearance and now death. Is there a reason for that?"

I stared at her. "I want a lawyer," I said.

"You're not under arrest, Mrs. Harper."

"Yet," I said.

I knew how it worked.

XVIII

Charlie doesn't call at the house for a few days. Outside, there are some journalists on the street, but not as many as before. You can't hear the dogs any longer, nor the helicopters.

You have been watching the journalists from the landing window, stepping back when they turn cameras on you. One day, you weren't quick enough. When your mum sees a photo of you in the paper the next day, staring out the window, the palm of your hand pale where it presses on the glass, your hair uncombed, she cries. "You look like a freak," she says. "It's all we need." Her tears make damp, spreading blots across the newsprint.

One day, you're in the kitchen with your dad. He is sitting still as a statue in the seat that has the best view down the front drive. Out of the blue, he slams his fist down on the tabletop so hard that your cereal bowl leaps and the spoon slides into the milk. You are frightened.

"What have you been saying to them, Lucy?" he says. "What have you been saying that makes them ask me whether anyone else apart from family saw Teddy the night before he disappeared?"

Your fingers grip the sides of your chair and you press your spine against the back of it.

"Do you know what that means? Why they're asking?"

You shake your head.

"It means they think me, or your mum, did something to Teddy and we gave you that story about going into the woods, to get you to cover up for us."

So many tears spill from his eyes at once that it's as if someone is inside his head, gently pouring a steady stream of them down his cheeks. A bubble of snot forms, then pops.

Your mum turns from the sink. "Don't," she tells him. "Don't blame her." But she doesn't look at you.

"We should have sat in on the interviews," he says.

"Don't tell me what I should have done," Carol replies. The washing-up brush in her hand is dripping suds onto the floor. "When my son is missing, and that man is constantly in my house picking through our lives and staring at me as if I'm a bad mother. Don't tell me what I should have done!"

Your dad's shoulders shake. Nobody touches each other. You stay where you are, pinned to the back of your chair. After a while he looks up and at you. His eyes are as red as the devil's, criss-crossed by veins.

"Have you been making up stories, Luce?" he asks. "Tell me, please. Tell me what you told them. Why don't they believe you?"

"You know why," your mum says. "You just said it yourself. It's because she's a fibber. Always has been, always will be."

37

They let me back in the house, handing over the keys in what felt to me like a parody of the day Dan and I had first turned up here together.

There were few physical signs of the police search but the sense that they'd been here, prying into my life, snooping through our stuff, touching things without leaving a trace, got right under my skin.

They'd taken some of the paperwork from Dan's office, I'd had to sign for it, but not everything. I found a record of the solicitor who had handled the house purchase. I called and got through to her assistant, introduced myself and was braced for sympathy, but he behaved as if he hadn't heard about Dan's death yet.

"How are you enjoying that magnificent house?" he asked.

I ignored the question. "I need a recommendation for a criminal solicitor," I added. "The best. Is there anyone at your firm who can help me?"

"Absolutely. I can put you through to someone." He paused. "Actually, our top criminal solicitor at the firm is a neighbor of yours."

"Who?" I asked, but I already knew.

"Ben Delaney."

Kate's husband. Of course. But I didn't want him. Barry had called him incompetent, and much as I disliked Barry, he struck me as someone both rigorous and intelligent. Plus, Ben Delaney was far too close to home.

I wanted the best. After a bit of persuasion the solicitor coughed up the name of someone from another firm.

"Thank you," I said. "I'll be in touch to arrange to come and add my name to the house deed."

"The deed?"

"Of the house. Dan said the paperwork was ready."

He cleared his throat. "I'm sorry but I'm not aware of that arrangement."

"Perhaps your boss knows about it."

"I'm aware of everything that my boss is working on, believe me."

I felt flustered. He must be mistaken. Dan had told me that everything was ready. Perhaps I'd used the wrong terminology. Dealing with people in offices was always a strain. They were so sure of themselves.

"I'll call you back about this," I said.

"Please do," he said. "And if you could send my regards to your husband . . ."

"He's dead," I said, and hung up and cried.

Vi sent me a text: How are you bearing up? Is there anything we can do?

I'd left their house abruptly earlier that morning, after DS Bright had called, and Vi had watched me from her doorstep, waving to me when I turned around, but I had felt as if there were darts in my back as I walked away. I felt conflicted about her offer. I didn't want to be anywhere near her, or Barry, but I needed help.

Please could you give me a lift into the city? I replied.

We followed the same routine as before, with me under the rug in her back seat. Before I pulled it over me, I asked, "Did Barry mind me staying last night?" I probably shouldn't have asked, but sometimes you want to press a bruise, and I thought if I pressed this one, she might confess to knowing about my past.

"Oh, don't mind Barry," she said. "He can be a bit curmudgeonly, but his heart's in the right place."

She draped the blanket over my head. "All set," she said. "A bit lumpy but it'll have to do."

The car rolled slowly down the lane. Every pothole jarred.

"Oh, my," I heard Vi say as we approached the end. "There are so many more of them." I heard her window roll down. Journalists began shouting questions at her. "Out of the way!" she snapped. "Piss off!" There was a loud thump on the side of the car. I flinched.

"She's in there! In the back!" a man shouted, and more voices joined his. I heard my name like an echo, amplified by the hot claustrophobia I felt beneath the blanket.

"Lucy, Lucy, can you tell us about Dan? What can you tell us, Lucy?" I covered my ears. Vi put her foot down and the car surged away.

"Bloody hell," she said after a few seconds.

I sat up cautiously. "I'm really sorry."

When we paused in the queue to pay the bridge toll, I climbed into the front seat of the car but Vi and I didn't speak much. I drank in the sights of the city streets as if they were nectar and I was parched.

Vi dropped me outside the solicitor's office. I put my hood up and ran from the car into the building. My new solicitor was waiting for me. Her name was Tamsin.

She was very corporate. In her business suit and heels she was intimidating to me, though her appearance gave me confidence in her abilities. Any woman who can wear a supersheer stocking with aplomb at her age must be doing something right. And her hair! A master class in that triumvirate of professional women's grooming: color and cut and spray.

But what was hard was the realization that I had just added another member to my handling team, and that she was likely to be an alpha member. What other choice did I have though?

I liked the way that even after I'd explained my situation, she maintained her bullish expression. She tapped the end of her pen on her desk and said, "Now, is that everything? It's important you tell me everything." I was emboldened by her and her confidence.

"There is one more thing," I said. My voice was barely louder than a whisper.

"Go on," Tamsin said.

I told her about Teddy. I felt Eliza becoming unbearably tense as I spoke, but I didn't tell Tamsin everything. Of course not. I only told her as much as anyone else knew, apart from Eliza and me.

Tamsin seemed to deflate a little as she listened, but not entirely. "That complicates matters," she said once I'd finished. "It's probably not something that's admissible if we ever find ourselves at trial, but it guarantees the police and the media are going to be all over you like a rash once they know. Thank you for being forthright about it."

There was something about the way she said it that made me wonder if I should tell her more. If perhaps I'd misjudged her, and this was the moment to unburden myself completely and confide in her, because holding that secret about the bunker for so long had been so, so hard and the urge to tell was suddenly very strong. And if someone else knew, would Eliza have so much power over me? Was Tamsin a safe person to tell?

Eliza kicked off, warning me not to say more, telling me to protect myself. She appeared suddenly beside me in an empty chair and leaned so close I flinched. Her jaw was clenched. I was afraid of her. I recoiled.

"You do not tell," she said. "You. Do. Not. Tell."

I had to squeeze my eyes shut and shake my head to get rid of her.

"Hello?" Tamsin said.

"What?"

"You kind of zoned out a little there. Are you all right?"

"Yes. Yes, I am. Sorry. It's all a bit overwhelming."

"I'm sure it is." Her words were kind enough, but there were new traces of concern in her expression. Eliza had lowered the temperature yet again. She had erected another barrier between me and the world.

"Do you mind if I ask?" Tamsin said. The pen was tapping on her desk again. "Do you have any medical conditions, either physical or related to mental health, that I should know about? I'm not being nosy. It's pertinent to your case."

"No," I said. "I don't."

She made a note. When she looked up at me, her eyes bored into mine, and I looked away.

"Let's keep in close touch," she said. "And by the way, I love your novels. That Eliza character, she's terrific. A real ball-breaker, isn't she? I wouldn't like to be working on the opposite side of her in real life."

I tried to smile, but my mouth felt as if it was full of gummy ashes.

XIX

There aren't any journalists out front of your house anymore and neither Charlie nor Karen has visited for ages, although they phone most days and your dad gets on the other line and you have to be as quiet as a mouse.

Your mum spends time in Teddy's bedroom every day, arranging and rearranging the toys on his bed, to make him smile when he gets home. "We can tell him they've been having a tea party," she says one afternoon. The toys are sitting in a circle.

"Like the people at the bonfire," you say.

Her head whips around.

"What did you say?"

"The bonfire people made a circle."

"Did you tell Charlie or Karen?"

You nod your head.

"Do you remember their faces? Anybody's face?"

She has asked this before. Your mother thinks one of the bonfire people took Teddy away with them and that you must remember seeing something. She's looking at you with such intensity that you quail. She wants you to describe a face, but the trouble is, you can't remember any of the individuals. Should you make one up, to give her hope? Or just describe the compound face that appears in your mind whenever you think of the features of those fire-burnished, shadowy people? She looks desperate enough to break if you don't chuck her a bone.

"A lady had a crown made from flowers."

"What kind of flowers?" She takes your hand, pulls you gently *toward her so you're both perched on the edge of Teddy's bed. Her other hand strokes the duvet cover as if it is alive and needs comforting itself.*

"Like a daisy chain," you say.

"What was her face like? Do you remember her face?"

Golden skin, flickering light, eyes like deep pools, hair in curls.

"She was pretty," you say.

"What color was her hair?"

You're not sure. It was impossible to tell in the firelight. "Probably brown," you say.

"Dark . . . light?"

"Light." It could have been. When you looked at photos of the summer solstice at the library, you saw a woman with light brown hair. Maybe she was in the woods, too.

The questions go on.

You answer as best you can.

You feel yourself growing closer to your mum.

She confides in you.

She says the police have only been able to find some of the revelers to question. They are not mainstream people, she says. Not local. They're pagans. Each word she speaks seems designed to snip the thread connecting them to the life you know, to make it clear that they are not people like us, and yet you feel you did know them that night. You shared something with them that ran deep.

She doesn't let go of your hand until she goes to phone the police to share with them the new details you've supplied. And you know that it'll probably only be a few hours before Charlie and Karen come back here to question you again.

38

I didn't want to go home after the meeting with Tamsin. I couldn't face it.

Afraid of being recognized on the street, I wrapped my scarf high around my neck, pulled up my hood, and found myself walking to my old neighborhood.

At the building we used to live in, our former landlady, Patricia, was sitting in her usual chair by the front window, smoking a cigarette, gazing vacantly at the street life, puzzle books stacked on the table beside her. She came abruptly to life when she saw me, as if a puppeteer had just jerked her strings.

She opened the front door wide. "Have you come to pick up those boxes?"

"I've come to see you."

I meant it. I wanted to be somewhere that felt like home, with someone whom I associated with safe, familiar things: cups of tea and cozy chats.

She said nothing about Dan. I saw no newspapers in her flat. I knew she didn't go on the internet and her television was mostly set to the channels that showed reruns of shows she loved. Perhaps she didn't know.

She made me tea and I told her about the new neighbors, how rich Sasha and James must be, how posh Barry and Vi were, and what a beautiful family Kate and Ben had. We watched her shows after that, and all the time, I thought: *I've got to tell her about Dan*. But she seemed so happy to see me, and I felt so grateful to cocoon myself with her for this little while, that I couldn't bear to say the words.

As credits rolled at hyperspeed down the screen, she said, "I miss you and Dan. It's not the same here with the new tenants. They're never home. I used to like to think of you up there, typing all day, dreaming up a whole other universe right here in my flat, while I was just below. It was a lovely feeling. Special. Do you want a tea cake, darling? I know you're partial."

It was getting dark outside. The lights in the bakery windows opposite had just gone out. I felt my tension melting, just a little. I wanted nothing more than a tea cake.

She toasted one for me. The edges were burned, but I didn't mind. As she sat back down beside me on the couch, she sounded as if the air had been punched out of her. She took my hand between hers and I felt the prickle of tears.

"Darling," she said, "I'm sure you don't want to talk about it or you would have said something, but I saw about Dan in the news. I know it wasn't all roses up there between you two because I could hear more than you think, but I am very sorry he's gone. He wasn't all bad, was he? They're usually not all bad. There's got to be some reason you love them, right?"

What had she overheard? She began to pat the top of my hand. When she didn't stop, the movement took on a sort of insistent quality.

"The police phoned me," she added. The patting stopped. "They're coming to talk to me in the morning."

"Oh?" I said, casually, but my heart thumped. What would she tell them?

"Yeah. They're coming in the morning, probably going to ask a whole lot of questions about you and your Dan. What I knew about you two, what I could hear, that sort of thing, which got me thinking—" She left her sentence hanging. My discomfort cranked up a gear.

"What's that?" I asked.

"Well, it's silly really, but do you know what I've always dreamed about? Having a book dedicated just to me. I think that would be really nice."

It took me a stunned moment to understand that she was blackmailing me. On the television a game-show host showed a mouthful of teeth. I found my voice as the screen filled with a shot of the audience applauding.

"It would be my pleasure to dedicate a book to you. It might be too late to get it into the next Eliza book, the one that's coming out later this year, but the book after that will be yours." I felt as if I might choke on my words. This was a small price to pay for her discretion, but I had trusted her when I shouldn't have and now I didn't know if I had anyone left on my side apart from Eliza.

Her face lit up. "Lovely," she said. "And can you put 'Thank you' . . . or maybe 'Thank you, Patricia,' or something like that?"

"Of course," I said. I felt queasy. I had to get out of there. It wasn't a refuge at all.

She settled back to watch the show, apparently satisfied. Except that she wasn't because she drew breath almost immediately, to say, "And then I expect there are journalists who will be interested to know about you and Dan, too. But we'll talk about that another day, darling, and I'm sure you and me can come to some arrangement because we all know journalists don't write very nice things and we wouldn't want that."

"No," I said. "We wouldn't."

I sat beside her, so angry I couldn't focus on the television, or hear it properly. It was a rush of noise and sensations. A crowding of my brain. My hands clenched tighter and tighter. My nails were digging into my palms.

Patricia, staring at the screen, oblivious to my mounting rage, said, "The saddest thing of all is that this happened when Dan was on the cusp of his big break."

"What do you mean?"

"I mean the project he was working on," she said. "Co-authoring," she added, as if that was a word that implied additional status. "With his good friend."

My blood ran cold.

"Which friend?" I asked, but Patricia didn't hear me. She was on a roll.

"It's a shame he was frustrated about elements of it. He said it was a challenge to work with somebody else and I can imagine that, I really can. Honestly, I'm not sure how you write a book using teamwork, you'd know more about that than I would, but what he said was the quality of her prose wasn't up to his. It really got to him, that did."

It sounded like Dan. She was quoting him, there was no doubt of that. I imagined him down here while I was working. Had he sat where I was now, drinking tea, eating tea cakes, and spouting this stuff to Patricia, loving the way she hung on his every word?

I badly wanted to know who "she" was. His "co-author."

"Did Dan mention the name of his friend?"

"Sasha," Patricia said. "And I remember because I used to have a cat called Sasha."

Sasha. Of course. I wasn't surprised.

But how could she not have mentioned this to me since he'd gone missing? How could he not have said anything either?

"I should go," I said.

"Well, don't forget them boxes Dan left here, God rest his soul. Or if you prefer, I could give them to the police?"

"I'll take them," I said.

"You be careful," she called out as I staggered down the

street with the two boxes in my arms. "And don't forget to keep in touch with Patricia, will you?"

When I was out of sight of the building, I dropped the boxes and heaved up my tea cake into the gutter, along with the last few morsels of trust I might have had left to offer.

39

I got a taxi home from Patricia's house. There was no way to hide from the waiting media as we drove into the lane; all I could do was pull up my hood, duck my head, and avoid eye contact. I worried about how they would caption the pictures I heard them taking. Would they say I was unfeeling? Not broken enough? Too broken? I had no difficulty imagining the sorts of things they would write about me.

I dumped the boxes in the kitchen and with a knife slit through the tape sealing them up. I wanted to know what had been so precious to Dan that he'd wanted to leave it in Patricia's safekeeping. I pulled out a few papers from one of them and saw they were some of his old, unpublished creative writing efforts. Short stories, a feature-length script, more than one attempt at a novel. Pages and pages of the stuff. Dog-eared and heavily annotated. I flipped up the lid of the other box. It was full of his old research notebooks. Years of fruitless work.

And obviously what he treasured most.

I felt a wave of sorrow, but it didn't overwhelm me. It reminded me that I wanted to find out what he and Sasha had been writing together.

I tried to remember if I'd seen an office in her home, somewhere she and Dan might have worked together. There had been the room she did the photocopying in, but I'd thought that was James's office. And would she have let me stay in the house if there were traces of the project there, when it was obviously important to her that I didn't find out about it?

I remembered the outdoor building I'd seen in the Morells' garden. Was that where Sasha and Dan had worked? Had she built herself a writing shed? It made sense. A dedicated shed was just the sort of thing Dan would have wanted, if he'd had the chance, and I was beginning to understand that he and Sasha had a great deal more in common than I had ever cared to consider.

I waited until it was late and let myself out into the garden, from where I made my way through to the Morells' house.

The route I took was more or less the reverse of the one Sasha had shown me, although I kept as far as possible from the houses so as to avoid being seen. I jumped at every shadow and shuddered with fear when a fox darted across my path. It felt as if my feet were sinking into the damp ground with every step, never to come back up, that eyes were watching me from everywhere.

I prayed that the Delaneys' old dog wouldn't bark as I crept through their garden, navigating carefully past the kids' toys on the lawn. One light glowed dimly from an upstairs window in their house, faint enough to be a child's night-light, and I thought of their children, safe in their beds, safe from the woods.

All the windows at Vi and Barry's house were black. From their kitchen plot, I slipped through the gap in the hedge and approached the Morells' garden building from the back, guided by its silhouette until I felt the rough wood of the cladding beneath my fingers. I looked into a window at the side of the shed, but the blind was drawn down. I peered around the front. There was a light over the door. I stepped out to see if movement triggered it, ready to dart back if it did, but it remained off. That was good. Lucky. I tried the door handle. It turned, but the door didn't open.

"Lucy? Is that you?"

The voice startled me. I saw no one. "Who is it?"

"It's James. What are you doing?"

I looked around for him. "You're on camera," he said. "See that device above the door?"

Not a light then, but an electronic eye. I should have known better. I'd heard Vi and Barry talking about James and Sasha's love of home security.

"I'm sorry," I said.

"Stay there. I'm coming."

I thought about running away but where would I go? He would find me in my home, and I was too afraid to run into the woods. The trees seemed fractious in the blustery wind.

My back slid down the shed wall until I was sitting on the deck. Cold seeped through my clothing. I wondered if Sasha would come out, too. I felt humiliated.

No lights went on in the main house, but after a few moments I saw James's silhouette approaching. He walked across the grass with a pace so measured that it seemed calculated and it frightened me. The closer he got, the faster my heartbeat raced. When he reached me, he stood right over me and I had the sensation of being subordinate to him. As if I were his victim.

But he sat down beside me, his back against the wall of the shed, just as mine was, his legs extended parallel to mine. He was wearing sweatpants and a light sweater. The woods rustled and a gusty breeze lifted some strands of my hair and dropped them again. James said nothing.

"I was snooping because I couldn't sleep," I said. "I'm sorry. I don't know why."

"I expect you do." He said it with resignation and shivered. It was catching, like a yawn. "Shall we talk inside?" he said. "It'll be warmer."

I studied him the way you always must if a man invites you into a space alone with him, but his expression was unreadable in the dark, his intentions unfathomable. I fumbled with my phone and shone the torch in his face. He covered his eyes with his forearm.

"Don't!" he said sharply. "She'll see."

I turned it off. I thought he'd sounded afraid.

"Let's go in," I said.

"He's not safe," Eliza warned. "Don't be stupid." I didn't care. I was starting to feel intrigued by him.

It wasn't much warmer inside, but at least the wind couldn't nip at us. James flicked a switch somewhere and we were buffeted by warm air.

"Take a seat," he said.

I felt my way into the room and took the desk chair. He sat on an easy chair opposite me. As my eyes adjusted, the rest of the room emerged slowly from the gloom. The walls had been fitted out with corkboards, and every inch of them was covered with photographs and printouts.

In the center of the display was a photograph that I knew better than my own face. It was Teddy. I felt as if I'd been punched in the gut.

Teddy's nursery-school photograph had been circulated far and wide after he disappeared. It was the image you saw first if you Googled his name. Someone had printed it out so large that his face was life-sized and I thought for a feverish moment that he might step out of the darkness and embrace me. I felt the pressure of his arms clamped around me, and the small-boy smell of him doused me like a perfume.

"Dan and Sasha did this," James said. "I'm sorry. I don't suppose you knew."

"I didn't," I whispered. But I still wasn't quite sure what "this" was.

"I thought they were having an affair at first," he said. "It wouldn't have been the first one Sasha's had."

"I'm sorry."

"Yeah, well, it was painful, but life can do that to you some-times. I know you know that."

I didn't respond, but what he said hurt.

"At first, I was relieved when I discovered that they were collaborating on a writing project. Obviously, I didn't approve of them doing it behind your back, but I thought it was at least a better use of Sasha's time than sleeping with Dan, but then I realized they were doing that, too."

I drew in breath, sharply. More detail emerged from the low-lit images around him. I couldn't keep my eyes off them.

"I expect you work hard," he said simply.

"He's trying to bond with you," Eliza said.

I looked back at him and wondered who we both were in this scenario, or could be. Betrayed and ruined spouses? Or, and this idea was just taking shape, did he want us to be some sort of team? Was he planning revenge on his wife for her affair and this collaboration? Had he already taken it? On Dan?

I felt a throb of fear.

"Didn't your husband get on your nerves?" James asked. "Banging on about writing all the time? Not understanding that people can't always get what they want? Was he jealous of you?"

I wanted to collapse beneath the weight of his words. Eliza spoke for me: "Do you actually want me to answer that? Or are you just getting your own marital problems off your chest?"

"You're right. Forgive me. Don't answer. I've actually read some of the stuff they've written together. They don't compare to you, you know."

But I didn't want James's compliments. Not here, not now.

"Were they writing about Teddy?" I asked.

He nodded. "Both of them fancied themselves as the next Truman Capote. They thought they were going to solve the mystery of your brother's disappearance and publish a big best-selling book about it."

"How could they?" I felt betrayed and I noticed that the anger in my voice had excited James.

"Do you want to trash this stuff?" he asked. "You can, if you want to. They deserve it. They should never have gone behind your back."

He didn't wait for me to answer but stood up and ripped a sheet of paper from the wall and I understood that it was he who wanted to trash the place, not me. I was his excuse. Both of us watched the paper he'd torn flutter to the floor, a tumbling shadow, and it triggered something in him. He launched himself back at the wall and ripped down the whole display in a frenzy of clumsy violence.

I stepped back and watched, too scared to join in with him, too compelled by the sight to leave. Once the wall was bare, he broke down, on his knees, head in his hands, the floor around him feathered with torn paper. Teddy's face stared up at me. I picked up his photograph and held it against my chest, flattened it there.

I let James cry alone. I didn't go to him. I didn't touch him. My own pain felt too immense, my emotions too raw, to offer him any comfort. I just sat with Teddy. It was quiet in the room apart from the sound of James's weeping.

After a while he stopped and made a choked apology. I sort of hated him for that. The betrayal I felt ran deeper than his. He was suffering as a result of the affair our spouses were having; I was suffering because of that, but also because I'd discovered that my husband was prepared to mine my carefully hidden past for his own profit.

A light went on in the main house. We both turned toward it.

"Sasha's going to the bathroom," James whispered, and even in the dark I saw something unexpected in his face, an echo of the fear I'd sensed in him earlier.

"Are you afraid of her?" I asked.

He turned toward me and got too close. It felt too intense. "I think she hired someone to kill me," he said, "but they killed Dan by mistake."

The world around us seemed to shudder a little.

"Have you said this to the police?"

"No."

"Will you?"

"No."

"You have to."

"I don't."

"Why not?"

"Because I love her."

And how memorable that moment was, in one particular way, because before then I had sometimes studied my own reflection, to see if I could detect madness there. It wasn't something I did all the time, only when I'd become worried that my storytelling and my imagination were not assets but a danger to me. Now, looking at James, I understood that it wasn't easy to see madness, to know whether someone was afflicted by it or not. It wasn't written on people's faces permanently. Instead, madness was something that sometimes swam to the surface and showed itself in our actions, or words, or expressions, then sank back down and away, until the next time. Its potential lived in all of us. This man was obsessed with his wife. But I hadn't seen it until now, and I wondered if Dan had. Sasha surely must have.

Another light came on in the house, downstairs.

"I've got to go," he said.

"James . . ."

"I won't talk to the police." He was halfway out the door, holding it open for me.

"Can I take the papers?"

He looked at the floor as if only just processing what he'd done.

"Take what you want. Shut the door behind you. I'll pretend someone broke in."

So, he and I were not a team, exactly, but neither were we enemies. And I wasn't sure if he was rational or reliable, mad or sane, or if, like me, he was no longer sure.

XX

You keep to your bedroom more and more, avoiding your parents and the traps they set for you because they want you to remember. Charlie and Karen haven't called for days. It might be weeks. You're not sure. Time is hard to track when the air in the house is as thick as jelly and you eat each meal alone at the table, every bite taking a lifetime to chew and swallow.

Teddy has not been found. You are your parents' only hope for a breakthrough. You can see it in their eyes. They watch you like hawks. They handle you differently. They still hold you sometimes, but not the way they did before Teddy disappeared. Now, the hugs don't last long enough for you to keep your ear pressed against their chests and count their heartbeats.

It's raining the day that Niall Wright comes. You've been hearing his name in the house for a few weeks. Your mum seems taken with him, your dad less so.

His voice isn't loud, but it is commanding. It brings you out of your room to peek through the banisters. Both his hands are wrapped around one of your mother's.

"I would prefer to work in the sitting room, Carol, if you don't mind," he tells her. "It's generally a more relaxed environment. And it would be lovely to have a few minutes to chat and get set up before we bring her down. Is she here?"

"Oh, yes," your mum says. "I'll call her when you're ready. But be warned, Lucy's quite a perceptive child."

"Perceptive is good. I often get the best results from people who *are more than usually perceptive. I'll bet she gets that from you, doesn't she?"*

You stick a finger down your throat as your mum says, yes, that's probably true because it sure as heck isn't from your father.

You go downstairs and open the door that they have just shut behind them. He looks at you the way the detectives do. As if you are a puzzle to be solved.

"Well, hello!" he says. "Just the girl I was hoping to meet."

You look at your mum. "This is Niall," she says. "He's come to help you remember."

"I can't remember," you say. "You can't make me."

"Nobody's going to make you," he says. "This is just a little game."

He's rearranging your mum's cushions, piling them onto the end of the sofa.

"Why don't you lie down here?" he says. He gestures flamboyantly.

You don't move. "What's the name of the game?"

"Well," he says, "I don't know if you've heard of it. In fact, it's a lot of fun. It's called hypnosis."

You look at your mum. She's got her hopeful expression plastered all over her face. You start to tremble.

"No," you say.

"It'll be fun," he says.

"I don't want to go to sleep."

"It's not sleeping, exactly, it's remembering. As if you were dreaming. Why don't we give it a go and then, if you don't like it, we can stop?"

"That's a good idea," your mum says. "Please, Luce. It's the only way we're going to get to the truth. I truly believe that, and Niall here—he's an expert at it."

"You're in safe hands with me," he says.

"Please, darling," your mum adds.

You lie down and listen to his words. At first you feel nothing apart from an acute sense of being present on the sofa, but it starts to slip after a while. His words are very soothing. Eliza whispers that you must stay in the here and now. You must keep the secret. It'll be even worse for you if you confess it after such a long while. They'll all think the very worst of you because what everyone has said all along, right from the first hours of Teddy being gone, is that the key to a missing child case is time. And a lot of time has passed now without them knowing about the bunker. They won't forgive you for that.

When Niall asks you to transport yourself back to the woods you lie as still as a fallen branch on the sofa and keep your eyes shut, but you hold every detail of the sitting room in your mind so he can't get you under his spell. His words build in a smooth curve and you ride along it for a while, almost lost, but when he talks you right to the moment when Teddy disappeared, you hear Eliza, and she tells you to give the answer you always give: "The fairy king took Teddy and he took him to his fairy land."

Your mum lets out a cry of frustration and leaves the room. You don't open your eyes, but you sense that Niall is very still. You feel him looking at you.

"Fuck," he says.

There is a rustle of clothing as he gets up. He takes a few paces.

"Oh!" he says a few moments later, as if it's an afterthought, as if he'd momentarily forgotten all about you because something else was on his mind. "You're back with us now, Lucy, okay?"

You open your eyes and sit up. Niall has gone but he's left a card on the coffee table. You pick it up, read the curlicue font: NIALL WRIGHT. HYPNOTIST. PSYCHIC. REFERENCES AVAILABLE.

From the hall, you hear your mother's sobs and Niall says, "This is not the end, Carol. If you were to take me to the woods, to the spot where the children were, there's a very good chance I'd be able to feel something. An exceptionally good chance. The auras will be strong. If we could bring something of Teddy's with us, that would almost guarantee it. It's not much of an extra cost."

In reply, your mother's sobbing sounds even more hopeless.

40

Eliza wasn't buying James's story about Sasha wanting him dead.

"He's protecting himself," she said. "It's too neat an explanation, too convenient. Too Hitchcock, frankly. James is the one who hurt Dan. He wanted Dan out of Sasha's life."

I wasn't so sure about that. James had appeared to be destroyed by his wife's infidelity, but he'd seemed truly frightened of her, too. Eliza went on all night, but I barely listened. She had her view and I had mine. And if James wasn't going to tell the police what he suspected, I would.

"Don't do anything hasty," Eliza said. "He might retaliate."

Or she might, I thought.

I drifted in and out of sleep, believing something different each time I surfaced into consciousness. My thoughts and dreams became increasingly scattered, until I no longer knew what I believed and all I could see were the torn papers carpeting the floor of Sasha's writing shed.

When I could no longer sleep at all, I got up and braved the frigid morning air to retrieve the papers I'd taken. I spread them out across my bed and huddled there, my duvet up to my neck, looking at them in batches.

As I flicked through them, my frustration built. I wanted to shake Dan. This was the work of amateurs. His and Sasha's "research" consisted of nothing apart from printing out every single thing about Teddy's case that was easily available online. As detective work went, it was pitiful. I couldn't believe he had betrayed me, for this.

I left it all on my bed and went downstairs. I rifled through the hamper in search of breakfast and found some florentines, which were good.

My new solicitor, Tamsin, called early.

"The police want to talk to you again," she said. "They say they have something new."

"What is it?"

"They'll tell us when we meet with them. And, Lucy?"

"Yes."

"Can we have a little talk first?"

"Yes. But can they come here, and can you? There are photographers at the end of the lane and every time I go in and out, they try to take a picture of me. And can you bring me some bread?"

She arrived about an hour later. She took off her coat in the hall and said, "Is this where they found the stains?"

"Yes," I said. "But it's my blood, not Dan's."

She nodded, a brisk movement. I took her up to my office, because the kitchen was in disarray. She was silent as she followed me upstairs and I could sense her taking in the state of the rest of the house.

"This is a lot of work," she said.

My office impressed her. She smiled for the first time. I invited her to sit on the sofa and took a chair opposite her.

"First thing to mention," she said, "is that a junior colleague in our office had a phone call from a solicitor called Ben Delaney who works for another firm. Do you know him?"

"He's my neighbor."

"Well, he tried to get information about you by intimating that you were thinking of moving to him for representation."

"I'm not. I haven't. I like you." And I didn't want Ben Delaney to represent me.

"Because I don't want to waste my time and yours if you are considering seeking alternative representation," she said.

"I'm not. He shouldn't have approached you."

"Honestly, I'm relieved to hear that. Full disclosure: he's not the best at his job."

I could imagine that, in spite of what I'd been told by his firm. There was something soft about him, guileless almost. It was hard to imagine him being effective in court. "Why do you think he did it? Do you think maybe he just wanted to know what was going on? He only lives there." I pointed out the window, toward the Delaneys' house. You could see a corner of the roof. Tamsin took a look.

"That's a nice house for a criminal solicitor," she said. "If he doesn't have his own firm, which he doesn't, he must already have money, or have married it. And that's what he'll be interested in if he's chasing your work. The money. It won't be the details. We've seen it all in our profession. He wants your business."

But I wondered if he'd seen me. Or little Lucy Bewley.

"Did you know you have a broken window?" she added.

"Don't touch it!" I snapped. "It's sharp."

The detectives arrived on time—two of them again—and they had a wolfish energy about them that I felt wary of. It expanded to fill my kitchen, which was where Tamsin and I met them. I didn't mind her being in my office, but I didn't want DS Bright up there again.

The detectives sat up straighter than usual and DS Bright held a notebook and some papers on her lap, propped against the edge of the table and angled so that only she and her colleague could see them.

She handed me a single piece of paper. There was some typing on one side. She nodded and I read it.

It began:

The stitch in your side feels like a blade, but you daren't stop or slow as you race through the woods toward home. Trees are gathered as far as you can see with the still menace of a waiting army.

Moonlight winks through the canopy and its milky fragments dot and daub the understory. The shifting light shrinks shadows, then elongates them. Perspective tilts.

The woods. I caught my breath. I didn't want to read on.

"Do you know what this is?" DS Bright asked.

The words crawled on the page.

"No," I said.

"Do you have any idea?"

I looked back at the paper and read the final few lines.

Limp in her tight embrace, you think, please can this moment last forever, can time stop, but of course it can't, in fact the moment lasts barely a second or two, because as any good mother would, yours raises her head and looks over your shoulder, down the path behind you, into the darkness, where the street lighting is inadequate, where the moonlight has disappeared behind a torn scrap of cloud, where the only other light is rimming the edges of the garage door of number 4, and every other home is dark, and she says the words you've been dreading.

"But where's Teddy?"

You can't tell them about your den.

You just can't.

Eliza would be furious.

Your mum is clutching you by your upper arms so tightly it hurts. You have the feeling she might shake you. It takes every last ounce of your energy to meet her gaze, to widen your eyes, empty them somehow of anything bad she might read in them, and say, "Isn't he here?"

I couldn't look up at them, I felt shame and terror. My hand shook as I replaced the piece of paper on the table and pushed it back toward DS Bright as if I didn't care, as if my heart wasn't pounding so hard that I thought it might deafen me.

"Where did you get this?" I asked.

"We removed some of your husband's papers from the house. It was among them."

Something clicked into place and it felt as if everything was crumbling at the same time. Of course. This was Dan's work. He was obviously experimenting with writing his "true crime" book in the second person, addressing me. It was so personal and so horrible.

"Is there more?" I asked.

"This is all we have."

Tamsin reached for the paper and began to read it. I pointed to it and didn't bother to disguise the tremor in my hand.

"I'll tell you what this is, this is bad writing," I said, "and if I'm not mistaken it reads like the kind of overwrought prose my husband would write."

"Do you know who Teddy is?" DS Bright asked.

"Teddy is my little brother. He disappeared when he was three years old."

"Were you questioned about the disappearance by the police at the time?"

"Everybody was."

"I have some of the notes from the original investigation here. Do you mind if I quote from them?"

I swallowed. She was further ahead of me than I had realized.

"This is a case note made by Detective Inspector Charles Cartwright: 'Lucy Bewley tells a constantly changing narrative concerning her brother's disappearance, to the point where it is impossible to separate truth from fiction.' What do you say to that?"

"I was a very imaginative child. I told them what I remembered but it wasn't good enough for them. They pushed me."

Tamsin cuts in. "How is this relevant to the current investigation? I must advise my client not to answer any more questions relating to this matter. Lucy, don't say anything else."

"I want to say something," I said. "You need to talk to James Morell. He told me last night that he knows Dan was having an affair with his wife and he thinks Sasha hired someone to kill him, and they killed Dan instead. By mistake. He's absolutely destroyed by it. And he was frightened, too. Really frightened."

DS Bright blinked. "Can you repeat that, please?"

I did. I told her what had happened in the writing shed. Her colleague, a young man, slim as a rake, hollow-cheeked, made notes.

DS Bright watched me carefully. I was so tired of that gaze. Tamsin's knuckles began to show white where she was gripping her iPad. The paper lay on the table between us all, taunting me.

When I'd finished recalling what James had said, and done, DS Bright didn't reply straightaway. She gave my words space, as if they needed to be carefully assessed.

"We'll look into that," she said eventually. She leaned forward and I felt hopeful that we were finally going to connect, that what I'd said had flipped a switch in her detective's brain, made her predator's eyes move away from me, to a different quarry, to James and Sasha.

"Lucy, did you lie about your brother's death?" she asked.

I laughed. It was from disappointment because she clearly hadn't believed what I'd said about James, and because I'd been asked this question before, so many times.

"Are you lying about your husband's death?" she added. "Did you get angry with him when you discovered he was researching your past, because you're clearly not happy about it? I know I wouldn't be, if my husband was working with his lover to write something that could ruin me."

"Detective!" Tamsin snapped. She turned to me. "Do not say another word," she said. "You're under no obligation to."

"Did you kill your husband because you wanted to stop him writing about your past?" DS Bright asked.

I shut down. I couldn't listen anymore. I hung my head and shut my eyes and covered my ears with my hands. The sound of the officers leaving was muted. They spoke in the hall with Tamsin and then she came and said goodbye to me. When the door had shut behind her, I lifted my head. I needed to know if Dan had written more and, if so, what he'd written.

I tore through all the paperwork the police had left in the house but found nothing similar. I was thinking of going to see Sasha to try to get it out of her when my eyes landed on the box I'd collected from Patricia.

I reopened them and emptied them out. Beneath the old notebooks, tucked right at the bottom of the box, where I hadn't been bothered to look before, I found a slender manuscript that had been carefully stored inside a plastic envelope.

I extracted it and read the first page. It was identical to what DS Bright had shown me. I sat down and flicked through the rest of it. My story was there, all of it, everything I'd ever shared with Dan in the safety of our own home, trusting that what I said was just between him and me. I read every word of it, right up until the last section, the twenty-first chapter, each one neatly labeled in Roman numerals. It was horrifying. I took a deep breath before starting the final couple of pages:

XXI.

Karen appears one day, out of the blue. Your parents interrupt a game you're playing with Eliza in your bedroom and ask you to come down to the kitchen, where Karen is sitting at the table with a cup of tea in the mug that she says she likes best.

"I got these for you," she says, pushing a bag toward you.

You remove a notebook from the bag. It's beautiful, with a hard cover. Holding it in your hands, you can feel indentations and the decorations shimmer like a peacock's wing. You open it and run your fingers over the paper, relishing the feel of it. It's perfect.

"There's something else in the bag," Karen says.

You tip it up and a slim case rolls out. Inside it you find a pen. It's bright yellow, tapered at one end, a hole in its plastic case through which you can see an ink cartridge.

"It's a fountain pen," Karen says, though you know that already. "Your mum says you're big enough to use one."

You've been coveting one of these for a long time.

"Thank you," you say. You're dying to try out the pen in the new notebook. You imagine how the ink might soak into the paper, how it will feel to watch words materialize on the page. To you, it's a thought as wholly satisfying as having a plate of your favorite food set in front of you.

"You can write some stories of your own with it," Karen says.

Your excited little heart beats rapidly. How did she know how much you would love to? You're unscrewing the cap of the pen when you get the sudden, skin-crawling feeling that this is too good to be true.

You stop what you're doing and look at the adults. Karen and your parents are studying you too closely, as if with breath held. Karen smiles. Your mother nods and smiles, too. Your dad is leaning against the fridge, a beer in his hand even though your mum doesn't understand how he can drink at a time like this, and he doesn't understand how she can be such a robot.

Dad raises the bottle to you, tries to smile like he's forgotten how to.

"You could write about the night Teddy disappeared, Luce," he says, as if he's just thought of the idea, but you can tell he hasn't. This is rehearsed. It's another trick to get you to remember what happened.

You put the pen down carefully beside the beautiful notebook, even though you are tempted to throw both of them as far away from you as you can. You place your hands on your knees. "Thank you very much," you say.

"Well," says Karen after a few moments during which you watch

her expression collapse from bright into saggy. "That's grand. You'll tell me when you've written your first story, won't you? I'd love to read it."

You ease yourself off the chair and leave the room as quietly as you can.

They don't start talking until you're at the top of the stairs. They think you can't hear from up here, but you can. Your mum lays into your dad.

"Why did you have to butt in like that and rush her? We were going to take it slowly. You've scared her off again."

"Me?" he shouts. "I'm not the one whose stupid idea it was."

You go into your bedroom and shut the door.

"Eliza?" you whisper.

"Yes."

"It was another trick."

"Did they fool you?"

"No."

"That's good," she says. "Shall we play?"

"What do you want to play?"

"Let's pretend."

It's your favorite game.

I felt sick by the time I'd finished reading. Betrayed. Wholly and completely.

Memories shimmered. I threw the manuscript across the room. The pages filled the air like locusts hungry to devour what was left of me.

Not only was Dan writing about my past, he was also pointing the finger at me.

"It's a hatchet job. They were out to get you," Eliza said.

She was right; my husband had believed me to be a monster.

41

I heard my phone ring as if from a distance but found it on the kitchen surface right in front of me. I was eating more food from the hamper. Noah was calling, the PR guy from my publishers.

"I'm so sorry about Dan's death," he said. "We are all so very sorry here. I can't imagine how hard it must be."

I pinched the bridge of my nose hard between my fingers as I listened. He was going to ask me for something, I could hear it in his voice, and I felt myself shrinking in anticipation of it.

"I hate to mention this to you now, but something unexpected has happened. We've been contacted by a journalist who has been working for a while on a long-form piece about something that happened in your childhood."

I sat down on the staircase. Above me, high above, in another place, a cloud passed over the light well.

"They've asked if you want to comment on the piece."

"No," I said.

He cleared his throat. "Can I ask . . . were you aware of the potential existence of this piece before now?"

"No." I felt pain. It was in my thigh. My fingers were digging into it.

"Okay," he said. His voice sounded as if it was being transmitted through molasses. "It's just that the journalist, um, has let us know that he's been working on this piece with your husband. Apparently, it was supposed to come out in advance of a publication your husband was involved with, based on your brother's disappearance. But given the circumstances, there is strong interest in publishing it now."

"Can't you stop it?"

"I'm afraid not. We can only try to get your version of the story out. Which is why we are suggesting another interview. We could expand the format to address the material in the article."

"I can't," I said.

"I understand. But will you think about it?"

"I really can't. You have no idea."

I ended the call and put the phone down. He rang back but I ignored it.

"I could do the interview for you," Eliza said. "It would be good if you did it."

"I need to see Sasha." I wanted someone to pay for this, or at the very least, to admit to my face how deeply they had tried to hurt me. And I wanted to look her in the eye to see if I thought there was any truth to James's accusations.

"That's a bad idea."

I didn't care. I cut through the gardens and leaned on Sasha's doorbell until she opened up. I put my foot in the door.

"How can you live with yourself?" I shouted.

"I don't know what you mean," she said. She was trying to sound cool as ice but there were nerves beneath the surface, I could tell. Her mouth gaped uselessly. For once she looked ugly. I jabbed a finger at her.

"You worked with my husband to write a book about me. You set out to ruin me and now he's dead!"

"That's nothing to do with me," she said. She tried to push the door closed but my foot stopped her.

Behind her, James appeared. I was surprised to see him at home on a weekday. He slipped his arm around Sasha's waist. Marital solidarity. It caught me off guard. It was the last thing I expected to see.

"Hello, Lucy," he said. "Is something wrong?"

He looked so blank-faced you'd think the night before had never happened.

"You know what's wrong," I said.

"I'm sorry. What do I know?"

"Last night. In her writing shed. You know what you showed me and what you told me."

The hot taste of blood filled my mouth. I had bitten my tongue.

"I'm sorry," he said, "but I've got no recollection of this whatsoever."

"Lucy . . ." Sasha's hands were trembling, but determination had set her face hard and there was an ugly curl to her lip. *I'm finally going to see the real Sasha*, I thought, but she flinched. James's arm had tightened around her waist so hard that she bent a little toward him.

"Darling," he said, in a tone that was light but very controlled, and she shut her mouth.

James smiled at me. "I think there's been a misunderstanding. Sasha wasn't working on anything with Dan."

I stared at him. "The writing shed," I said. "Their stuff was pinned up on every wall. Teddy's photo. All of it. You ripped it down. You went mad. You can't deny it."

"You're welcome to have a look at the shed if that'll help us settle this confusion. Shall we go around the side?"

I took off ahead of them, walking and then running as if arriving first would change anything. The shed door was open. The inside of it looked completely different. The corkboards were on the wall, but there were no pins in them, no torn shreds of paper, just two posters of tranquil landscapes, neatly pinned. A yoga mat was spread out on the floor, more equipment sat tidily in a corner, a small table was home to a cluster of candles, and a lemon tree stood proud in a terra-cotta pot in one corner. It was pretty. Peaceful. A world away from what I'd seen here just hours before.

Sasha and James arrived right behind me. I didn't dare look at them. If they had done this, what else were they capable of?

"Sasha so enjoys doing yoga in here," James said. "Don't you, darling?"

"It's a terrific space," she said. "Very relaxing."

"You're both lying," I said.

"No," James said. "I don't think the mistake is ours. You must be confused."

"I have proof! I took the papers from this shed."

"Proof of what?"

"That—" But I wasn't sure.

He nodded. "I think you'll find it's proof of nothing apart from the fact that somebody printed out materials related to Teddy."

I was shocked. He was lying so brazenly. I focused on Sasha. "The police have some of the paragraphs you and Dan wrote," I said.

"I didn't write anything," she said, and I thought she looked genuinely surprised. Perhaps Dan had written those pages I'd read without Sasha. He would have considered his writing skills superior to hers, of course. Patricia had told me that, and knowing him as well as I did, I should have assumed it anyway.

"It strikes me," James said, "that you might be having an episode."

"What?"

"Well, Daniel did confide in us that your behavior can be erratic. That you have mood swings and memory lapses. That it was sometimes frightening."

"No," I said.

"We have told the police."

I backed away from them, onto their lawn.

"Do you want me to walk you home?" James asked. "Is there someone we can call?"

"Lucy," Sasha said. She looked uneasy and I thought for a

moment she might be about to throw me some sort of lifeline, or perhaps she was just intending to confuse me more, but James took a step between us and extended a hand toward me as if he wanted to offer help. It dissolved and re-formed before my eyes.

"Stay away from me!" I said. I began to run. It was difficult on the muddy grass.

I didn't stop to think about the media until I burst from the end of the Morells' drive and came face-to-face with them. There were more of them than before; they began to shout questions at me and I could only stand there, panting, staring blankly into their pleading expressions and down their bottomless camera lenses.

"Turn around and walk away," said Eliza. "Say nothing."

I did what she told me to do and only the fact that she was walking with me kept me going.

42

There's a playlist I made to get me in the mood to write and if you listen to the very first song you can hear the artist taking a breath before they start to perform. One breathy inhalation, and on that soft rush of air I imagine I can hear the nerves of the performer, the preparation, the hope, the talent, the precious time invested, all of it pent up and ready to be expelled in a single performance.

To me, that breath might just as well represent the baring of the writer's soul in the instant a reader turns to the first page of their book and begins to read. It begs for a meaningful connection between writer and reader. In my profession, we write alone, but it's that connection we long for. I write for my readers.

Then why did I take Eliza out of my books? you might ask.

You know why now.

You might like the idea that a writer lives with their characters, talks to them, sees them. But would you want that to be your life? Would you be able to hold it together? Who would you trust? Yourself? Your creations? The real people around you?

I paced through the crumbling spaces in my house. I went from top to bottom. I avoided windows. The shutters and blinds were still closed and I made no effort to open them. It was twilight I moved in. I was just one more shadow among hosts of others. I was trying to avoid going online. The lure of it was so hard to resist and because I write for readers, because they are the most important people to me, the hardest thing was not to look at the Eliza Grey fan page. I resisted social media and media sites, I ignored the incessant ringing of my phone and the ping of notifications. But I longed to look at the Eliza Grey page and I realized I had always thought of it as a cord that connected me to the world. Umbilical, if you like. Severing it would be a brutal cut.

But I resisted it.

I put on the television and watched a person so fat they couldn't wash themselves talk to the camera. I changed the channel. Click. Fires raged and wildlife burned. Another channel change: talking heads oozed sarcasm. Click. Commercials for charities in which people starved. Click. Competing models. Click. Buy a new car now the easy way. Click. Competing chefs. Click. Click. Click. I felt disoriented. I didn't know where I fit in with any of this.

I raided the hamper and found a fruitcake. It was delicious, but dry. I left crumbs on the kitchen island. I picked at the wrapping around the flowers that had been delivered until all of it came away. The stems were drooping. Scraps of tissue paper landed around the base of the vase among discarded petals.

There was a card tucked deep into the bouquet. I hadn't noticed it before. I plucked it out and opened it.

Dear Lucy,
So, you got what you wanted. Eliza is out of the book. I hope you're happy now. Some of us are not. I have lost a spouse. And what do people commonly want in revenge? It's an eye for an eye, Lucy. You know that.

Yours, disappointed to the core,
MrElizaGrey

I wrenched open the door to the garden and threw out the flowers, the vase they had come in, the card, all of it. The vase shattered on the patio; the lilies, blooms of death, lay strewn over the stones, as haphazard as if they'd been tossed onto a coffin, their sticky orange pollen clinging to the stone where it fell like some kind of baneful, unnatural lichen.

How did they know about Eliza?

As I stared at the wreckage, a figure stepped out of the hedge, onto the lawn. It was the boy. The little boy from next door.

"Hello," I said.

"Hello." He held a ball. "I heared a noise." That's not a typo. It's how he said it: "hear-ed."

"I dropped my flowers," I said.

We stared at each other.

"Uh-oh," he said.

I felt myself blinking back tears. I blinked faster and faster. "You should go back to your own garden now," I said. "Go on home before your mum gets worried."

He didn't move.

"Go on!" I shouted.

When he had slipped away, back through the gap in the hedge, I went inside, slid the door shut behind me, and locked it.

I had no hesitation about going online now. I intended to find MrElizaGrey. I had thought Dan might be behind the name before, but now I wasn't sure. Had he sent me those flowers before he died because he wanted to scare me into keeping Eliza in the books? Or was someone else targeting me?

There was another question I had, too. It had been building in my head since I'd read what Dan had written. Had he moved us here because he thought it would lift the lid on my memories and encourage me to spill my guts for his book? Did he hope this place would strip back my defenses and reduce me to my rawest, most vulnerable state? Was that what he had intended?

The header on the Eliza Grey site had been changed. It now had a black border around it. "RIP Daniel Harper" it said. I wanted to spit at it. At him. For what he had done to me. But it also made me feel horribly low and sad. Because I also missed him so very much.

I scoured the site for new posts by MrElizaGrey and quickly found one dated just a day ago, so it couldn't have been written by Dan. I sat back and stared at it. The title was "Divorce?"

It described a row between MrElizaGrey and Eliza, and it was a passionate row, a semiviolent one. I was disturbed by the descriptions in it. They were alarmingly vivid. "Write what you know," Eliza muttered as we read, and I nodded. Pain and pent-up emotion sprang off the page. It was explosive and I couldn't help thinking of James Morell trashing Sasha's writing shed.

If I sent a message to this person, would I be communicating with James? Had he found out about Eliza via Sasha and Dan? Would he be the next person to step through the gap in my hedge? To retaliate?

"Take a moment," said Eliza. "Don't do anything rash."

I thought about calling DS Bright, but I was worried that it would make her doubt me more than ever. I knew she was starting to consider me a fantasist and I couldn't forget how things had gone when I was under police suspicion as a child. How the detective who had interviewed me for hours and hours had started to burn with frustration when we talked, and how his frustration had morphed into suspicion.

I clicked on the comment button beneath MrElizaGrey's post and a slim window opened. The cursor inside it blinked. My fingers settled onto the keyboard, poised to type, feeling the familiar little plastic bumps on the "F" and "J" keys beneath my fingertips, the hum of the machine beneath that.

I typed, "Who are you?" and hit "Send." My heart began to thump like a jackhammer.

A reply box appeared below my message.

The doorbell screeched.

I couldn't tear my eyes from the screen. The box disappeared.

The bell rang again.

43

I peered through the spyhole in the front door. Ben Delaney was there, dressed casually. I opened up.

"Hi," he said. "Kate made you a lasagna."

He handed over a casserole dish covered in foil. A meaty sauce had dried on the sides of it.

"I'm so sorry," he said. "If there's anything we can do to help, please give us a shout." He ran his hand through his fine hair, mildly self-conscious, but sweet, too, and I thought, *He's so beautifully ordinary; why didn't I marry an ordinary guy?* But then he said, "You might remember that I'm a solicitor. Criminal solicitor. So, if you need any advice, or just to chat through things, don't hesitate to ask. It would be as a favor to you, of course."

"Thanks," I said, and I remembered that he'd phoned my solicitor to try to get information about my case, but people have money troubles, and he had a family to support, so I didn't blame him for chasing my business. I added nicely, "I'm fine. I have representation."

"Yes, of course. I'm sorry. Kate told me to offer whatever you need. So, there you go. Anyway . . . We're here if you need us. Enjoy the lasagna."

He started to move away.

"Wait!" I said. "What do you know about James and Sasha?"

He looked as if he had to think about it. "Um, nice couple. Moved in about the same time as we did. We've always got on great with them. If you want to know more, Kate's the person to ask. She's had much more contact with the neighbors than I have." He lowered his voice. "The ones you actually want to watch out for are Barry and Vi. She's all right, but he's very tricky. He's got a rod shoved right up his you know where. He made it very difficult for us when we were buying The Lodge." He looked up suddenly. "Do you hear that?" he asked.

It was a humming, like the sound of a small lawn mower, but coming from somewhere high up, and it was getting louder.

We watched as a small object appeared above the top of the tree line that could be glimpsed from our driveway.

"It's a drone!" Ben said. "Wow."

It approached us and flew lower. The noise level increased. I felt as if it was filling my ears, swelling inside my head. I backed into the house. "Do you want to come in?" I beckoned to him. I didn't care which side of the door he was on, but I wanted to get inside.

"No," he said. As the drone swept lower, he pulled the hood of his coat over his head and headed home. I shut the door, but I could still hear it. The frequency seemed tuned specially to torment.

I put the lasagna in the kitchen and peered beneath the foil. The cheese had crusted onto the pasta sheets. The sauce was deep red and oily. I knew I couldn't eat it. It reminded me of Dan's cooking.

I returned to my laptop and moved it out of the kitchen, to the sitting room, where I'd closed the shutters.

The noise of the drone faded in and out as it circled my home. I could see when it passed over the light well because the light in the hall faded momentarily and every time it did, I caught my breath. I cowered as it hovered right outside the windows. I knew it couldn't see me, but it wasn't difficult to imagine it crashing through the glass and the shutters, its little camera approaching until it hovered right in front of me for a close-up of what I knew the press would love to call my evil face.

It went, eventually, but I remained where I was, in case it came back, and it felt like I stayed there forever. Time bent and swayed. I sat stiff and still, and my legs were sore by the time I finally got the courage to move. I straightened them out and opened the laptop, and being in the glow of the screen made me feel like I was waking up after a fever dream.

I checked my emails. Max and Angela had written messages of support, but I felt dissociated from their words, as if they were meant for another person, in another time and place. I skimmed over them and didn't linger because I was drawn to the Eliza fan page.

There, I found a reply to my message to MrElizaGrey.

44

I don't want to say who I am, the message read. But you need to talk to Naomi Dent.

Who is she? I typed.
No. 10 Charlotte Close.

I paused when I saw that. It took a moment for my fingers to find the keys again.

You need to tell me who you are.
I can't. Ask Naomi about the traps.

MrElizaGrey disappeared offline.

"I'm not sure I want to know who this is," Eliza said.

"It's somebody who knows something about Teddy."

"We need to leave that alone."

"I can't."

"Lucy!" Eliza shouted and it shocked me. "This is the very worst thing you could do. You must understand that." She appeared, standing in front of me, pulling herself up to her full height, the way she did in the books when she needed to.

"Don't try to stop me," I said.

I knew I would have to go through the woods to reach Charlotte Close if I wanted to avoid the media. I put on more sensible clothes this time. Walking boots and one of Dan's coats that was waterproof. I checked the time. It was after seven and would be getting dark soon. The lawn squelched as I walked down it.

Sawdust from the felled cedar stuck to my boots and cold needles of rain drove into me relentlessly, stinging my cheeks and my hands, drenching everything, erasing sharp edges, making the foliage lurk and loom.

The sky was empty of drones, though a bird of prey dove through the murky sky and screamed before disappearing into the trees. As I approached the boundary of my property, I watched carefully for signs that journalists were there. I didn't see anyone, or the dark glint of a lens. I hoped that the lateness and the weather had driven them home for the night, but I knew I could be wrong. That they were tenacious. That there could be eyes on me covertly.

I parted the barbed-wire fence and stepped into the woods, moving carefully in what I hoped was the right direction for Charlotte Close. I felt disoriented. I'd never known this part of the woods. I wasn't sure quite how to reach where I wanted to go. I would have to follow my gut instinct. Everything dripped. Rain-slicked leaves drooped, the tops of branches wore dark blemishes from the creeping damp, and all the sounds were strangely muted, the usual echoes curtailed and concentrated. I blinked moisture from my eyelashes and had the sense of being in an altered world. I used the torch on my phone to guide me.

I made it close to the woods' car park but didn't enter because I could see vehicles there. A pair of headlights sent beams of light searching into the undergrowth. I kept back, creeping from one pool of shadow to the next. I knew this part of the woods very well. It wasn't difficult for me to make my way to the backs of the gardens and from there to the road.

I stood at the end of Charlotte Close. I could see every home. I hadn't set foot here since my parents and I moved and now that I was back, I wasn't sure if I could. Some of the properties had lights on and people hadn't drawn their curtains yet. The familiarity felt disorienting, like seeing a face you think you recognize before realizing it's your own. Aged, subtly changed, but bearing traces of everything you ever lived through, even the things you want to forget.

The first step was an effort, and so was each one after that. The houses sat squat and ordinary, looking harmless, just the way they had every evening of my childhood before Teddy disappeared.

My old home didn't look too changed after all these years: a different car in the driveway, fresher sets of curtains in the windows, the front door a pale blue where it had been white when we lived there. The little window that punctuated it looked the same. The most startling thing was that it looked loved. Everything my parents had let go after Teddy had gone had been taken care of. It was painful to see. A life we could have lived if things had been different.

The doorbell on number 10 trilled with an optimistic electronic jingle when I pressed it. "Who is it?" called a voice.

"It's Lucy Bewley," I said. Hearing my old name spoken out loud after all these years was a shock. "I used to live at number seven."

The door opened. I pulled down my hood. Naomi Dent squinted at me. I recognized her immediately. She wore the same hairstyle as she had years ago, though her hair was granite gray now. "I don't believe it," she said. "Is it you?"

"Please, can I come in and talk to you?"

The layout of her home was identical to my family's at number 7. Naomi and I sat in the sitting room at the back. An outside light over the French doors lit up the garden. It was smaller than my parents' garden had been. She had no lawn. Rain bounced off her deck and a bare rotary washing line protruded from a patch of earth. She made me a cup of instant coffee and served it with a plate of the same biscuits she used to give our family at Christmas. I felt time lurch.

"I saw you on the news," she said. "I'm sorry about your husband. He was a lovely man."

"You met him?"

"He came here to talk about when your brother disappeared."

I tried to control my expression. I didn't want my anger with Dan to show. "Do you remember that night? When Teddy went?"

"I'll never forget it."

"I've come to ask you about traps. Did something happen that had anything to do with traps? Do you know about that?"

"You're the first person to ask me about it. I mentioned it to Daniel, but he didn't seem that interested. I had a journalist come here, too, but he was very rude, so I told him where to put his checkbook."

I remembered her pride. How the other neighbors had complained about her stubbornness.

"I'm interested."

"You remember it was the summer solstice, the night Teddy disappeared? Well, local people didn't like the partygoers using the woods to celebrate. That year a few of us got a petition organized to try to force the police to do something to stop them gathering there. The Forestry Commission didn't allow it then, but nobody enforced it, that was the problem. They were underresourced and the police didn't want to take responsibility unless there was a crime being committed. They didn't care if a few folks on this side of the bridge were kept up at night. They had bigger problems to deal with in the city. But what a racket those pagans or whatever they liked to call themselves made and what a mess they left there, and we were afraid the fire would spread."

My vision flickered as if flames were dancing at the backs of my eyes.

"So, we got organized on the Close and went around to the lane to see if we could get some support from the big houses, too. Are you living there now?"

"I am."

"Your husband said you were planning to move there. I was surprised you'd come back here, if I'm honest." Her eyebrows made careful arches.

"Did anyone on the lane offer help?"

"We didn't have much luck. The house near the road was empty, and the one down the very end—"

"My house," I murmured, and she nodded.

"Your house was home to a man who spent half the year in France, so he was never there."

"And Barry and Vi Kaplan?" I said.

"Right. We talked to Barry and Vi. She wasn't too bothered, she's more of a live-and-let-live sort of person, I always thought, but Barry cared. I'm not sure he would have if they hadn't lit the bonfire on such an important historic site, but he really cared about that. It's his area of study, isn't it, history, so it wasn't surprising. What bothered him most was the risk of damage to the site, mostly from fire. And as it turned out, Barry was prepared to go further than the rest of us to stop it. He wanted to patrol the woods on solstice night and keep the pagans out physically, but there weren't enough of us and some of us were afraid to do it. What were we going to do if they challenged us? Get in a fight?"

I remembered Dad raging about the police failure to pursue the individuals who had been in the woods on the night Teddy disappeared. "What can they do?" Mum had screamed back at him. "Those sorts of people aren't going to help the police. They're secretive. They close ranks."

Naomi Dent was studying me the way she used to stand on her front lawn and stare at us while we were playing. She spoke again, more softly this time. "I should say sorry, I suppose. A few of us on the Close thought you did something to Teddy. I don't know why we thought that now. I suppose we humans like to look at the dark side of things, don't we? At the most twisted things. We like that feeling of shock and horror. It makes addicts of us. Though you were a strange girl—not your run-of-the-mill little thing. But, anyway, I'm sorry for that now."

"Thank you," I said.

"Did you know?" she asked. "I have sometimes wondered if you knew what we thought."

"Yes, I knew."

I looked down at my knees, at the half-empty cup of coffee I was resting on them. The surface of the liquid shimmered.

"The thing is, Barry set traps in the woods on the night of the solstice," Naomi said. "They were only small ones, meant for animals, but he said they'd do enough damage to an adult's foot to be a deterrent. He wanted to teach those people a lesson."

I stared at her. "What are you saying?"

"I always worried," said Naomi, "that Teddy got hurt in one. It's stupid of me because we'd know if he had, they'd have found him, but I dream about it sometimes. Even now."

"Did the police find out about the traps?"

"I don't think so."

"You didn't tell them?"

She shook her head.

"Why didn't they find them when the search parties went out?"

"Barry collected them up before the police started properly searching. Someone called him to tell him that kids had been in the woods and one of them was missing. Barry was the one who knew where all the traps were, you see, because he set them. He bolted out there and took them back. Thank goodness there was nothing in them! He called to let us know. We were beside ourselves worrying until then. You wouldn't be able to live with yourself, would you, if you thought you'd hurt a little boy?"

"Who called Barry to tell him?"

"My Eric did, my husband, right after your dad rang our bell to say Teddy was missing and could we help look for him."

I thought of my passage through the woods with Teddy. How we had been looking up at the canopy, talking about the spirits, imagining the wild dance up there, while beneath our feet the ground had been littered with traps. I imagined their cold metal teeth, the horrible force with which the sprung hinges would have clamped shut, how much damage that could have done to a person as small as Teddy.

I wondered how close we had passed.

"Did anyone else know about the traps?"

"My husband knew, obviously, but he's passed away now, and I always assumed Vi knew. Though I never asked her because they moved away so soon after it happened."

"Do you know why they moved?"

"Barry got a teaching position at a university in Australia."

"And no one else knew about the traps?" I was badgering her by repeating the question, but I wanted to be sure.

"Just the people I told recently, which would be your husband and the young woman who came here with him."

"Do you remember her name?"

"Sasha. Your neighbor, I believe."

Sasha.

"Did you tell Sasha and my husband everything that you've just told me?"

She nodded.

We said our goodbyes and as I walked away from Naomi Dent's house, I put my hood up. The rain had worsened, glazing the pavements of Charlotte Close, reflecting the lights so the street looked daubed with vivid color.

My head ached from everything I didn't know.

Was Teddy hurt, or even killed, in a trap? What had happened to him? Had Barry buried his small, sweet body?

Had Dan discovered this, and had it put him in danger? Was Sasha in danger, too, or was she dangerous?

And was it Sasha who had tipped me off about Naomi Dent, or Vi?

Finding the answers was imperative. The prospect was terrifying.

45

I walked back through the woods using the torch on my phone again. It had grown darker.

The rain felt like a gift now. Memories of heat, fire, and sparks flying on the night Teddy disappeared threatened to burst into life with every step I took but were extinguished by the damp veils of foliage, the wet air. I came across the path. It was deserted in both directions. I couldn't help turning onto it instead of sticking to the undergrowth. I felt drawn toward the redwood copse, and what lay beyond it, as if it would bring me closer to Teddy.

Eliza's voice ran around my head. "Go home," she said. "You're driving yourself crazy." It was like an echo of Dan.

But I wanted to be close to Teddy, here in the woods. Being near him would help shut out the other voices. I followed the route back to the bunker, walking slowly and steadily, my hood fallen back, too focused on my goal to care about who might notice me or be following me. I ignored Eliza's words; they were background noise, just like my heavy breathing and my footsteps, and the myriad sounds of the woods around me. I only wanted my brother.

I found the bunker door again easily and ran my fingers over it. I examined the padlock. I wanted to go in. To see where I had left him. I wanted to feel that pain again. I had avoided it for so long, but what if feeling it jogged my memory and told me something important?

"How do I open this?" I asked Eliza. I shook the padlock.

She said nothing.

"Tell me!"

"You need two wrenches," she said. "Or a lock-picking set."

"No. You did it without wrenches once." I remembered researching it for one of the earlier Eliza novels. I was sure it involved hitting the padlock with a hammer. I searched around for a stone and began to strike the lock with it, bashing it harder and harder, but it didn't break. I put my phone in my pocket, took the stone in both hands, and kept at it, sometimes not even making contact with the padlock at all, until I broke the almost-healed skin on my knuckles.

"Stop!" Eliza said. "Try this. Take hold of the shackle, the metal loop."

I slipped my fingers beneath it.

"Now pull it up and away from the base as hard as you can and when you've done that, hit the side of the padlock with a few sharp taps. Keep going. You want the side where it's fixed. It's only going to work if it's a certain type of mechanism."

It was difficult to get the right angle. Water dripped down my forehead; damp hair stuck to my face, crept between my lips. I pulled on the shackle and tapped it with a stone, again and again, and just when I thought it was never going to work, the padlock sprang open.

I pulled it off, dropped it to the ground, and tugged on the door. Its metal edge cut into my fingers, but it opened inch by inch. When the gap was wide enough, I got out my torch again and peered through, the drumbeat of my heart picking up tempo. But I saw nothing. Or, rather, I saw a blockage, just a foot or so from the doorway. Confused, I wrenched the door open farther, tugging it and swearing at it, because this was the last thing I had expected. I was sweaty by the time I had created enough of an aperture for the beam of light to fall onto what was behind it.

It was a wall constructed from cinder blocks and it sealed off the bunker entirely. There was no door in it. No way past it.

Beneath my fingertips the texture of the rough concrete blocks felt harsh enough to skin me. I ran my hand all the way around the edge of the wall, feeling for some sort of gap, but it was impregnable.

The place had been sealed like a tomb and this created a sense of horror in me, a living, crawling fear that felt bigger than me, and capable of swallowing me.

I turned and ran back toward the redwoods, almost falling with every step I took, trying to keep ahead of the horror, dodging the tendrils it threw out, which unfurled at breakneck speed behind me, grasping for my ankles, trying to pull me back there, deep into the darkness, to that place where traps were laid and where a small boy could disappear without a trace.

46

Once I'd gotten back to the path, I couldn't run anymore. I could only stand, doubled over, and wait for my breathing to slow down. I still felt disoriented, as if the woods were changing shape around me. I realized for the first time that there must have been a more direct way home from the bunker, but I hadn't thought of that when I was fleeing. I only knew the woods well if I stuck to the routes I'd taken as a child.

I headed back toward my house. I hoped I was going the right direction, but I was exhausted and felt as if I had nothing left in the tank that might help me make a single rational decision. I tripped a few times more. The torch beam bounced off the tree trunks. My head spun. Close to home, I stopped abruptly, sensing someone else. I turned my torch off. The person was to my right, heading in the opposite direction, walking behind a much more powerful beam of torchlight than mine. I stepped behind a tree and leaned against it, feeling the bark scrape my back. A moment later I heard a voice.

"Hi," he said. "It's me. Just checking in." He spoke startlingly loudly. He wasn't afraid of being overheard. "No. . . . Nothing. . . . I don't think she's in. . . . No, mate. . . . I'm going back to the car. . . . I'm fucking soaking. . . . I got lost." He muttered to himself as he walked, swore again as he stumbled, and I stayed pinned to the tree as he passed by. A journalist, I thought. He must have been trying to approach my house from the back.

"It would serve him right if he stepped into a trap," Eliza said.

It was a relief to reach the end of my garden. The barbed wire caught my hair as I slipped through the fence. I wrenched it clear and relief coursed through me as I walked up the lawn, free from the trees and no sound of a drone.

I pulled everything out of the hamper in search of the last of the food. There was wine and a packet of fudge. I had some of both. Tamsin had brought me bread, so I made toast and took it upstairs, afraid of who else might be creeping outside.

I couldn't help peeking out through the shutters. It was as if I had unfinished business in the woods. I was curious about where exactly the bunker was in relation to my home. I had the feeling it was closer than I'd ever imagined but my tired brain could not figure it out. My sense of direction was wholly unreliable. My memory, well, you know. I stared out. It was almost completely black out there now.

The bunker cannot move, I told myself. *It cannot close in on me.* Thinking otherwise was fantastical. I should not be seeing and feeling things that were not there.

"You should not," Eliza confirmed. But still, I could not chase away the feeling that it was close.

I secured the shutters and took refuge in a lit screen.

I input Dan's name and added "article" and "Lucy Bewley" to the search. I wanted to see if I could find the piece that Noah had referred to. A result came up immediately. It was a tweet by a journalist.

Coming soon: Teddy Bewley disappearance (look it up if you haven't heard of it). Dramatic new evidence. You won't believe it.
#lucybewley #lucyharper #teddybewley #disappeared #coldcase
#watchthisspace #solvethecase #elizagrey

I clicked on the journalist's head shot and recognized the white-blond hair. This was the man Dan had described to me as a structural engineer, who had come to our house the night my husband disappeared. The police had wasted time looking for him. I copied a link to the tweet and emailed it to DS Bright. This is the engineer, I wrote. Except that apparently he's actually a journalist. I would leave it to her to pursue him. I didn't expect she'd think he was involved with Dan's death. I didn't think he was. But I liked the idea of him being paid a visit by the police. It would be some payback for the article about me that he and Dan had been working on.

I considered replying to his tweet, asking how he felt about exposing my story to the world, but before I could type this, I started to cry. I had no fight left in me. What did this man care about me anyhow? He wouldn't have been writing the article if he had a shred of decency.

I visited the Eliza Grey fan page. MrElizaGrey was not online. I added another comment to our previous communication: Sasha, is this you? I thought she was more likely to be doing this sort of stuff online than Vi was. I'd only noticed a dated desktop computer at Vi's house. No smartphones, no laptops.

I thought about James taking over as Sasha stood at the door when I visited them and I remembered how he'd looked as he'd lied about what had happened in the writing shed. Was he really controlling her? Or she him? There were twists in that relationship that I could only guess at, but which left me feeling alarmed for myself and for one of them, I just didn't know which one.

I researched James online. The results, only a few of them, brought up nothing more than some links full of corporate speak about projects he'd been involved with and two glossy head shots of him in a suit and tie. It was very anodyne, and he didn't appear to have any social media presence.

I searched for Barry next. He wasn't on social media, either, but there were pages of links to publications he'd been involved in and university positions he'd occupied. I wanted to know where he'd gone right after Teddy disappeared. And why.

It wasn't difficult to find out. He'd taken up a post at the University of Melbourne just a little over a month later. I found a mention of him on an old alumni forum.

Anyone know why Barry Kaplan lost his job? one of his former students had asked some years ago.

Had a nervous breakdown right after he arrived, another wrote.

No way! Bored himself to death? I know I slept through most of his lectures.

Ha! No one knows why. My academic mentor said she heard it happened like the moment he got off the plane. He never really functioned properly so he taught on a reduced schedule and left soon afterward. Basically, threw away the biggest opportunity of his career. Weird.

I scrolled down looking for more, but the chat ended there. I typed "Barry Kaplan nervous breakdown" into the search engine, but nothing more came up. Why would he break down as soon as he arrived to take up a prestigious position? Was it the result of something that had happened just before he moved?

Could he have discovered a little boy in one of his traps, a fatally wounded little boy? The idea was horrific, but it was impossible for me to unthink it. And it was possible to believe it. If Barry knew what had happened to Teddy, it could explain why he'd been so unhappy to have me in his house. If he was at all human, he would be feeling unbearably guilty. And he would also be feeling under pressure. If he knew what my husband and Sasha had discovered about the traps, perhaps it had worried him enough to take action against Dan.

I thought about all the hours the detective had spent grilling me about Teddy's disappearance. Had he ever talked to Barry?

"Don't you dare," Eliza said.

"I need to ask him."

"You have more than enough to worry about already."

She leaned over me and typed my name into the search engine.

Recent photographs of me filled the screen side by side. To the left was the latest shot of me, just emerging from the woods, looking crazed, like a vagrant. In the middle was a still from the TV interview, looking relatively groomed and self-possessed. On the right-hand side was the old photograph of me as a child that had horrified my mother, the one where I was staring out of our landing window, my hand on the glass pane, as creepy-looking as any character you've ever seen in a horror film.

THE MANY SIDES OF LUCY HARPER? screamed the headline. ONE WOMAN. TWO IDENTITIES. TWO LOVED ONES LOST ran beneath it.

It was bad. But I wasn't going to be distracted from contacting Charlie Cartwright, the detective who had investigated Teddy's case.

"Don't," Eliza said.

"I have to."

I clicked the little X that closed the photographs and typed in "Retired Detective Inspector Charles Cartwright."

I looked through the spyhole. Retired Detective Inspector Charlie Cartwright was smaller than I remembered.

"Come in," I said. I'd made contact with him by email. It had been surprisingly easy. It turned out he was the secretary of a local golf club. I was surprised that he'd responded immediately and had suggested he meet me the following day at my home, but grateful, too. The media will be all over you, of course, he'd written, so I'm sure you won't want to come out. And I'm not comfortable answering queries via email.

I showed him into the kitchen, where I'd rigged up a sheet over the windows, and I made tea. He'd brought milk, as requested.

Every time our eyes met, decades disappeared and we were a much younger man and a young girl. I gave him his tea. He still took it with milk and two sugars. When I stirred the sugar in, it was my childish hand I saw, momentarily, and my mother's cup.

"Thank you for seeing me," I said.

"Of course." His hands were liver-spotted. One clasped the other, as if disguising a tremor. I wished it were as easy to disguise the hatred I felt for him. I needed to, if I wanted information.

"I'm sorry I can't offer you some Battenberg cake," I said. It had been his favorite. For a while, before she started to lose hope, my mother had kept some stocked for him.

"You remembered."

I nodded.

"Congratulations on your writing success."

"Thank you."

"I've read all your books."

I was disconcerted by this. The idea that he'd followed my progress from afar, that he'd still been watching me when I thought he'd given up long ago.

"Thank you," I said.

"Spotted one or two typos." He winked.

"You and all the other pedants." I summoned up the smile I use in publishing meetings when my editor has asked me to do something that I'm going to decline.

"I saw in the acknowledgments that you talk to Tim Partridge for research," he said.

"Do you know him?"

"We were partners for a while."

"Tim never mentioned it."

"I expect he doesn't want to put you off."

I almost laughed.

"He enjoys talking to you."

"I enjoy talking to him." Or I thought I had, when I'd assumed that he didn't know who I was. It was an intensely creepy feeling, realizing that he might have been reporting on me to Charlie.

"I wanted to ask you about the old investigation," I said. "Did you speak to any of the people who lived in the houses here on the lane at the time?"

"We did."

"Do you remember a couple called Barry and Veronica Kaplan? They live two doors down. Actually, it was one door down back then. The Lodge hadn't been built."

"The investigation into your brother's disappearance is still open, technically, so there's not a great deal I can tell you, but if I remember correctly, I think we spoke to them briefly, immediately after Teddy went missing, but they left the country very soon afterward, just a few weeks later, as I remember it. Their trip was prearranged, so there was nothing suspicious about it, if that's what you're asking."

"I heard that Barry set traps in the woods that night. To deter the summer solstice partygoers."

"Uh-huh," Charlie said slowly. I couldn't tell if he knew already or not. But he didn't seem to consider it important. He changed the subject.

"It was interesting to see Eliza in the books, transformed into a detective no less."

It almost sounded as if he wanted to take some credit for that and I was incredulous.

"Do you still talk to her?" he asked, and I didn't like the way his eyes had narrowed. I'd seen that look before. It was the expression his face had settled into over the weeks he spent talking to me after Teddy disappeared, as hope collapsed and undisguised suspicion grew in its place.

"What did Barry Kaplan tell you about the night Teddy disappeared?" I asked. "Because I think he's been lying. I think he knows something. He had a breakdown right after he left Bristol."

Charlie slurped his tea. "We ruled him out."

"How? Did he have an alibi?"

"I can't discuss details like that."

"But you discussed me and the case with my husband! I know you did. I've read what he wrote about it. There's stuff in his book he could only have gotten from you."

"I didn't tell Daniel anything that I wasn't allowed to. How's the investigation into his death going, by the way? Are you being helpful to the police?"

The glint in his eye was nasty. I realized I had been stupid to think he might feel any impulse to help me. He was here because he still hated me; because he wanted to turn up the pressure on me; because he, like DS Bright, thought me a murderer, twice over. I had been so stupid. But I was also angry with him.

"Did you think I was going to confess to you if you came here today? Is that what you were expecting? How exciting that must have been." I laughed. "Or, and I don't know which is worse, did you just come here to gloat because my husband is dead? Could you stoop any lower?"

"One day, you'll tell the truth and then everyone will know what you did."

"The truth is that you were an incompetent detective."

He got to his feet. I recognized the twitch in his jaw. I'd seen it plenty of times before. He took two paces toward the door but turned back suddenly and in one swift movement swept his arm across the table, sending my mug and his crashing to the floor.

I scrambled up from my chair and backed away.

He stared at me; his fists clenched, and his face twisted. The scale of his anger was terrifying, and unexpected.

"That little boy," he said. "My whole career . . . my whole life, I haven't been able to forget him." He choked up before composing himself. "How could you? How do you sleep at night?"

He slammed the door shut after him and I slid to the floor among the broken mugs and the slick of spilled liquid, and felt myself unraveling. I don't know how long it was until I found the words to answer his question.

"I don't," I said.

48

DS Bright arrived I didn't know how much later. I had to get up off the floor to answer the door. I was so very tired. I offered her some fudge, because it was all I had, and she declined. Her colleague followed in her wake again.

"You've blocked the window," she said.

"There was a drone."

"Has something happened here?" She pointed to the broken mugs on the floor.

"I dropped some tea."

"Don't wring your hands," Eliza said. I stopped.

"I think we need to clear that up," DS Bright said.

I looked at the mess. I didn't care about it. I didn't have the energy. Her colleague stepped in. "Two mugs," he said as he retrieved the shards. He put the pieces in separate piles beside my kitchen sink. "Be careful. They're sharp."

"Did you have an altercation with someone?" DS Bright asked.

"I dropped them," I said, but wondered if she already knew what had happened. I had no way of knowing how far Charlie Cartwright's reach was.

"We have a couple of quick questions, if you don't mind."

"Do I need my solicitor?" I felt exhausted by the thought of even calling Tamsin. I just wanted them to go away.

"Of course, you're welcome to get in touch with her, and we can wait for her to join us. Otherwise we could just do this quickly and leave you in peace."

"Have you talked to James and Sasha?" I asked. "There's

something bad going on there. Really bad. And I think my husband found out something about my little brother's disappearance that might have put him in danger. Have you talked to Barry and Vi Kaplan?"

"We've talked to all your neighbors," she said. "And we went to the building you described as a writing shed. What we found was a yoga studio."

Her tone was flat, but one of her eyebrows arched, and I remembered James and Sasha had told her that Dan considered me unstable and now she had proof. "Don't reply," Eliza said.

"Actually, we're here because of something one of your neighbors told us," DS Bright said. "We wanted to have a quick chat about a report we received from one of them that you were seen being dropped off by a vehicle at the end of the lane in the early hours of the morning on the night your husband disappeared. What do you say to that?"

"Say nothing," Eliza said. "Not a word."

"Which neighbor?" I asked.

"I'm not at liberty to tell you."

Her voice echoed in my head. My hands shook. I looked DS Bright straight in the eye.

"No comment," I said.

"You don't want to comment?"

"No."

"Are you sure you can't clear that up for us?"

"No comment."

As they left, she said, "By the way, tomorrow we should be getting back the results of the tests on the blood we found on your hall floor. So, we'll be in touch then."

49

I tried to call Tamsin, but she was in court. I didn't want to leave a message.

The kitchen was a mess. I could see it now. Broken crockery beside the sink, the floor sticky from the spilled tea, packaging from the hamper spread out over all the surfaces, the shopping list so crammed with words that it was illegible. The sheet I'd hung up to block the window was drooping. I found packing tape and secured it better.

I didn't know what else to do except gather together all the papers I could. I retrieved from my bed the ones out of Sasha's shed, lugged in the boxes I'd gotten from Patricia, and opened the folder containing bunker research from the history man.

I was hungry for anything new. Beneath the clinical blaze of the halogens I began to sift through the papers, but found nothing at first.

Eventually, only Rupert's folder was left. Dan had never seen this but it still seemed worth revisiting.

The plan of the bunker lay on top of the other papers.

The first time I'd looked at this diagram, I had been transported back by it so vividly that I hadn't paid much attention to the annotations, but now I saw they were possibly by another hand, and extensive, written in cramped lettering that was hard to read, so I used my phone to magnify them.

At the far end of the bunker, opposite the place where Teddy and I had made our way into it, there had been another door, smaller, and so jammed that you could neither close it nor widen it more than the centimeter or two it already stood open. This was shown on the diagram. I had peered through that slender gap more than once, raking my dad's torch beam over what lay beyond it, but all I had seen was earth and rubble. Whatever had been behind there had collapsed at some point, filling in the space completely.

On the plan, that space was shown as a small, separate room and labeled "ammunitions storeroom." At the far end of it, there had apparently been another door. I found this unsettling to see. On the diagram, a hand-drawn arrow, confidently parabolic, pointed to this door. Beside it were the words: ESCAPE TUNNEL ACCESS. IT IS BELIEVED THAT THE TUNNEL EXTENDS SOUTHWEST. IT IS OF UNKNOWN LENGTH, BUT TYPICALLY ESCAPE TUNNELS IN SIMILAR BUNKERS RANGE IN LENGTH BETWEEN 30–100 M.

I sat back, shocked that I had never known about this.

I studied the annotations once again, looking for a way to orient the bunker so I could understand where the escape tunnel might have led to. Arrows pointed both to the Iron Age fort and, in the other direction, to a line marked "private boundary."

The air stilled. I felt goose bumps. There were only two private boundaries I knew of that bordered Stoke Woods: the gardens of Charlotte Close and the gardens of the houses on this lane.

I brought up a map of the local area on my phone and zoomed in, turning it to try to orient it with the plan of the bunker, but I already knew which boundary this referred to. It had to be our gardens, here. Even with my hazy sense of direction, I knew Charlotte Close was too far away and I also knew I could easily have missed the fact that the bunker was close to here when I was a child. I had never explored beyond the bunker and as far as the lane.

What I saw now was that the escape tunnel could very easily

have extended far enough for the end of it to have been in the garden of a nearby property, and from what I could tell, that garden most probably belonged to Vi and Barry.

I had to make sense of what this meant.

"Don't put yourself in danger," Eliza said.

"But nothing else matters anymore," I said. And it didn't. I had to know what had happened to Teddy.

50

No," Eliza said. "Stop. You have to pull yourself together and concentrate on protecting yourself from the police investigation. This is not the time to be trying to find out what happened to your brother."

"The police don't believe anything I say. You know that. They never have and they never will. But what if Dan discovered something about Teddy that got him killed? What if we can find out what happened? Did you think of that?"

It was such a tantalizing prospect. I thought that if I knew what had happened to Teddy, I might find some peace.

Eliza appeared in front of me, crystal clear. I could have touched her. The sight of the damage to her neck made tears spring to my eyes and I reached toward her, wanting to give her some comfort, but my hand went through her, because she wasn't there. Not really.

"Protect yourself, Lucy," she said. Her hand went to her neck. Her fingertips traced the outline of her bruises. They hadn't gotten any better.

"I can't help you unless you help yourself," she added. She sounded terribly sad.

I found myself copying her, touching my own neck, as if we were the mirror image of one another. My fingertips were electric with sensation, and from my neck came a duller feeling, the impression of the lightest of touches, the smooth skin of my fingertips, followed by the harder line of my nails. Eliza tightened her grip on her neck, and I did the same to mine until I felt the constriction on my windpipe. She squeezed tighter. I felt the blockage of air as a hardness. She released her grip, and I did, too. We both inhaled sharply, the rush of air into our bodies like a gasp for life, a release from horror.

Our fingers settled on our jawlines, where they explored our chins, the softness of our cheeks. I took the ends of my index finger and thumb into my mouth and then the next finger and closed my eyes instinctively because this was what I'd done as a child. It was how I had mourned my brother. Alone in my room. Sucking my fingers like a baby. Tears wetting my pillow, slicking my face and hand, sealing strands of hair to my skin. I had to wash those tears away before I went down to face my parents, and the police. I was ashamed of them.

The only witness to my sorrow had been Eliza.

When I opened my eyes, she was gone.

51

I felt quite alone.

I said to Eliza, "There's no point in protecting myself. They're going to arrest me anyway. You know they are."

I wanted to justify myself, but she did not reply.

I said, "All I can do is find out about Teddy."

I thought I heard her reply then, in a hopeless-sounding whisper. "No," she said.

But I couldn't be sure I'd heard anything at all.

I checked online but there was no reply to my most recent message to MrElizaGrey. I walked up the drive and down the lane to Sasha and James's house. The journalists and photographers roused themselves again. Now they weren't just calling my name but Teddy's, too. They knew about him, and who I was. I ignored them as best I could but my heart beat so hard I believed they'd be able to hear it if they would just stop shouting for a moment and listen.

Sasha's car was in the drive, but only hers. I rang the bell, but there was no answer. I leaned heavily on it but still nobody came. I wondered if Sasha was on the other side of the door, not wanting to open it to me, waiting for me to go away.

"I want to know what you and Dan discovered," I called out, in case she was there, but my voice dissipated like smoke.

"What do you know?" I bashed on the door until it hurt. When nobody answered, I stood back and looked at the property. I had the strong sense that it was empty, that there was no breath of life inside it. That James and Sasha were gone.

I went around the side. I wanted to see if she was hiding in her writing shed, but it was empty, too, and still set up as a yoga studio, as it had been when they showed it to me and when the police saw it. Only I knew that it was no more real than a stage set.

I slipped around the back of the shed, into Barry and Vi's property. If the end of the tunnel was here, I would find it myself.

It wasn't dark enough for me to search their garden unobserved as yet, but it wouldn't be long before I could risk it. I crouched at the back of Barry and Vi's kitchen plot, behind the raised beds. The woods were only a few feet away from me. The fairy-tale woods where the spirits liked to play. As darkness fell, I felt the tug of them, just as I had when I was a kid. It would never go away, I knew that. The feeling I was part of them, and they were part of me. That their beauty and their horror were mine. They existed inside me, part of the fabric that made me, our roots intertwined.

It was cold. I huddled against the wall and used the time to think about where the entrance to the bunker might be. My memory of the diagram was hazy, my ability to interpret it limited. When a light went on in Barry and Vi's house, not at a back window but deep inside it, the glow came from the hallway and barely penetrated the garden at all. I unfolded my stiff limbs and stood up.

I walked the length of the back wall, looking for signs that it had been built over a tunnel, looking for any access point. I imagined it might be some kind of trapdoor. I scraped back the gravel along the path with my bare hands and they began to ache as the stones bruised them and dislodged my scabs, and my fingers became clotted with the earth I found underneath.

I dug slowly because of the need to be quiet. I worked around the edges of the vegetable beds. There was no sign of any access point to a tunnel. I moved on to the compost beds. These were waist-high, both had rotted down over winter and were humming with the stink of decayed plant matter. I found a spade and began to dig, dragging everything out. Heaps of compost piled up on the stones behind me. It covered me. I kept going until I reached the bottom and found bare earth again. I scratched at it with my hands.

I didn't spare the vegetable beds. Every muscle in my body was screaming, but I plunged the spade into the beds repeatedly, pausing only to catch my breath. I wanted to hear the clink of metal or the duller thud of wood. I got nothing and was running out of strength.

Was I in the wrong spot? The lawn stretched out toward the house; the trunks of the cherry trees were dark sentries. Moonlight touched the blossoms on the branches and the ground, and they glowed. I walked among the trees, waiting to feel something beneath my feet that wasn't grass, but there was nothing and I was afraid to get too close to the house.

Despondency settled into my bones, in lockstep with the cold. Another light came on in Barry and Vi's house and I knew I had to leave their garden, go home, think again, before they saw me out here.

I crept into the driveway they shared with the Delaneys. For a moment, I imagined I saw police cars crawling past the end of it, on their way to my home, to inform me that the evidence against me had built up incontrovertibly, that they were there to arrest me, that I had the right to remain silent.

52

I made myself breathe deeply, shutting my eyes tight, and when I opened them again there was nothing but darkness. No police cars. No slow crackle of tires as they rolled down the lane.

I was considering whether to leave via the front drive when the Delaneys' front door opened. "Go on!" a voice ordered. It was Ben Delaney. I watched from the shadows as their old dog shuffled out into the darkness. It moved in measured circles around the lawn, getting closer and closer to me, tracking a scent . . . my scent? I stayed where I was and hoped its senses were too dulled to allow it to find me. The dog approached me but stopped suddenly, and backtracked, then ate something it found on the lawn before nosing its way back in through the door to the house. I exhaled my relief. Through the open door I saw a child in pajamas, the younger boy. He embraced the old dog. "What are you doing downstairs? You should be in bed by now," I heard Kate scold him as she shut the door.

If only my mother had done that to Teddy. If I had. If I'd left him to cry, refusing to let him come with me. If I'd not gone to the woods at all. Then the rest would never have happened.

I thought about the Delaneys living their nice family life here, in a home carved out of the garden of Barry and Vi's property. And I wondered, was Barry so touchy about their build because he knew the bunker tunnel ended here somewhere? Not in his garden, but in theirs? Was that why there had been so many covenants attached to what the Delaneys could do?

Their house stood in the middle of the plot. Logically, Barry wouldn't have wanted any digging to take place near the tunnel, so it was probably near the perimeter fence. I walked to the end of the Delaneys' garden. Half of this boundary was identical to Barry and Vi's, walled to chest height, but in the middle of their plot the wall ended where it butted up against a large tree. This was an area of the garden out of sight of my property and Barry and Vi's. From the tree to my boundary the perimeter was marked by a barbed-wire fence, just the same as mine, to which Ben and Kate had attached further wire with a small mesh, to stop the dog and children escaping, no doubt.

The tree looked as if it had stepped right out of the woods and into their property. Its roots had exploded from the ground and grew intertwined with one another, thick and greedy, spreading a few feet in every direction. It was a monster. The Delaneys had constructed their wire fence around the tree in an elaborate way. They had even wrapped it around the back of the trunk, onto property I was sure wasn't theirs but belonged to the public, as if to discourage anyone who walked outside their perimeter from touching it. It was a strange construction. More than they needed to do to secure their boundary.

I ran my fingers along the wire. One end of it was simply looped over another section. It was easy to detach and step through. The roots were mossy, slimy to the touch. Leaf debris and twigs lay among them, as if it hadn't been cleared away for seasons. I walked around the trunk. Where it almost butted up against the stone wall, my footsteps sounded different. There was a sharper crunch, as if something inorganic lay beneath the debris. I kneeled down, sank my fingers into it, and felt metal beneath them.

It was easy to shove the debris aside. There was only a thin layer of it, and beneath that a metal door, square, hinged, set into a larger bed of concrete. I glanced back at the house.

Through the sitting-room window, I could see the Delaney family on the sofa. Their heads were bent over a board game.

The parents and their two older children, a boy and a girl. The little one wasn't there. I was certain they couldn't see me.

I lifted the trapdoor. I felt as if I had finally reached the end of a very long story, one I'd been reading for most of my life, and I was terrified. Beneath the door I could just make out a ladder made from metal hoops set into the wall. I opened the trapdoor as far as it would go. I turned on my phone torch and clambered down into the tunnel. I couldn't reach the trapdoor to close it so left it open, grateful as I descended for the patch of gray evening light above. There were twelve steps to the bottom. The rungs were cold and slippery and the air chilled by the time I reached the bottom. It also seemed thicker, as if it had hung there undisturbed for years.

The tunnel led off in the direction of the woods and the beam of the torch danced a crazy pattern on the walls as I tried to steady my hand. The tunnel was formed from corrugated iron, sheets of it bent into uneven arches that were held up at intervals by steel supports. The floor was of dry earth, strewn with dead leaves and rubble.

I saw a light switch on the wall and tried it. It illuminated a single bare bulb that hung over the middle of the tunnel from one of the supports. What dim light the bulb gave off gathered around it like a cloud of midges, but it was better than nothing. I put my phone away and used both hands to steady myself as I picked my way toward the bunker.

At the far end, more corrugated iron blocked the way, but I saw a panel had been cut from it, to give access. It was propped up rather than hanging.

Walking down the tunnel felt as if it took forever. I ran the fingers of one hand over the waves in the corrugated iron. I wanted to see what was behind that door, but I was so afraid that my chest seemed to tighten with every step and I swallowed compulsively. My head swam. Images of ancient underground tombs came to mind. Darkness, a final resting place. Somewhere a little boy might have lain lonely for far longer than he had lived.

The panel was rusted at the edges and heavy. I inched it carefully to one side. It revealed a crooked aperture just high enough for a man to duck through. My shadow fell into the space before me. The air here felt even denser than before.

I stood just inside the new space and my hand found my phone in my pocket, but before I pulled it out, my eye was caught by a glint to one side of me. It was a slow, golden glint, like the blinking of an amber eye. And right beside it, I saw another. It was mesmerizing. As my eyes adjusted, I saw more flashes of brightness to either side of me. They vied with one another for my attention. They were dancing sparks from a fire. Here one moment, gone the next. Gold, yellow, amber. They were glitter, fireflies, constellations. This was a place where spirits lived.

"Teddy," I whispered. Was this how we were to be reunited? In this beautiful, sad way?

53

I pulled my phone from my pocket. Light from the screen lit my face and it felt warm, as if I could bathe in it. I flicked the screen and the torch came on.

There was no sound apart from my ragged breathing. I raised the beam, bringing it up from the rubble-strewn floor.

The room I was in was small and lined with shelving on three sides. A doorway only a couple of paces ahead revealed a similar space, but bigger. This was the doorway that had been blocked up when I used to visit. The area beyond it was my bunker, except that it wasn't recognizable.

At the far end of it was the new cinder-block wall.

In front of this were more shelves. And things were not just glinting at me from the darkness now, they shone as their forms emerged into the inquisitive beam of my torch.

Every shelf was stacked with objects. There were candelabras, religious artifacts, sculptures. Too many objects to categorize. A cornucopia. A plastic box with lid ajar contained a hoard of golden coins from another time. There were jewelry cases and also money. Bundles of cash were stacked one on top of the other in teetering piles. On one wall racks had been built from floor to ceiling and paintings slotted into them, the edges of their ornate frames catching and reflecting their own dull golden glow.

This was an Aladdin's cave, a treasure trove. A wonderland. I touched a candelabra. It was beautiful, old. My fingertips sank into the box of tiny coins, feeling their hammered surfaces ridged with motifs. I picked some up and examined the angular face of an ancient king. I pulled a painting from the rack and recognized it. I'd seen it on the news. It had been stolen from a famous collection and nobody had seen it since. I looked at another and saw both beauty and enormous value in the traces of deft brush marks.

Inside a jewelry box, a necklace sat fatly, gold filigree nestling around a huge emerald.

I shut the box.

Teddy wasn't here.

This place was a storeroom, its contents beyond valuable. It was, if I wasn't mistaken, a storeroom for a criminal fence.

I stood in the middle of my bunker and turned in a circle, trying to take all of it in. What was here, what it meant . . . and as I did so, a man's voice said from behind me, "Don't move, and turn off your torch. Now!"

54

Now!" he shouted again when I didn't comply immediately.

I swiped at my phone's screen. I had to do it twice before the torch was extinguished. As soon as it was I heard a click and the light in the tunnel went out. Another click sent a strong beam of light into my face, blinding me. Whoever was there was shining a powerful torch into my eyes.

"Who is it?" a woman's voice said.

The man shushed her, but not before I'd recognized the voice.

"Kate! It's only me," I said.

"It is Lucy," Ben Delaney's voice confirmed. He swore. "Put the light on. You might as well now."

"She'll know it's us anyway," Kate snapped.

The light in the corridor flickered back on and he turned off his torch. I watched them approach. When Ben reached the inner room, he pressed another switch and the two rooms were flooded with bright light.

"Sit down," he said.

I hesitated, but the expression on his face was grim. He was barely recognizable as my affable neighbor. I sank to the floor, almost in the very spot I had left Teddy.

"It's okay," I said. "I'm sorry. I don't want your stuff—if this is yours. I don't care whose it is."

Tension was etched across Kate's face also.

"How did you find this place?" she asked. "Dan couldn't have . . ."

Her words trailed off and the expression on her face betrayed the fact that she'd said too much. I stared at them both and I felt it then, the terrifying certainty that they were prepared to use violence to prevent others from knowing what was down here, and also that they had been violent toward Dan.

"Did you hurt Dan?" I asked.

Ben tensed, but looked upset by the idea. I was working hard to make sense of it all, to decide what to do, how far they would go. Eliza wasn't helping me.

"He found this place, didn't he?" I said.

"Now, look," Ben began, but I could see it in Kate's face. Guilt. And a resolute hardness.

She stared at me and it was as if shutters were coming down over her eyes, removing any trace of humanity, any empathy, until all that was left there was the simple decision she had reached.

That I had to be dealt with.

I was in danger.

I started to scramble up.

"Stay down!" Kate said. "Ben!" she snapped.

He reached around to his back pocket and produced a small revolver. He pointed it at me.

"I will sit . . . I will! I promise," I said. I lowered myself slowly back down. "I just want to talk to you."

"Is there any point?" Kate asked her husband, and I shut my eyes for a moment, thinking, *Would it be so bad if this happened?*

When I opened them, the gun was still pointing at me, but there was something else to see, too, something unexpected.

Behind Kate and Ben, at the far end of the tunnel, stood a small person. A boy. He must have climbed down the ladder and now stood facing me. He wore pajamas.

I smiled. A tear slid down my cheek.

The boy walked down the corridor toward us, not making a sound. Neither Ben nor Kate was aware of him.

"Stop smiling," Ben Delaney said, but I didn't. "What's wrong with her?" he asked Kate. She didn't respond.

The boy stopped just behind them.

"I saw a light and I climbed down the ladder," he said.

He startled his parents. They both swung around to face him.

"What are you doing?" Kate said. The transformation in her was instant. Ben moved the gun so his son couldn't see it. Kate became a mother again, her whole being focused on her child. She made a grab for his arm, but he was quicker. A naughty boy. He slipped past her, and his dad, and me, and reached out to touch a small and beautiful sculpture, a golden elephant with ruby eyes that stood on a shelf at his height.

I was the closest person to him. I was between him and his parents. I saw Ben struggle to decide whether to get the gun back out or not.

"Can you show me that elephant?" I asked the boy.

"Come here now!" Kate snapped at him.

She moved toward her son again, but he was on an adventure, and not in any mood to listen to his mother and father. He came to me and I pulled him onto my lap, and he brought the sculpture with him.

"That's a nice elephant," I said to him. I could smell his just-washed hair.

Ben looked as if he might rush me. He stepped forward. "Don't," Kate said.

I stood up, slowly, keeping the child close. I slipped my arm across his chest so it would require only a small, swift movement to pull it upwards and throttle him.

"What did you do to Dan?" I asked his parents.

Their eyes were on the boy. He began to struggle. I felt a flash of irritation and whispered in his ear, "This is a game. And I bet you're really, really good at games, so let's pretend I'm capturing you because I'm the pirate, and Mummy and Daddy can't win you back because they're rubbish at fighting." And he stopped moving and laughed.

I didn't have to hold him tight after that, but I held him close, and he and I took a step back, farther out of his parents' reach.

"What did you do?" I repeated.

"You can't get me!" the boy trilled at his parents.

Kate blinked fast. Ben licked his lips. Neither of them spoke.

I knew what they had done, and I felt my anger build.

"Did Dan find this place?" I asked.

Ben nodded.

"And, what? You murdered him?"

"Not us," Ben said.

I pulled the boy back farther.

"Who, then?"

He exhaled. "Tell her," Kate said.

"When Dan drove away from your house that night, he found himself parked in. Two of our associates had blocked the lane with their van. They were loading up goods from here. It's not something that happens very often. In fact, it was a very unfortunate coincidence. The people we work with don't use our drive for that sort of thing because obviously we share it with Barry and Vi and we don't want to arouse their suspicion. We try to be discreet. Anyway, Dan got out of his car. We were in the house with our associates, but Dan didn't ring the bell. Instead, he must have noticed light at the end of the garden, because the tunnel entrance had been left open, and decided to take a look. We found him in here. Or, rather, one of our associates did. Your husband can't have been down here for long, but sadly it was long enough that he'd gotten some unfortunate ideas about how he and we might work together in future, which was never going to be possible. Our associates would not contemplate it. A row broke out. Dan was struck and he died. It wasn't meant to happen. It was very regrettable."

"Regrettable?" I said. Dan had not deserved this, but I could easily imagine his excitement when he found himself down here, among the treasures, and how he'd have naïvely assumed he could handle the situation and even try to work it to his advantage.

"It was tragic," Ben said.

"And the blood in my hall?"

He hesitated and Kate replied for him. "They put it there while you were asleep. They had Dan's keys. It wasn't difficult."

I tightened my grip on the boy and felt his fingers grip my forearm where it lay firmly across his chest. He squirmed.

"Now listen," I said. "You both know who I am. You know what happened to my brother. It'll take me one second to snap this child's neck and, believe me, I know because I've done it before."

Kate stifled a sob. Panic glazed her eyes. "Ben," she said.

"You'll go to jail if you harm him," he said.

"I didn't care about that when I was nine years old, and I don't care now."

I felt as if the bunker was feeding me words. They came out of my mouth with absolute precision. Total clarity. The Delaneys shrank away. Kate was stooped over now, covering her mouth in horror. "Mummy," the child said. He held out his arms toward her. I didn't even know his name.

"Here's what you're going to do," I said. "Ben, get out your phone."

"I don't have it on me."

"Kate?"

She pulled hers from her pocket.

"You're going to phone the police and tell them what happened to Dan. And you're going to tell them about this place and what you use it for."

"It was Ben," she said. "Not me. Jackson needs his mother— all the children do. I can't go to jail." She started to cry.

I could feel her son's heart beating. The last time I'd been this close to a little boy was down here, all those years ago. That boy had trusted me, too.

"Give Ben the phone," I said.

She held the phone out to him, her hand trembling.

He looked at it.

"Take it!" I said, and he did. Kate turned her face from him and covered her mouth with her hand.

I looked at Ben. "Make the call. Tell the police that you're responsible for Dan's death, and exactly what happened to him. Tell them everything about this place, about who you're storing stuff for and who you're working with. I want to hear names and details. You can make it clear that Kate knew nothing. And tell them to come immediately."

I watched his finger tap three times on the screen as he dialed emergency services. His hands shook.

"Put it on speakerphone," I said.

"Emergency. Which service?" The operator's voice was loud.

"Police," Ben said.

The child was completely still, watching his parents. His father looked at him, and then away.

There was one short tone before a new voice came on the line. "Police. What's your emergency?"

Ben looked me right in the eye with undisguised hatred as he said, "I have an urgent confession to make with regard to a murder."

When I heard a siren approaching, I let go of the child and walked away from him and his parents, down the tunnel.

I didn't look back.

A silence fell. Minutes, hours, days, weeks it lasted, and Eliza said not one word to me.

Things got done.

People did things.

Ben Delaney was charged. I discovered it was he who had told DS Bright that he'd seen me being dropped off at the end of the lane on the night Dan died. He'd wanted to add another little nugget of evidence to the case the police were building against me. His attempts to get closer to what was happening at the time made perfect sense now. Ben pleaded guilty to a list of offenses including handling stolen goods, assisting an offender, and perverting the course of justice. The charges would take him to prison, where he would doubtless encounter some of his former clients. Whether they would be pleased to see him or not was debatable.

Two weeks after Ben's confession, we buried Dan. His mother wrote the eulogy. She was surprised when I suggested it, and grateful. She had no idea of our difficulties.

We asked the officiant to read out her words. He was a stranger dressed all in black. A raw shaving cut on his neck. Shiny shoes. He did a good job. His voice was enriched with pathos. I felt dissociated from it all. I barely recognized Dan in the words he spoke. Dan's mother had reimagined his childhood as a utopia.

Fewer people attended than I expected. It seemed as if Dan, too, had forgotten to maintain his friendships over the past few years. The empty chairs were painful to see.

I cried hard for what he and I once had and for what might have been and threw a rose onto the lid of the coffin once he'd been lowered into his liar's grave.

Max and Angela were there among the mourners. They brought that whiff of London with them again. It lurked in the folds of their dark wool coats.

They stayed overnight and I met with them the following day. No champagne on this occasion. We drank rich coffee in a hotel drawing room warmed by a real fire. They spoke carefully as they reported good news.

"We've been talking internally," Angela said, "and we feel that we would like to publish your most recent novel, as it is."

"The novel you rejected?"

"Yes."

Max was sitting forward, smiling, his body language telling me that this was unequivocally a good thing, but I needed to clarify. "You want to publish the novel without Eliza in it?"

She nodded. "If you'll let us." It was a masterful display of submission.

"Well, that would be lovely," I said.

"Fabulous," Max said.

"And we would also like to talk about you doing some more Eliza novels going forward," Angela added.

Now they watched me even more closely, waiting for my reaction. Angela's eyes were on me even as she stirred milk into her coffee. I felt mesmerized by the motion of the spoon, the liquid.

I said, "Can I think about it?" and the stillness in the room shattered, scattering dust motes. The flames in the fire flared. They hastened to assure me that of course I could think it over, that I should take all the time I needed, that they were very keen to make this work for me, that my continued relationship with the publisher was extremely important to everyone.

Max and I waved Angela off in a cab. He didn't go with her this time, but held open the door of the next taxi, for me. "I'll call you tomorrow," he said, once I was in, "and we'll talk. I'm not going to lie to you; they're publishing this novel now to capitalize on the publicity around Dan's death. You know that, don't you?"

"I do."

"But it gets it out into the world."

"Right." I felt a small flicker of happiness.

"And the Eliza books? How do you feel about that?"

"I don't know yet. I don't know if I'll know tomorrow."

"It's okay," he said. "You've got some time. But, you know, she's a terrific character."

"Bye, Max," I said.

The silence stretched longer.

Max did call. He kept calling until I had decided what to do and stopped after I'd finally made the decision. It was an obvious choice.

I tidied up my house and found a shopping list crawling with words so unintelligible that they might have been hieroglyphs, or some other communication from another time and place. I chucked it out with all the other mess.

The woods burst with life. It was a beautiful thing to see. Acid-green leaves began to unfurl, making a start on filling the gaps between the evergreens. At ground level, they cast an ethereal emerald glow over burgeoning carpets of bluebells.

Sometimes, I walked in the woods, usually at dawn, when I had them to myself. I was looking for Teddy.

I got the builders in to renovate the house. I could afford

it now. Payment for the book they didn't want to publish then did want to publish had landed promptly in my account. More money was to come imminently from the new deal Max had negotiated for me. Much more. Oodles of it. Because I had agreed to write the next two Eliza Grey books.

When the men downed tools, through windows thrown wide to let the endless choking dust escape I could sometimes hear the squeak of the trampoline as a child bounced in the garden next door.

Another delivery of cloudberry jam arrived, left outside my door, as before. I ate it.

I wasn't the only person on the lane to have the builders in. The Morells did, too. Sasha and James's property became slowly more fortified that spring. Gates went up at the top of their driveway, perimeter walls were built higher, a security system was installed. It was hard to know whether they were trying to keep the world out, or to contain each other.

I didn't see James at all, except once in his car, when he carefully avoided looking at me, but Sasha came to my door one day and admitted to being MrElizaGrey. She hadn't written all his posts, many of them had been posted by Dan, but she was responsible for some of them. She made the admission to me tearfully, on my doorstep. Dan put me up to it because he wanted to shake you up, she told me, because he thought it might help you remember material for his book. She was so very sorry because she knew what it was like to be with a difficult man and she wasn't sure what she'd been thinking.

She tearfully explained how bad she felt and asked for my forgiveness, mentioning the tipoff she'd given me about Naomi Dent as if it was leverage.

"So, you and Dan were gaslighting me?" I asked.

"Yes," she said, and that someone would finally admit to this after all the times Dan had denied it brought me a surprisingly powerful feeling of relief. But I didn't thank Sasha. She didn't deserve it. I closed the door in her face and felt exhausted, the type of profound physical lag you experience after an illness. Or at the end of a book. I knew it would pass.

Barry and Vi I did see. One long night we met and talked in sentences that were sometimes as broken as our hearts and that struggled to convey meaning with any fluency, but we could see in each other's eyes that each one of our souls had bled for Teddy.

After my brother's disappearance it was Barry's horror at what he'd done, and what might have been, that shattered him. When he rushed out to collect his traps that night, sickened with fear after hearing a young boy had gone missing in the woods, he found he'd caught nothing worse than a young rabbit. Its soft, warm body and eyes bulging with pain and fear left Barry with haunted dreams in which my little brother suffered horribly in the brutal embrace of the trap's teeth.

We kept our distance after that night, the three of us. We shared tentative smiles and raised our hands in greeting when we glimpsed one another, but we didn't approach any nearer. I didn't mind. I planned to sell Cossley House once the renovations were done. It could never feel like home.

One evening, during the silence, I stepped outside. It was almost dark, and bats spilled from the eaves of my house. They looked pretty against the darkening sky. Pitch-black confetti thrown against the inky blue.

The severed cedar stump looked different now. The once fresh wood of the cut had weathered to a deep gold. I sat on it and waited for Eliza. When I felt the back of my neck prickle, I shifted a little to one side and she sat down beside me.

Her neck had healed beautifully. There was no trace of the bruising, and she had rebuilt her strength. It had been the work of moments to make it happen. I'd simply started the first chapter of the new Eliza novel that I'd agreed to write for Angela. The words had flowed, were still flowing. I thought this would be my best Eliza book yet. My fans were ecstatic. They flooded my social media accounts with their enthusiasm.

I sipped my wine.

"Look," Eliza said.

She pointed to the very end of the lawn, where a section of my boundary fence had fallen and I had not yet repaired it. Though I would, before the house went on the market. A doe had come into the garden and with her, her fawn. The doe raised her head and stared at us, and we at her, all of us perfectly still until she turned tail and disappeared into the woods and darkness fell across her like a veil.

"Did I hurt Teddy?" I asked Eliza. I had to know. The silence hadn't given me any answers.

"You were nine years old. You could never have disposed of a body. You didn't do it. You couldn't have."

"Are you sure?"

"You weren't a killer then and you aren't now."

I felt something at that, but it was hard to define what. Relief? Maybe, but also an ache because of all the answers that still needed finding. "Then who did it?"

"We don't know. We'll probably never know."

The woodland sighed, as if so much time had passed that it, too, could no longer remember what had happened to my brother.

"But you know," Eliza said, "it's not necessarily the worst that happened. Perhaps one of the people by the bonfire took him. Perhaps someone else did. They could have raised him as their own and he might have been happy with them. He would have forgotten his family after a while. He might have felt loved."

"I don't know," I said. "I don't want to think about someone taking our place. What if he's still in the woods? I want an ending. I want to know."

Eliza shrugged. "You and I are always honest with one another, yes?" Her voice was gentle.

"Yes."

"Then you might never know, and they might never find him. But here's how you live with it. Think of it like this: At midnight on the summer solstice, the spirits crossed from their world to ours. They roamed the woods, playing tricks on one another and on the adults they found there. It delighted them. But they were even more delighted to find a child, lying in a bunker, because everybody knows that children make better playmates than adults. They coaxed Teddy awake and took him with them. He played with them, dashing through the woods, somersaulting between the tops of the trees and the stars. Teddy had never had so much fun in his life. He was one of those sparks you saw, rising so high it hurt your neck to look. The spirits were having so much fun with him that they forgot to bring him home when the sun rose. And, in fact, it wasn't just that they forgot, but that they didn't want to give him back. They loved him too much already, so they took Teddy with them."

"Because he was perfect," I said.

"Yes."

I lay back on the cedar stump and felt the contours of the wood press into my back, thinking about it all until the sky blackened and the first star appeared.

I wouldn't miss this place, when I sold it. I couldn't wait to get back into the city, to immerse myself in Eliza's world. She had always been with me, and she always would be.

She lay down beside me. The way she moved now was effortless; strength coursed through her.

"You tell the best stories," I said, after a while.

"I know," Eliza replied, "we both do."

ACKNOWLEDGMENTS

Helen Heller's belief that I could write this book and her unwavering personal and creative support are the reasons it exists. Thank you for loving Lucy.

Warmest thanks to my editors, Emily Griffin in London and Emily Krump in New York, whose patience, enthusiasm, and editorial suggestions improved this manuscript immeasurably. Thanks to Julia Elliott and Jess Ballance for all your input and hard work on the manuscript. The support of Selina Walker at Century & Arrow and Liate Stehlik and Jennifer Hart at William Morrow is much appreciated, too. Thank you.

At HarperCollins Canada, thanks as ever to Leo MacDonald and Sandra Leef for everything you do for my books, and I'm very grateful to Mike Millar, Cory Beatty, and Kaitlyn Vincent for all your hard work, and for looking after me in Canada.

Thanks to Camilla Ferrier and Jemma McDonagh and all at the Marsh Agency. You are a joy to work with.

For wonderful marketing and publicity campaigns, thanks must also go to Camille Collins and Kaitlin Harri in the U.S. and to Sarah Ridley, Natalia Cacciatore, and Isabelle Ralphs in the UK.

I am forever grateful to the exceptional sales and production teams who get my books onto shelves. Raising a glass to you, Linda Hodgson and Mathew Watterson in the UK, and to Carla Parker and everyone else in the sales department in the U.S.

Huge thanks to Ceara Elliott in the UK and to Elsie Lyons in the U.S. for your terrific cover designs.

Thank you to the publishers who translate my books internationally and to the editors and teams who work on them. It's a privilege to work with you.

Readers, booksellers, bloggers, and reviewers are all part of the generous and supportive community that makes my job a pleasure. Thank you for your warm and fun interactions online and in person. It means the world.

Support from fellow authors is such an important part of my life. I daren't try to name you all in case I forget someone, but you know who you are, and please know that I'm deeply grateful to you personally and professionally.

Thank you to the two retired detectives who have advised me on police matters since I wrote my first novel and are terrific company as well as fonts of knowledge and inspiration. Any mistakes or liberties taken with police procedure in this novel are mine alone.

To friends Annemarie Caracciolo, Philippa Lowthorpe, Abbie Ross, Claire Douglas, Shari Lapeña, and Tim Weaver, thank you for your support, encouragement, and wise words this year.

My family has been incredibly supportive and patient during the writing of this book. Thank you, Jules, for the garlic chicken, and thank you to my children, Rose, Max, and Louis.

GILLY MACMILLAN is the internationally bestselling author of *What She Knew, The Perfect Girl, Odd Child Out, I Know You Know,* and *The Nanny.* She lives in Bristol, England.